THE MULLAH'S STORM

ALSO BY THOMAS W. YOUNG

The Speed of Heat:
An Airlift Wing at War in Iraq and Afghanistan

THE MULLAH'S STORM

THOMAS W. YOUNG

G. P. PUTNAM'S SONS / NEW YORK

PUTNAM

G. P. PUTNAM'S SONS
Publishers Since 1838
Published by the Penguin Group
Penguin Group (USA) Inc., 375 Hudson Street, New York, New York 10014, USA •
Penguin Group (Canada), 90 Eglinton Avenue East, Suite 700, Toronto, Ontario M4P 2Y3,
Canada (a division of Pearson Penguin Canada Inc.) • Penguin Books Ltd, 80 Strand,
London WC2R 0RL, England • Penguin Ireland, 25 St Stephen's Green, Dublin 2, Ireland
(a division of Penguin Books Ltd) • Penguin Group (Australia), 250 Camberwell Road,
Camberwell, Victoria 3124, Australia (a division of Pearson Australia Group Pty Ltd) •
Penguin Books India Pvt Ltd, 11 Community Centre, Panchsheel Park, New Delhi–110 017,
India • Penguin Group (NZ), 67 Apollo Drive, Rosedale, North Shore 0632, New Zealand
(a division of Pearson New Zealand Ltd) • Penguin Books (South Africa) (Pty) Ltd,
24 Sturdee Avenue, Rosebank, Johannesburg 2196, South Africa

Penguin Books Ltd, Registered Offices: 80 Strand, London WC2R 0RL, England

Library of Congress Cataloging-in-Publication Data

Young, Thomas W., date.
   The mullah's storm / Thomas W. Young.
      p.   cm.
   ISBN 978-0-399-15692-2
   1. Soldiers—Fiction.   2. Afghan War, 2001—Fiction.   3. Survival after airplane
accidents, shipwrecks, etc.—Fiction.   4. Prisoners of war—Fiction.   5. Taliban—Fiction.
6. Afghanistan—Fiction.   I. Title.
   PS3625.O97335M85   2010   2010003110
   813'.6—dc22

Printed in the United States of America

10   9   8   7   6   5   4   3   2   1

BOOK DESIGN BY GRETCHEN ACHILLES

IN MEMORY OF CHIEF MASTER SERGEANT FRED WILLIAMS

CHAPTER ONE

A leaden overcast covered the sky above Bagram Air Base, Afghanistan, hanging so thick and low that the afternoon became a long twilight. Peaks of mountains surrounding the Shomali Plain disappeared into the cold, gray mist.

Inside the C-130 Hercules transport plane, Major Michael Parson blew into his cupped hands to warm them, then pulled on his Nomex gloves. He donned his flight helmet and turned up the interphone volume at the navigator's panel.

The rest of the crew strapped in. The pilot and aircraft commander, Lieutenant Colonel Fisher, adjusted his boom mike and said, "If we don't get out of here soon, we won't get out at all."

Parson's weather sheet told him why. The coded forecast read: "+BLSN, PRESFR." Heavy blowing snow. Pressure falling rapidly.

At the flight engineer's station, between the pilots and just forward of Parson, Sergeant Luke tapped on his calculator. With his grease pencil, he wrote numbers on a laminated takeoff card, then handed the card to Fisher.

"They need to get that son of a bitch out here now," said the loadmaster, Sergeant Nunez. Nunez was back in the cargo compartment; Parson heard him on the interphone.

A blue van stopped in front of the airplane.

"Here he is," said the copilot, Lieutenant Jordan. He tapped his fingers on the side console.

Two security policemen bearing M-4 rifles escorted the prisoner, a high-ranking Taliban mullah. They guided him out of the van and steered him toward the crew door, just downstairs from the cockpit. Shackles bound his hands and feet; he had just enough length of chain between his ankles to mount the steps. He wore blacked-out goggles. Long beard more gray than black. Desert camo coat and prison overalls.

Parson thought the mullah looked smaller and more frail than he had on CNN. But that had been just brief clips of the man exhorting crowds at Friday prayers, or older footage of him when his hair was all black, hoisting a Stinger launcher triumphantly over the smoking wreckage of a Soviet helicopter.

A woman in an Army uniform followed the prisoner. An interpreter, Parson assumed. A middle-aged, bald man in civilian clothes accompanied her. Agency, Parson guessed.

From the cargo compartment, Parson heard chains clanking as Nunez and the security police seated the mullah. Nunez was singing loudly, *"Guantanamera, guajira guantanamera, guantana-mehhhhhra. . . ."*

"Don't do that," Parson said over the interphone.

"Why not?" Nunez asked.

"It's not professional. And they're closing Gitmo, genius."

"That's all right. We got other places to put these *pendejos*."

"Ready for checklists?" Fisher said. An order, not a question. "Let's get these engines started."

Terse, clipped commands crossed the interphone and radios, and the roar of spinning turboprops split the winter stillness. Parson scrunched his nose at the odor of jet fuel exhaust until Nunez closed the crew door. Large snowflakes splattered onto the windscreen and turned to running droplets on the glass. The cargo plane began lumbering, and Parson noticed the snowflakes getting smaller and flying sideways. The mountains off the far end of the runway dissolved in a white haze.

"Flash Two-Four, Bagram Tower. Clear for takeoff, Runway Two-One."

Fisher lined up on the runway and advanced the throttles. Parson felt the vibration in his shoulders through his flak vest, and the acceleration pushed him back in his seat. The runway centerline stripes grew shorter and shorter until Jordan said, "Go," and the ground fell away. A moment later, the windscreen went solid gray as the C-130 entered the cloud deck.

"Positive rate," Fisher called. "Gear up."

Parson watched his radar screen as the airplane climbed. In terrain-mapping mode, it showed the mountains ahead as if they were a green photograph.

"How are we doing, nav?" Jordan asked.

"You're good as long as you stay on the departure procedure," Parson said. He cross-checked the radar screen with his chart, monitored the plane's progress. On the pilots' instrument panel, he saw the digital numbers on the radar altimeter running down, then up, then back down. A mountain, then a valley, then another ridge.

Parson looked forward to breaking out above the cloud layer.

Fisher would level off and put the Herk on autopilot. Nunez would make coffee. Luke would probably want to borrow Parson's copy of *Shooting Sportsman*. Easy mission from then on.

Just as Parson turned back to his radar screen, missile warning tones shrieked through the cockpit.

Fisher whipped the yoke to the right, rolled the C-130 into a steep bank. Parson's arms grew heavy with the pull of G forces.

"Flares, flares," Jordan called. "Missile three o'clock."

Parson grabbed the pistol-grip trigger for the antimissile flares. Punched off a salvo. The flares torched across the sky, trailing parabolas of smoke through the clouds. Parson hoped the fast turn and the flares, burning hotter than the engines, would fool the heat-seeker.

It was not enough.

An explosion rocked the airplane. Impact somewhere out on the right wing. Fragments slammed against the fuselage, sounded like thrown gravel. The aircraft yawed to the right. Then it began to vibrate hard. On the instrument panels, white needles inside black gauges trembled into unreadable blurs.

"Fire in number three," Luke called. A red light glowed in the number three engine's fire handle. Then the light next to it came on.

"Fire in number four."

"Oh, fuck," Fisher said. "Shut 'em down."

Jordan and Fisher began running emergency engine shutdown checklists. Parson took over the radio calls. He flipped the wafer switch on his comm box to UHF1.

"Mayday, mayday," he called. "Flash Two-Four is an emergency aircraft. Taking fire. Two engines out. Ten souls on board." He hoped his voice didn't give away the fear he felt.

Jordan pulled the fire handles. Luke's hands played across the overhead panel, shutting down fuel pumps and generators on the burning engines. The airplane was already half dead.

"Flash Two-Four, Bagram Departure. Say intentions."

"Stand by," Parson said. The altimeters showed a slow descent. Could be worse, Parson realized. Fisher still had some control. Parson saw him shove the two good throttles all the way up.

"That's all she's got," Fisher said, pushing hard on the left rudder pedal to keep the nose pointed straight. "We're going down, boys. It's just a question of where."

"Right turn zero-six-zero for a heading back to Bagram," Parson said.

"I don't have enough speed to turn into the dead engines."

"There's rising terrain to the left," Parson said. "We can't climb over it now."

"Damn it. Just find me someplace to set it down."

"Come left five degrees," Parson said. "I'll try to get you into a valley." Mountains blocked a full turn left, and physics prevented a bank to the right.

Parson could see nothing out the windows except cloud. Inside, the radar showed more lines of jagged ridges. His heading took the plane between two of them. Farther from Bagram with each second, but maybe the landing would be survivable.

"Bagram, Flash Two-Four," he called. "We won't make it back to the field." Parson transmitted coordinates for where he predicted touchdown. Nearly fifty miles from the base.

Jordan flipped a red guard from the alarm bell switch. He gave six short rings: Prepare for crash landing.

"I can't see shit," Fisher said. "I'll just try to keep the wings level."

"Stay on this heading," Parson said. The numbers on the radar altimeter counted down as the plane neared the valley floor, but Parson saw only mist and swirling snow. He rotated his seat to face forward for the crash. A smell like burned oil filled the cockpit.

"Loadmaster," Jordan said, "give us a scan on that right wing."

"Heavy smoke from number four," Nunez said. "The whole turbine section's blown off number three. Fuel misting out of the external tank."

"I'm keeping the landing gear up," Fisher said. "Engineer, pull the breaker for the gear warning horn." Luke leaned from his seat to trip a circuit breaker.

The C-130 broke through the cloud deck, revealing the stark terrain ahead. A scattering of evergreens stood among boulders and shale dusted with powder. Fine snow roiled in the air like a spray of milk. Parson felt a spike of fear deep in his chest. He'd hoped for a nice, flat field.

"Strap in tight," Fisher ordered. "This is really gonna suck."

Jordan gave a long ring on the alarm bell: Brace for impact.

"Flaps to a hundred percent," Fisher called. "Feather one and two."

Just feet above the ground, Jordan shut down the two remaining engines so they wouldn't burn on impact. Eerily quiet now, the wounded airplane glided back to earth. No sound but the whistle of the slipstream until Parson felt the first wrenching jolt of a wing striking a tree. Then another, and another.

A scraping noise came from the back of the airplane as the tail crashed into rocks. The fuselage slammed to the ground. Parson jerked against his shoulder straps. His arms flailed. He felt stabs of pain as he bit his tongue and cracked his right wrist against the edge of the nav table.

The left wing separated with a grinding crunch, the sound of metal ripping like the aircraft itself roaring in pain. What remained of the plane swerved hard, sent up an arc of flying dirt and snow.

Then, for a moment, stillness and silence. Parson closed his eyes and braced for the fireball, fearing his flameproof flight suit would just prolong the agony. He smelled JP-8 fumes from ruptured fuel tanks. Breathing the kerosene odor was like inhaling needles.

But no fire came. Parson exhaled, felt cold air rushing into the broken flight deck. Shouts came from the back.

"*Allah-hu akbar! Allah-hu akbar!*"

Then a dull thump. Metal against flesh.

"Shut the fuck up!" Nunez yelled. "Do you fucking understand me? Bet you understand this." *Whack.*

Then the woman's voice: "That's enough."

Parson unbuckled his harness, took off his helmet, spat out a mouthful of blood. Still stunned, he saw tiny points of silver floating across his eyeballs. He heard Fisher groan.

"I think my legs are broken," Fisher said. "Somebody check on the others."

"I'm all right," Luke said. "I'll look in the back."

Parson stumbled to the copilot's seat, leaned on it with his right hand. That launched waves of pain that brought him to his knees.

"I fucked up my wrist," he said through gritted teeth. He cradled the wrist with his left hand and examined it. Maybe not broken, but sure as hell cracked and bruised.

The copilot didn't move or make a sound.

"You okay?" Parson asked, nudging Jordan's shoulder with his good hand. No response.

Parson pulled himself to his feet. Now he saw Jordan's open eyes staring lifelessly at the floor. He checked for a pulse at the carotid artery, and when he did he felt an odd bulge at the side of Jordan's neck.

"I think his neck's broken," Parson said. "He's dead." It still hurt where he'd bitten his tongue, and the pain slurred his words.

Fisher closed his eyes and grimaced. "See if you can get somebody to help me out of this seat," he said.

Parson descended the flight deck steps. He found Luke and Nunez pulling first-aid kits off their wall fasteners, and he swallowed hard when he saw the mess in the cargo compartment. The civilian spook sat slumped to one side, his seat belt still holding him in the troop seat. A gash in his skull revealed spongy tissue. One of the security policemen held a compress on the other's chest. The injured SP was on his back, blood streaming under and through the gauze pad. The blood ran across the floor and pooled in the tie-down rings.

"What happened to them?" Parson asked.

"Shrapnel, I think," Nunez said.

"Jordan's dead. Fisher's legs are broke. Can you help me move him?"

The prisoner sat quietly, silenced at least for now by Nunez's blow. The woman guarded him. The uninjured SP checked his partner's pulse and placed an ABU jacket over the man's face.

Parson climbed back to the flight deck, then supported Fisher's thighs as Nunez carried him down the steps and into the cargo compartment. Fisher cried out with each bump. His fingers clawed into Parson's arm. They laid him down across the troop seats.

"Let's see if I can get outside," Luke said. He rotated the handle on the crew door, kicked the door hard. It opened about halfway, and the flight engineer turned sideways to crawl through. "I'm going to make a radio call," he said.

Parson watched him let go of the bent door frame and drop to the ground. Luke pulled his PRC-90 from his survival vest, extended the antenna, pressed the transmit button. He squinted against the stinging ice pellets.

"Mayday, mayday, Flash Two-Four down. Any station, Flash Two-Four down."

"Flash Two-Four, Bookshelf. Say location."

Parson gave Luke a thumbs-up, relieved that the engineer had already made contact with the AWACS bird orbiting far overhead. Parson handed Luke a scrap of paper with the crash site coordinates, which Luke transmitted to the AWACS.

"We'll relay to search-and-rescue forces," the AWACS controller said. "But be advised weather conditions have everything grounded in your sector."

"We kind of figured," Luke said. He stared at the murk above.

Parson heard what he thought was the *pop, pop* of burned metal as it cooled. Blood spurted from the flight engineer's throat. The radio dropped from Luke's hand, and he crumpled to the ground. Then came a burst from an M-4 firing out a troop door behind Parson in the cargo compartment. A man in a black turban ran toward the airplane and fell.

Nunez scrambled for the dead SP's rifle and covered the other open troop door. He fired a trio of shots. The brass casings flipped through the air, rattled as they dropped.

The interpreter kicked the prisoner to the floor, held him down with her foot, aimed her rifle at him. *"Peh zmekah tsmla,"* she ordered. *"Chup shah."*

With his good hand, Parson drew his Beretta from his survival vest. Burned gunpowder stung his nose. He heard someone grab the partially open crew door and try to pry it farther open.

Parson felt he couldn't turn fast enough. But he raised his arm as an insurgent squeezed through the door. He fired two shots from his pistol. The intruder neither fell nor advanced. Parson fired again. The man's torso jerked as it absorbed the rounds. He still didn't fall, wedged in the crew door. Parson was pumping bullets into a corpse.

He moved to the crew door, pushed the dead man back outside. The body slumped and lay still in the snow. Parson forced his way through the door, jumped down to check on Luke. The bloodied face seemed like that of a stranger. No breath, no heartbeat. Wounds to the chest as well as the throat.

The broken remains of Luke and the insurgent rested within feet of each other. Flakes melted instantly as they touched warm blood. Beyond the wreckage, Parson saw only trees and rocks diffused by the swirling powder.

"See any more?" Nunez called.

"Not now," Parson replied. He climbed back into the cargo compartment.

"Negative," the security policeman said, peering out the troop door across from Nunez. The SP ejected a spent magazine and pulled a fresh one from his vest.

"Where's Luke?" Fisher asked.

"Luke's dead," Parson said. "And search-and-rescue isn't getting here anytime soon. The weather—"

"Sirs," the security policeman said, "we need to get ready for another attack. Every hajji within ten miles heard this plane go down."

"They know we have their preacher guy," Nunez said.

Parson saw Fisher looking at what was left of his plane, crew, and passengers. Then Fisher's eyes seemed to rest on the mullah.

"We need to get him out of here," Fisher said.

"That's crazy," Parson said. "You can't travel with two broken legs."

"No, I can't. And the smaller the party, the easier it will be to evade. You're the highest-ranking guy standing. I need you to take the prisoner and the interpreter, and go."

"Forget it. I'm not deserting my crew."

"You heard the briefing," Fisher said. "This mullah is about as high-value as any detainee we have. We can't risk him getting freed by his buddies."

Parson felt dread flow into him like a toxin. Every instinct told him to stay with his crewmates. He looked out into the snowfall. Evade? Here, with a prisoner?

"Mike," said Fisher. "I just gave you an order."

"But—"

"We'll stay with Fisher," Nunez said. "Leave us some weapons and ammo, and the SP and I will take care of him till they can get a helicopter in here."

Parson could hardly believe it. He'd always thought Nunez was a drunk whose life amounted to flying from one party to another. But now this. Setting up for an onslaught like a pro.

"You okay with that plan?" Parson called to the interpreter.

She was a master sergeant. Maybe thirty-five, blond hair. Accent sounded like New England, but not when she spoke Pashto. Her name tag read: GOLD.

"Yeah," she said. "Let's do it."

"Then get your stuff and keep it light," Parson said. "Just your rifle and ammo. Layer up your clothes as much as you can." He hated what Fisher wanted him to do, but now this sergeant and the prisoner were his responsibility.

Parson went to Fisher and held out his left fist. Fisher tapped it with his own fist. It was the same gesture they used when they ran the Combat Entry checklist.

"I got the first round when I see you again," Fisher said.

"No cheap stuff, either," Parson said.

He put on a desert parka and pulled a black watch cap over his head. He wished he had snow camo now, but C-130 crews flew over so much varying terrain, it was impossible to dress for all of it. On the flight deck, he retrieved charts from the nav table, folded them into small squares. He found Luke's backpack filled with flight manuals. Parson dumped out the books and put the charts and two first-aid kits in the pack. He also picked up two sets of night-vision goggles, Luke's binoculars, and three Meals Ready to Eat. From his own flight bag he took a package of charcoal handwarmers and three bottles of water.

He looked around the cockpit for anything else that seemed useful. He noticed Jordan's pistol still holstered on the copilot's survival vest. Parson took the handgun. He looked down at Jordan one last time as he shouldered the backpack with his good hand.

In the cargo compartment, he found Gold searching the pockets of the dead civilian. She took some paperwork from the man's coat, looked into the lifeless face. Then she unshackled the mullah's feet. Parson had no training on how to handle prisoners, but he knew he and Gold and the mullah had to move. Right now.

"Tell him he's going for a little hike," Parson said as he sat beside the mullah.

"I did. He says he's not going anywhere."

Parson felt a jolt of anger hit him like voltage. My friends are dead because of you, he thought, and you're going to give me an attitude? I don't fucking think so.

He pulled up the left pant cuff of his flight suit. Reached down to his boot knife, unsnapped the leather sheath. He withdrew a four-inch dagger as he grabbed the prisoner's right thumb.

Using his injured hand, Parson jammed the blade deep under the mullah's thumbnail. The mullah shrieked, shouted something in Pashto. Parson swore. He felt as though he'd rammed a white-hot nail through his cracked wrist. He twisted the knife and ground his teeth as his own pain tripled.

"Stop it," Gold said. "Sir."

The prisoner jerked his hand away and began jabbering and sobbing. Gold tried to examine his bleeding thumb, but he wouldn't let her.

"He says he'll go with us," Gold said, "but it matters little because the flames of hell will consume you."

Easier than I expected, Parson thought. Everybody understands pain. Bet he's inflicted his share of it.

Parson could see Gold didn't like what he'd just done. It probably violated all kinds of laws. And it was the first time he'd ever really hurt someone. But it was hard to care about that with people dying around you. Parson looked back at Fisher. He seemed satisfied enough. Parson nodded at him, turned to Gold: "Time to move."

Gold took the chain from the prisoner's legs and locked one end to her wrist. She spoke in Pashto, but the mullah did not respond. She picked up his right arm and fastened the other end of the chain to his wrist. Parson could not see all of the man's expression because of the black goggles covering his eyes, but he did notice the mullah's lips curling as if he'd inhaled some foul odor. Guess you don't like a woman putting you on a leash, Parson thought. Serves you right.

"He's going to have to see to walk with us," she said.

Parson removed the goggles from the prisoner's face. The mullah blinked but did not look around. One eye seemed dull and focused on nothing. It was blue. The other eye, black and alive, glared at Parson with undiluted hatred.

"What's wrong with his eye?" Parson asked.

"It's glass," Gold said. "He lost it fighting the Soviets."

"Tell him he'll lose the other one if he doesn't do exactly what I tell him."

"Don't get carried away."

Who did this sergeant think she was? Parson decided to let it pass. He needed her.

He jumped out the paratroop door at the back of the cargo compartment. The three-foot drop jarred him, sent pain throbbing through his wrist. He reached up with his left hand and helped Gold step down with the prisoner. The move came easily to him since he was so much taller than they were. When the mullah reached the ground, his head came up only to Parson's chest.

This son of a bitch inspires the people who shot us down, Parson thought, and now I have to look after him. For an instant, Parson wanted to grab him by the hair and slam his face into the side of the airplane.

"Good luck, guys," Nunez said. "Major, if I'd known you was this hard-core, I'd have been more respectful."

"You're all right, Nunez," Parson said.

Ice pellets made ticking noises as they fell, gathering in the folds of Parson's coat like spilled salt. He opened his compass and took a bearing, then sighed. The mist of his breath rose in the cold air, only to get torn away by the Afghan wind.

CHAPTER TWO

The snow fell in thick flakes. That relieved Parson a little. It would cover their tracks after they holed up for the night.

The three walked for about half an hour along the valley floor. Mountains loomed on either side, and Parson knew the old man couldn't make any time uphill even if he wanted to. The mullah looked well over seventy, with white eyebrows and a face as lined as a terrain map of his homeland. Right now Parson just wanted distance from the airplane.

"What do you give our chances?" Gold asked.

"Wouldn't bet money I couldn't lose."

Gold nodded and tugged gently at the chain that attached her to the prisoner.

The light began to dim, but with the snow and heavy cloud cover, evening brought no sunset, just a slow fade to gray. Parson heard two shots register in the distance. He stopped to listen. Then an eruption of automatic-weapons fire. A mile away. Sounded like popcorn cooking off.

"It's happening," Parson said. "That's at the airplane." He wished he knew who was winning. Then he realized he did know. Too late to think about it now. Just follow Fisher's order.

"You did well to get going so quickly," Gold said.

"We better keep going. In a minute or two, they'll realize their mullah's not there."

A forest of Afghan pines covered the ridges to the north. Their boughs drooped with snow, and Parson thought the scene might look pretty if he weren't running for his life with the devil in tow.

"Let's get into those trees and find some cover," Parson said.

He led the way through snow now ankle deep, and just as he pulled a branch aside for Gold, the prisoner shouted, *"Mrastah wukray!"*

Parson clapped a hand over the old man's mouth and pushed him to the ground. Gold pointed her rifle at the mullah and scanned the mountains.

"There," she whispered. "Five or six men coming down the ridge. He just yelled for help."

Parson saw them a couple thousand yards off. He dug a handkerchief from his pocket, unfolded it, and twisted it into a gag.

"Tell him to open his mouth," Parson said.

Gold said something in Pashto, but the prisoner gritted his teeth. Parson pulled his boot knife.

"Tell him to open his mouth or I'll gut him like a deer."

Gold said what sounded like two or three words.

The old man obeyed, and Parson tied the handkerchief as tightly as he could. The man's face jerked as Parson closed the knot down hard. The prisoner grunted in protest.

"Damn it, I should have thought of this before now," Parson hissed. "Let's move." He yanked the prisoner off the ground and pulled him uphill at a trot, with Gold pushing from behind. Matted snow slid off the mullah's back and shoulders. The three stumbled through the trees until they reached the crest of the rise. The mullah wheezed with each breath. Saliva soaked the gag and oozed down his chin. Parson looked downhill.

"God, I hope there's a stream down there," he said. "Do you see them behind us?"

"Yeah."

Parson grabbed the mullah's coat and pulled him down the back side of the ridge. The man fell to his knees, and Parson dragged him up again. Parson knew they were leaving a path through the snow like a herd of buffalo. They slid down to a creek bank, the mud frozen to iron. Panes of white ice covered pools in the stream, but the water ran fast and clear over rocks in the middle.

"Get in the water and try not to break any ice," Parson whispered. He thought if they walked in the stream, they could make some distance without leaving tracks in the snow. He just hoped the creek was as shallow as it looked.

It was getting dark quickly now, and in the creek bed he could barely tell the moving water from the frozen. He felt stones rolling under his boots as he splashed through the riffles—then he stepped into a deeper section and nearly lost his balance. Parson felt the water soak him to his hips. He gasped as the cold closed on him like a vise.

He slogged through the deep pool, shivering. He stepped up onto a gravel bar where the water ran shallow again. As he waited for Gold and the old man to catch up, Parson reached into his pack for a set of night-vision goggles. He flipped the little silver switch and looked through the NVGs. Evening became full daylight, as if viewed through dark green sunglasses.

Parson studied the terrain and did not see any pursuers. The stream wandered through a narrow valley, and he feared that if he followed the creek too long he'd come to a village. Hypothermia was setting in, and he tried to force his hand to stop shaking and steady the NVGs. He saw that the center of the stream ran ice-free for a few hundred yards. Above the stream and to the right, drifts enveloped the trunks of trees. In the pixels of the NVGs, snowflakes skittered down like green moths.

"Let's stay in the river just a little longer," Parson said. "Then we'll find a place to stop." He turned off the goggles and placed them inside his flight suit to keep the batteries warm.

The three staggered downstream in the last natural light, boots crunching over icy mud and creek-bed stones. Parson hoped whatever tracks they left would get washed away or covered by snowflakes he could no longer see falling. He stopped when he could distinguish nothing around him, no shape or form, nothing but the deep black of night in a country without electricity under a sky without moon or stars. He feared the next step might plunge him into an unseen pool deep enough to drown him, so again he looked through the NVGs.

The brook widened a little but still ran shallow. On either side of the water, the ground sloped upward, studded with boulders and pines. The wind had piled drifts against the rocks, and Parson sloshed out of the creek, pulling Gold and the mullah by the length of chain between them. He felt the chain pulsing with rhythmic tugs, and he realized both of them were shivering uncontrollably.

"Just hold him still," he whispered. "I'll get us out of the wind." The cold numbed his face, and he formed each word by force of will.

Parson selected the biggest boulder he could pick out, though in night-vision green he had trouble telling rock from snow. The big stone would form the back wall of the snow cave he wanted to build. He dropped to his knees and dug blindly in the drift that had formed against the boulder. That hurt his right wrist so much that he had to dig with his left hand alone until he finished hollowing out the cave. The effort soaked his cloth gloves, and twice he made fists inside the gloves to keep what little feeling remained in his fingers.

He found the second pair of NVGs in his pack, put them in Gold's hand, and said, "Look through these. Pull him inside."

Parson followed them in and sat cross-legged with his back to the entrance. He pulled at his wet gloves, and they peeled off inside out like reptilian skin. Then he felt in a coat pocket for his light.

Covering the lens with his hand, he thumbed on the flashlight. The grooves between his fingers lit up red, and he parted two fingers just enough to let out the narrowest shard of light. He saw Gold's face, eyes hollow, lips blue.

"If we don't get warm," she said, "we won't live through the night." Parson detected no panic, just a statement of fact. The mullah stared at the ground. Probably hoping for martyrdom, thought Parson, and he's not far from it.

Parson opened his pack and buried the flashlight in it. In the glow, he found his wad of handwarmers. He tore the cellophane wrapping from several of them and handed the charcoal packets to Gold.

"Put these under your pants legs and anywhere else your clothes are wet," he said. "Don't let them burn you."

He opened several more and placed them under the mullah's soaked prison overalls. He put others under the prisoner's coat. The mullah glared at him silently.

Parson saved the last few for himself. The packets heated with exposure to air, and when they touched his skin, he realized this was a poor solution. The handwarmers might keep his core temperature high enough to stave off death, but they did nothing to dry wet clothes. Just a recalibration of misery, keeping Parson and his charges barely this side of the grave. He clicked off the light and rubbed his legs.

"I never should have left them," Parson said. "They're probably dead by now."

"You had to decide quickly," Gold said, her voice now disembodied by the blackest darkness Parson had ever seen. Like a conversation with God, if you believed in God and He was a She.

"With all of us shooting, we might have fought them off," Parson said.

"You can't second-guess yourself now," Gold said. She paused a moment. "Civilians pay us to make decisions they can't handle."

Civilians pay me to fly, thought Parson. Two hours ago, I was in my world. I should be up there somewhere, warm and sipping coffee at twenty-seven thousand feet. When we got shot down, what if I'd been scanning out a window instead of sitting in my seat? Could I have seen the missile before the sensors picked it up? Could I have called a break in time for Fisher to out-turn that fucking SA-7?

In the Air Force survival school, they'd told him despair comes first after a shootdown. A few pounds of propellant and high explosive have taken you from your environment to the enemy's,

and the realization hits hard. But this went beyond Parson's imagination. Evading the enemy on your own was bad enough. No one
had ever said anything about carrying him with you.

More than a decade had passed since Parson completed the
Survival, Evasion, Resistance, and Escape course. In what amounted
to a final exam, he hid from his pursuers/instructors during an
evasion exercise in Washington State's Colville National Forest.
Deep in a thicket, covered with leaves, camo paint on his face, he
smiled when he heard Southern and Midwestern accents shouting,
"We find you soon, American pig!" But they didn't. As a country
boy, he felt as comfortable in the woods as his SERE instructors.
However, that had been the Pacific Northwest, not the damned
Hindu Kush. And there, the weapons fired blanks.

Parson's shivering eased some, and he began digging away the
snow on the ground just inside the entrance. He piled snow to
close the cave's opening down to a narrow slit. Moving the snow
also served another purpose—by digging a second, slightly lower
layer of floor, he created a sump for the coldest air. Once, when
he was seventeen, a surprise blizzard caught him miles from his
family's Colorado ranch while he hunted elk. He dug as his father
had taught him. When the deputies found him walking out of the
trees the next day, his Winchester slung over his shoulder, they
told him they hadn't expected to find anyone alive.

"Anybody spent last night on top of the snow," the sheriff had
said, "we'd have carried them out frozen in the position they died."

Gold's voice brought Parson back to the war.

"Can we take the gag off him?" she asked.

"Yeah, tell him we'll let him drink some water and sleep without the gag," Parson said, "but if he speaks above a whisper, it goes
back on."

Gold clicked on her own light, shading it with her glove. She spoke to the mullah as Parson unknotted the gag. When the handkerchief came away, the man exhaled hard and worked his jaw and chin. Then he began speaking softly.

"He says the lions of jihad clawed you from the sky, and Allah sent a mighty storm to ground all your aircraft," Gold said.

"So he fancies himself a poet?" Parson said.

"He probably does. The Pashtuns love to recite poetry and tell each other stories."

"Well, good for them." Parson wasn't interested. Gold seemed to want him to know there was more to Islam than terror. He knew she was right, but cold and pain and anger made it hard to care.

Parson handed Gold a water bottle from his pack and pulled out his NVGs again. He looked through the slit he'd left open as an air vent. He saw nothing moving but snowflakes seemingly energized and pulsating in the electronic image of the goggles. The trees and rocks and stream appeared as varying shades of green, the world viewed through a glass of absinthe.

He'd either lost his pursuers or he hadn't, simple as that. He could go no farther tonight. And if he hadn't lost them, they'd probably kill him and Gold within the hour. He'd have to work with stealth and wits, since his circumstances sure as hell denied him speed. And all because of whatever was in this old man's head. Parson remembered how the intelligence officer at the mission brief had been vague about why the mullah was so important. The intel guy said only that the old man's followers would do anything he said, and he had some pretty scary ideas.

Parson thought he heard voices. It was just the creek's gurgling, water whispering in the gliding vowels of Pashto as it purled into eddies and pools. Calm down, he told himself.

At the edge of his field of view he caught some flicker through the trees, then another and another. His pulse rose. The movement came nearer, and he saw the beam of a flashlight sweeping right and left. Parson held his breath. He wanted to signal Gold to keep the mullah quiet, but he didn't dare so much as blink. Better the prisoner not know, anyway.

Two men. No, three. Four, five, six. Parson held faint hope they were coalition until he saw the ragged clothes and AK-47s. Some wore the flat-topped Chitrali cap seen everywhere in Afghanistan, and others wore what Parson took to be Taliban turbans. Black ones, he guessed. In night vision, everything was green. And that damned flashlight was not a good sign. Either this area was so securely Taliban that they didn't need to be careful, or they wanted their mullah bad enough to take crazy chances.

One carried something that didn't look like an AK. The man walked more slowly than the others, emerged last from the emerald gloom. He stepped deliberately, seemingly intent on a different task. As he drew nearer, Parson recognized his weapon. A Russian-built Dragunov sniper rifle topped with a PSO-1 scope. In the right hands, that thing could place a 7.62-millimeter bullet within a five-inch circle out to a thousand yards.

Parson hoped to hell that guy didn't know how to use such a weapon. But the Taliban wouldn't waste a rifle like that on any moron. Based on what he had seen in the news, those bastards usually killed cruelly, publicly stoning people for various offenses, or mortaring whole villages deemed insufficiently pious, raking survivors with automatic fire. Death by long-range precision represented a new level of artistry.

Parson could find no advantage in his situation, even though he saw the insurgents and they didn't see him. The element of surprise would disappear with the first shot from his pistol, and then there would still be five or six AKs against his handgun and Gold's M-4. No winning that firefight.

The mullah coughed. Parson silently cursed him and all his tribe and all his religion. But the guerrillas wandered past, the noise absorbed by the snow walls and the distance. Parson sighed slowly, not wanting even his breath visible.

After a time, he turned away from the air vent.

"An insurgent patrol just came by," he whispered. "Maybe a half dozen of them."

Gold nodded, didn't seem surprised.

"If you want to sleep," Parson added, "I'll take the first watch."

Gold leaned against the stone slab that made one wall of their sanctuary, and she passed her rifle to Parson. The mullah slept in a fetal position. Parson touched the prisoner's back, not out of sympathy but to check for shivering. No movement, and that was good. Didn't want to lose him to hypothermia. Parson felt the snow cave getting warmer with body heat.

He continued scanning outside, saw nothing but snow coming down as though it always had and always would. The red low-battery light began blinking, so Parson turned off the goggles. He decided not to flip the power switch the other direction and use the backup battery. No telling when and how often he'd need these again. Instead he decided to call home.

Again working by shaded flashlight, he turned on his GPS receiver. The screen read ACQUIRING SATELLITES for several minutes, then displayed his position, not by his present coordinates but in relation to a fixed, secret reference point. Parson could transmit that in the clear and still not give away his position to the wrong people.

He plugged in the earpiece to his radio and rolled the thumb-wheel switch. Static fried in his left ear as he extended the antenna.

"Bookshelf, Flash Two-Four Charlie," he whispered. No answer. He called again, and they heard him this time.

"Flash Two-Four Charlie, Bookshelf. Have you weak but readable. Go ahead."

Parson gave his location and asked, "Advise status of search-and-rescue."

"Bagram weather is zero-zero and they can't launch helos. Meteorology advises this front has turned stationary, so we don't know how long it will be. Buddy, I wish I had better news."

Parson ground his teeth. "Tell Bagram command post I have my cargo intact," he said.

"Copy that. Anything else we can do for you?"

"Have you had any other calls from Flash Two-Four?"

"Negative."

Parson turned off the radio, closed his eyes. Never should have let Fisher make me do this, he thought. We'd have beaten the enemy or died together. You don't leave your comrades.

Much of the night passed in silence until Gold nudged him. "I'm not really sleeping," she said. "Want me to take watch for a while?"

Gold unlocked her end of the chain and fastened it on Parson's good wrist. They traded places, bumping into each other's limbs and gear. Parson made sure Gold still had the night-vision goggles he gave her, and he told her to use them sparingly. Then he leaned against the stone and tried to rest.

He fell asleep immediately, but not for long. The pain in his wrist woke him whenever he moved his hand. Sleep came in inter-mittent moments instead of hours, and Parson's waking thoughts and fears mingled with dreams and nightmares. Through both sleep and wakefulness, the stream outside spoke to him in a lan-guage he could not understand. Its currents murmured of wars long past and wars ongoing. You're hallucinating, Parson thought, still listening to the water.

CHAPTER THREE

Parson hovered in the murky consciousness between sleep and waking, the logical part of him trying to separate nightmare from reality. You will wake from this and go have an omelet, some corner of his mind reasoned. Then he came to full awareness, as if rising from the bottom of a pool. He opened his eyes to the gray light of the snow cave and inhaled air stale with body odor. For a moment he fought panic. You're an officer of the United States Air Force, he told himself. Deal with it. Deal. He worked the fingers of his right hand, and the cracked wrist still burned.

The mullah sat cross-legged, chained to Gold. He spooned food from a brown packet marked: BEEF STROGANOFF.

"Hope you don't mind me going into your pack," Gold said. Her voice had a resin in it, either from cold or fatigue, though she sounded better than last night. Parson thought she might have been attractive in more normal circumstances, but even before the crash she'd seemed all mission: shoulder-length hair tied tight, no makeup, no nail polish. No tattoo that Parson could see. Eyes deep gray as a whetstone.

"Can't let him starve," Parson said, "but I'd have given him the pork."

He looked outside and saw only a few light flakes falling. But in the distance, veils of snow trailed from looming clouds the color of a deep bruise. He considered whether to move or stay put. Neither held much to recommend it. He knew the insurgents were looking for him in the immediate area. But any movement would leave tracks and make the three of them easier to see.

The shivering tipped Parson's mind toward moving. He had no more handwarmers, and his wet clothes still clung to his limbs, sapping away heat. Gold and the mullah could be no better off. Parson decided they had to find better shelter somehow. Probable death by gunshot versus certain death by cold.

He unfolded a tactical pilotage chart and marked his location by creasing the map with a thumbnail. No dots of towns appeared anywhere nearby—just the curving contour lines of rising terrain, along with the notation "Numerous Scattered Villages." The map told him little of use. It was meant for fliers moving five or six miles a minute, not foot soldiers slogging through snow.

Parson wanted to find an abandoned village. He'd seen enough of them from the air, the tic-tac-toe patterns of roofless mud walls where mortars or Katyusha rockets had exploded. The ruins stood as silent, shrapnel-scarred witnesses to hardscrabble lives cut short in places that did not even merit a name on an American map. Parson needed just one roof, or part of a roof still intact, to get out of the weather and wait for the clouds to lift.

Peering out, Parson watched and listened for any sign of pursuers. He saw no one, so he kicked away the snow from the entrance and crawled outside. He looked around and saw nothing moving but snowflakes, swirling fog, and stream water flowing clear as vodka. By the creek, he found what he needed.

The limbs of a leafless shrub reached over the water like a claw. Using his left hand, Parson broke away some branches and shook off the snow. Then he sat by the cave entrance, drew his boot knife, and shaved away twigs and bark until he had two smooth sticks as big around as his fingers and about ten inches long. He rummaged through his pack for a first-aid kit, unzipped it, unrolled a bandage. Holding the cloth with his teeth, he cut off a three-foot strip. Parson tried to wrap the sticks over his injured wrist, then realized he didn't have enough hands.

"Gold, can you help me?" he asked.

The sergeant spoke softly in Pashto, and she and the mullah emerged from the snow cave.

"I need to splint my wrist," Parson said.

Gold admired the splint sticks he'd improvised and said, "I'd have done this for you." She wrapped a layer of bandage over his wrist and forearm, then arranged a stick on top of his arm and a stick underneath, leaving his fingers and thumb free to move. Gold wrapped more cloth over the sticks and secured the splint with medical tape.

"Good work," Parson whispered. "Let's go. We'll try to stay in the trees. If we run into villagers, we'll just have to take our chances."

"Charlie Mike," Gold said.

"How's that?"

"Army talk. CM, for continue mission."

"You got it," Parson said, trying to sound better than he felt. He realized this soldier Gold was, professionally, a distant cousin. The Army and the Air Force had different cultures and lingo. However, as a C-130 crewman he'd had more contact with the Army than most blue-suiters. He had air-dropped many loads of paratroopers in exercises, and he admired their warrior spirit. Sometimes on the run-in, doors open, red light standing by for green light, he'd heard them psyching themselves, chanting and growling. Nowadays it wasn't unusual for a load of about sixty airborne troops to have one or two women. They weren't infantry; they were admin, medical, or interpreters. But they were all part of the airborne division. And he noticed Gold wore jump wings.

He took his handkerchief from his pocket, still wet with the prisoner's spit.

"Tell him to open his mouth again," Parson said.

The mullah obeyed, and Parson tied the gag, this time not so roughly.

"He seems cooperative today," Gold said.

"Wonder why?"

"Maybe *inshallah*. Whatever happens is the will of God. Or maybe he thinks what we're trying to do is hopeless."

Or maybe he's seen enough of his own captives made to suffer, thought Parson, that he knows he doesn't want to be on the receiving end.

Parson took a compass bearing, surveyed his surroundings. Tendrils of mist ghosted through the trees, branches laden with snow. He heard nothing but his own breathing and the faint clink of chains as Gold and the prisoner moved. Well, navigator, he said to himself, find your way.

He walked uphill from the stream, hoping to disappear into woods and underbrush. Boulevards of pines provided some cover, but little other vegetation grew in the crumbling shingle rock beneath the snow. When the three had gained some elevation above the creek, Parson looked back on where they had spent the night. He felt relieved to see that the snow cave did not stand out at all, though the tracks leading from it were pretty apparent. But the placement of other tracks across the stream unnerved him. The insurgents he'd seen through his night-vision goggles had come a lot closer than he'd realized. *Inshallah.*

The three continued up the rise until it flattened into a narrow plateau. The pines gave way to terraced fields now left to nature, planted in what Parson guessed were apricot or mulberry trees. Survival instructors had briefed him about food sources in country, but most of those sources came in summer. The old fruit trees stood bare like ranks of skeletons, broken branches glazed with ice. Parson could hardly imagine them ever sprouting leaves and bearing fruit. This Afghan winter seemed permanent, designed to extinguish life in all its forms.

The heavier snow he'd seen in the distance advanced across the valley and began showering the orchard. The flakes blurred the vista across the fields, and it seemed to Parson as if he were looking through gauze. He avoided the open mulberry grove and kept to the woods. The pines gave way to junipers at the edge of the field, and the junipers grew in stands closer together and provided better concealment. Parson headed northeast, roughly back toward Bagram. He held little hope of walking that far, but he thought it made sense to go in the direction of a big American base. The nearer they got to it, the more likely they'd run into friendlies.

After a time they stopped to catch their breath and let the mullah rest. It was snowing so hard now that the flakes made a hissing sound as they sheeted against Parson's coat. He leaned against a poplar and looked through the binoculars. At the edge of visibility through the snow and fog, he saw a large, dark mass, something clearly out of place. He rolled the binoculars' focus knob with his middle finger, but he still could not identify the thing. He turned to Gold and placed an index finger to his lips, then pointed two fingers to his eyes, then gestured toward the object.

They kneeled in the cover of the evergreens, and Parson watched the black shape from less than a hundred yards away. He worried that it was a Taliban truck or maybe a mobile rocket launcher. Parson passed the binoculars to Gold. She raised them to her eyes for a full minute, then handed them back and shrugged.

Silently, Parson mouthed, "Stay here," and Gold nodded. He drew his Beretta from his survival vest. His right hand still hurt and the splint felt awkward, so he held his pistol with both hands as he crept forward. The weapon could fire double action, one trigger pull both cocking the hammer and firing at a stroke. Still, Parson clicked back the hammer with his thumb, to fire a tenth of an instant faster.

Whenever he gained ten feet or so, he hid behind trees or drifts and scanned the object and the woods. The shape lay in a clearing that seemed part of a disused road, or more like a goat path. Eventually the object materialized as a T-72, a Soviet tank left rusting for more than two decades. One of its tracks had been blown off, the metal links tangled like some fossilized reptile frozen at the moment of violent death. Parson stood and motioned with his arm. Gold pulled the mullah along, and she held her M-4 pointed up at a ready angle, her index finger inside the trigger guard.

They caught up with Parson, and Gold loosened the prisoner's gag to give him water. The mullah mumbled something in Pashto.

"He says his people defeated the Russians with American weapons, and now they will defeat Americans with Russian weapons," Gold said.

"Tell him to go to hell," Parson said, as he uncocked and holstered his pistol. He imagined what must have happened to the tank and its crew. He had seen an old videotape taken by the mujahideen, the good guys then, as they ambushed a Russian truck on a road like this. Dust flew from under the vehicle as a land mine exploded and the truck jerked to a stop. A voice off-screen, perhaps the cameraman himself, shouted, *"Allah-hu akbar!"* Then the quick thumps of AK-47 fire. The picture shook as the cameraman ran forward. For a moment, a close-up of dirt and rocks became visible, maybe the camera held at the operator's side. The final image showed a Soviet soldier crawling in a ditch, dirty and stubble-cheeked, eyes wide, one hand raised against the inevitable.

Parson approached the tank cautiously, wondering what to do. It might contain something he could use. It might also be booby-trapped. He saw no footprints in the snow, however, so nobody had gone near it recently. Not necessarily the kind of thing you'd booby-trap, anyway. Screw it, he decided.

He stepped up on the broken track and wiped snow from the lid of a toolbox mounted on the outside of the tank. Beneath the snow, he uncovered a layer of rust that caked on his glove. He raised the lid and found wrenches, a hammer, a screwdriver, nuts, and washers, some of which lay encased in ice at the bottom of the toolbox. He also found a roll of cord, synthetic line much like American 550 parachute cord. Parson put the roll in his coat pocket, hoping the rope wasn't too rotted.

He crawled atop the tank, peered through an open hatch. He saw a tattered seat cushion and unfamiliar controls, two tillers like antique farm equipment, all dusted with snow. A metal data plate on the panel carried a serial number and some writing in Cyrillic. Parson recognized none of it except CCCP. A rod of some sort rested at an angle against a seat back. On closer inspection, Parson realized that its white color came not just from powdery snow. The thing was a bone, a femur. Parson saw no other remains, and he guessed animals had scattered the rest.

He jumped down from the tank, rubbed his hands together to brush away the rust.

"That was stupid, sir," Gold said.

"Probably."

They crossed the path, ducked under juniper boughs as Parson led deeper into the forest. The wall of a steep slope stretched in front of him, but the only way to easier walking led to sparser woods where they might be seen. He kept to the sharp grade, stopping every few yards to let Gold and the prisoner catch up. He wanted badly to take off his flak jacket. The extra weight bore down on him and made him feel claustrophobic. But he'd heard too many stories of flak jackets discarded by people now in wheelchairs.

The snowflakes hardened into sleet, though the overstory of evergreen shielded Parson, Gold, and the mullah from the worst of it. Now that he walked under the trees, only rarely did Parson feel ice stinging his face, but when he did, it burned like birdshot fired from a twelve-gauge. They kneeled under an ancient Himalayan yew, its lowest branches forming a tree well that concealed them entirely. The black trunk glistened, laminated by ice. Gold shivered, and the old man looked at the ground.

"How's he doing?" Parson asked.

"Better than I thought," Gold said. "He's been walking these mountains all his life. But he can't do it all day."

"We'll stop when I find some shelter."

"Heaven help us if it's the wrong village."

"I know. What kind of reception do you think we'll find around here?" Parson asked.

"Tough to say. There are some hard-core Taliban in this province, but maybe they've made some enemies. And what makes things even harder to predict is that allegiances tend to go on sale in Afghanistan."

Parson considered whether he should just build a fire outside. He decided that might not get them dry, and it would attract attention. And when it did, he figured, we'd be right back to the coin toss of local loyalties. He felt relatively safe for the moment, though.

The yew hid them so well that Parson decided to take advantage of it.

"We can rest here," he said.

Parson glassed the mountainside with his binoculars, but he couldn't see far and he liked it that way. Good cover for now. No sign of another human being. The mist made it hard to tell, but he thought the rise leveled out just above him. He'd grown up in the Rockies and he believed he had a sense of terrain. He remembered a thousand moments alone on a ridge with a .270 and his spotting scope, the gray rocks under his boots, the cold air in his lungs, and the blue sky clear and pure as eternity.

The contrast with now made him so homesick it moistened his eyes, but the similarities gave him strength. He looked at the mullah. I'm a mountain man, too, hajji. You have no idea who the fuck you're dealing with.

Parson watched his breath drift through the air like smoke signals as he exhaled rhythmically. He'd hoped the hiding place might trap a little warmth, but he felt no relief from the cold. He pulled off his gloves, examined his hands. The reddened skin stretched tight across the pads of his fingers, which had no feeling at all. No frostbite yet, but he worried about it. He'd heard stories of people pulling off their gloves and leaving their fingertips inside.

He put his hands in his coat, under his armpits. They felt like blocks of ice against his body. Parson looked at his gloves now draped across his knee. He considered cutting off the right glove's index finger to better feel for his pistol's trigger. No, he thought. If I do that, I'll lose that finger. He put his gloves back on and looked at Gold and the mullah.

"You can hitch him to me for a while if you're tired," Parson said.

"I'll take the pack," Gold said. She unlocked the cuff on her wrist.

They crawled from under the yew boughs, white dusting on their knees and shins. The rise turned nearly to a sheer cliff, but when Parson topped it, he found that his instincts were correct. The land smoothed into a clearing grown over in brown grass about knee high, like the broomsedge back home. The grass stems stuck up through the snow like long whiskers. At the far edge of the clearing, Parson saw a building obviously not put up by tribesmen.

Corrugated metal lined the shack, and its steel door stood open and twisted from the frame, hanging by only the top hinge. A stovepipe rose from the flat roof, edges softened by a coating of snow.

Parson inspected the structure through binoculars. Built by the Russians, he figured. Maybe a Spetsnaz camp at one time. God, I hope that stove works.

He pointed to the shack as Gold joined him.

"Let's just watch it for a while," he said.

Gold whispered one word: "Mines."

Good point, Parson thought. Soviet special forces troops almost certainly would have protected some of the approaches by burying land mines, and they'd never been too particular about removing them. Plenty of Afghan kids with missing feet could tell you that. Still, he tallied the odds a little better than just walking up, with zero intel, to the first village he found.

Parson shivered as he surveyed the old campsite. He pondered whether to use the woodstove if it remained, since the smoke might draw notice. Then he thought, Just use it after dark, dumbass. He figured the cold was affecting his mind if it took him that long to think of the obvious.

He eyed the tree line around the clearing. Fog obscured the tops of the trees, and Parson imagined their trunks rising forever. The wind had calmed now, and it was so quiet he heard the swish of a pine needle cluster as it fell from above him and impaled itself in a drift.

In the corner of his eye he saw movement at the far end of the clearing. A low bough sprang back from something that had moved it, releasing a shower of dry, crystalline snowflakes like pulverized glass. Parson drew his handgun and lowered his head, trying to disappear into the sedge. He pulled the mullah flat to the ground. Gold thumbed the safety on her rifle.

Through the grass stalks, Parson saw a patch of dun-colored fur. It's over, he thought. Can't run from insurgents on horseback. I'll shoot the prisoner like I should have done yesterday, and then I'll take as many of them with me as I can.

Then a strange animal stepped into the clearing, alone and riderless. Parson stopped his thoughts of killing and dying, and he tried to think of the word for that thing. Yeah, ibex. Asian mountain goat. Curved horns curled back over the creature's shoulders, and its black nose emitted twin plumes of mist when it exhaled.

Good left shoulder shot from here, thought Parson. Could take him down like a mule deer or a Dall sheep. Nah. I wouldn't hurt that ibex. Besides, the shot would draw attention.

The animal sniffed the air, then lowered its head and pulled a mouthful of brown grass. Parson regarded it through binoculars. Thicker fur at the base of its neck, a point of ice at the end of each hair. It stared in Parson's direction and munched as if in deep thought, ears twitching. Then it looked away and resumed feeding. The ibex grazed across the clearing and nothing startled it, so Parson felt safe enough to move.

He unlocked the chain attaching him to the prisoner and handed the cuff to Gold. Then he pulled the radio from his survival vest and gave that to her as well. She frowned like she didn't understand.

"We don't need this radio getting blown up," Parson whispered. "Stay behind me and try to walk where I walk. If I find a mine, just backtrack and get out of here."

Gold shook her head.

"Yes," Parson said. He raised his eyebrows: This is not a suggestion, Sergeant.

Bent at the waist, he crept through the junipers and pines at the clearing's edge, taking an arcing path toward the shack. The evergreen smell made him think of childhood Christmases. If it's the last thing I smell, maybe except explosives, that's all right, he thought. A small mercy.

Parson stepped around a tangle of razor wire, a tuft of snow gracing each blade. He nicked his thigh in the man-made thicket of thorns, and a spot of blood appeared around the rip in his flight suit. That figured. A little gift from the Russians. Why the fuck did they want this place to start with?

He glanced behind him and saw Gold and the mullah keeping their distance, well clear of the kill radius of any mine he might detonate. The tree line took him within fifty feet of the shack, and Parson let out a long breath. Made it, he realized. They'd have put mines farther out than this. Nothing left to do now but take a look.

He pulled his Beretta and cocked it, and he tromped to the door, snow crunching as he made deep bootprints. Parson entered the cabin gun first, sweeping the barrel across the room as he watched for movement. He saw little in the dark shack until his eyes adjusted, and he figured he might as well have kept his pistol holstered. Anybody in here, he thought, would have drilled you before you got two steps inside.

A cast-iron stove sat in the center of the room, its pipe extending to the ceiling. Steel bunk frames along the walls, sleeping places for eight troops. Only two contained mattresses, and they smelled of mold. Wooden ammunition boxes with Cyrillic lettering lay scattered across the concrete floor. A metal cook pot rested upside down on a table. Another door at the back of the cabin, fully closed. Two steel chairs between the bunks. Everything gone to rust and rot.

He leaned outside and gestured to Gold with a thumbs-up. When she led the prisoner inside several minutes later, she said, "Looks like a bunch of men have been living here." She unlocked her end of the chain, closed the cuff around the steel crossbar of the bunk nearest the stove, locking the prisoner to the bed frame. She put down the pack and leaned her rifle against the table. The mullah kneeled on the floor and began to pray, the gag muffling his words.

Parson wondered about the soldiers who had lived here. If they really were Spetsnaz, they'd have been bright, thoroughly trained, and politically reliable. How had they suffered? Did they make it home? They'd served a misguided government that had done some awful things, but he found it hard to despise them. Yeah, some committed atrocities, but most were like me, he thought, professionals trying to complete a mission.

The cold war had come before his time, but he remembered his late father's stories about flying as a navigator and weapons systems officer in F-4s. The Phantoms screaming off the runway at Eielson, twin spikes of flame from the afterburners. Climbing through the thin air to meet the Bear bomber. Rocking the wings and waving to the tail gunner. Okay, Ivan, you've made your point. Now turn that thing around before I send you into the Arctic Ocean in pieces. Let's not do this again real soon. Fly safe, boys.

His dad once quoted some line from Yeats: "Those that I fight I do not hate."

Unlike that motherfucker on the floor.

CHAPTER FOUR

Parson hoped they could stay in the shack until the weather lifted, but he knew they couldn't count on it. Might as well make the most of it while we can, he thought. He looked around and found a dull ax. Its handle was splintered along the grain, ending in a sharp wooden point like some nasty prehistoric weapon.

"Keep a lookout, will you?" Parson said. "I'll make some kindling and then light a fire when it gets dark." He placed rags over the single, cracked window.

Gold lay prone on the floor in the doorway's shadow, leaving little visible to the outside but the barrel of her rifle. The tip of the barrel danced as she shivered.

Parson took the ax in his good hand, held it near the head. He swung it into an empty ammunition box, and the slats split with a sharp cracking sound. Thin nails held the slats together, and Parson pulled and twisted the slats apart until the box became a stack of firewood. Any torque on his right wrist produced a stab of pain, so he began holding down the slats with his foot and working them apart with his left hand. He chopped up four other boxes, creating a three-foot pile of kindling. Then he pulled off his gloves and picked at a splinter that had gone through the fabric, deep in the heel of his good hand. Now both hands hurt.

He opened his pack and saw that all the water bottles were empty. That gave him another problem to solve. He emptied his pack and took it to the door.

"All clear?" he asked.

"Yes, sir," Gold said. "What are you doing?"

"We're out of water."

Parson stepped outside, scooped the backpack into a drift, filled the pack with snow. Then he hung it from a bunk frame and placed the old cook pot underneath it. The pot contained some kind of residue, but he had no better container. He searched the pockets of his survival vest until he found a small pillbox. He shook out two water-purification tablets, his red fingers fumbling, numbed by the cold. Dropped the tablets into the pot, faint clinks as they landed. Parson thought about putting some of the snow in his mouth, but he knew that could lower his core temperature.

In another pocket he found waterproof matches, and he wanted very badly to light the stove right now. Wait, he told himself. Don't get yourself killed with impatience. Think. He could remember nothing, not a fine car, not a beautiful woman, not one thing that had tempted him like those matches and that kindling.

He pulled at the woodstove's handle, but the grate would not budge. He turned the handle the other way. Still nothing. He picked up the ax and hammered the flat of the blade against the stove handle, and the grate clanged open. The mullah startled at the sound, then resumed looking out the door as if waiting for salvation.

Gray ash spilled from the firebox, powder fine as graphite. Some drifted in the air and put Parson in mind of a genie released from a lamp. He didn't bother to empty the ash pan, and he placed several sticks of kindling in the stove, stacked them at angles to each other for quicker burning. Took out his matches and stared at them for a moment, then set them by his woodpile. Parson decided another task might keep his mind off the cold, so he turned on his radio.

"Bookshelf, Flash Two-Four Charlie," he called.

No answer.

"Bookshelf, Flash Two-Four Charlie."

A British accent answered him: "Flash Two-Four Charlie, Saxon. Go ahead."

So the Royal Air Force was on station. Probably took off from Kyrgyzstan or as far away as Oman. Parson imagined the Nimrod jet orbiting in the stratosphere above him, the blizzard that trapped him just a cottony undercast to the RAF crew.

"Saxon, Flash Two-Four Charlie. Have you been briefed on my status?"

"Affirmative, mate. Search-and-rescue on alert for you at Bagram and Kandahar. Both aerodromes still fogged in."

Parson fought an urge to fling his radio into the wall. He walked in a circle, cursing, then took a deep breath. "Stand by to copy my position," he said. Parson turned on his GPS and gave them his new coordinates. Then he asked, "Can you advise on position of friendlies in my vicinity?"

"We can. Stand by for authentication." Then, after a pause: "Flash Two-Four Charlie, what's the sum of the first two digits of your authenticator number?"

"Five," Parson called. Do I sound like a fucking raghead to you, Nigel?

"Copy that. Right, then. You have enemy force movement reported to your west and southwest. There is an ANA unit operating to your east, but they're not in communication with us."

Great, thought Parson. This province is filthy with Taliban, which I already knew. And somewhere in Asia there's the Afghan National Army without a radio.

"Flash Two-Four Charlie copies all," he said. Parson turned off the set, stuffed it back into his survival vest.

He wondered if he'd ever feel warm and dry again. There was still a little too much daylight for him to start the fire. But once it got dark, even insurgents with night vision would have trouble seeing the smoke, since the goggles would have so little ambient light to amplify. The bad guys could still smell, but he could do nothing about that.

The gray outside deepened, and night began to gather at the bases of the trees. The darkness seemed to creep up from the ground. Parson took from his survival vest some fire starter of his own making: cotton balls soaked in Vaseline. Never expected to use these, he thought as he placed the oily cotton under the kindling.

When blackness at last submerged the highest branches, Parson lit a match. The yellow flame flared out like wings, hissing as it consumed the chemicals at the tip. Parson felt the heat on his face. His cold fingers shook, and the flame jittered like an injured firefly as he tossed the match into the stove. The fire leaped into the cotton and embraced it, white strands going black and curling in the orange glow. Runnels of flame illuminated the lettering on one piece of wood, and Parson saw the numerals "7.62" until the fire obliterated them.

The heat infused Parson's flesh like a narcotic, and for a moment he thought paradise itself, if there were such a thing, might consist purely of warmth.

The mullah held out his hands toward the stove. Parson watched him. Do you expect seventy-two virgins for all the hurt you've caused—in the name of God, no less? Why should this fire comfort you the same as me? Parson wondered. Only because my mission requires me to keep you alive.

He needed Gold alive, too. "Sergeant," he said, "why don't you let me take watch for a while? Get dried off over here."

Gold stood up immediately, walked to the stove, handed Parson her rifle. She closed her eyes and inhaled deeply as she removed her soggy gloves and spread her fingers.

Two steps placed Parson back in frigid agony. He weighed whether to stay in the heat, to hell with keeping watch. No, no, no, he said to himself, keep your wits, you idiot. That's just the cold and exhaustion talking.

He sat on the floor where Gold had lain, and he turned on his night-vision goggles, using the backup battery. Green snowflakes floated into an emerald clearing. Parson heard nothing but the crackle of fire and the shuffle of wood as it burned and shifted. The stovepipe didn't draw well, and smoke hung in the room and burned Parson's eyes a bit. He got up and pulled the back door halfway open for ventilation, then resumed his watch at the front.

Gold moved two chairs near the stove. She placed her coat across the back of one of them, and she used it as a screen as she unbuckled her belt and pulled down her trousers. White long johns underneath. The mullah tried to mumble in Pashto through his gag.

"Oh, be quiet," Gold said. She tied her coat around her waist and placed the wet trousers across the chair to dry.

The snow in the backpack began to melt, and Parson felt a moment of satisfaction when he heard the dripping of his make-shift water generator. Gold opened a meal and placed a food pouch inside its heating packet. When the cook pot had collected a few inches of water, she poured some into the heating packet to activate it. A few minutes later, she handed Parson a pouch of boneless pork ribs so hot it burned his tongue.

He hadn't realized how hungry he was until he took the first bite, and then he could not stop himself from eating despite the burns. He scanned the clearing and forest, licking his fingers. Gold brought him a water bottle dipped from the cook pot, and he took a long drink. The water tasted of metal and medicine. Awful, Parson thought, but at least the tablets will make sure we don't get giardia or something.

Parson watched Gold eat as greedily as he had, devouring a pouch of banana bread and collecting crumbs from her shirt by dabbing at them with a fingertip. He realized that after these MREs they'd have nothing left but what they could scavenge. Pine needles and twigs. Survivor salad.

Gold untied the prisoner's gag and gave him crackers and

water. Parson listened to them speaking in Pashto, and he wondered what they could be chattering about.

"He says he won't undress in front of infidels," Gold said. "He sure won't in front of me."

"That's all right," Parson said. "If he sits there long enough, he'll get dry. Just hang his coat up near the fire and tell him to take off his boots and socks."

More chatter in Pashto.

"He won't take off his boots," Gold said. "These guys don't like any kind of nakedness in front of strangers."

"I don't want to drag his ass after he gets trench foot," Parson said. "Tell him to dry his damn socks or I'll give him another manicure."

Gold spoke to the prisoner again. The mullah removed his boots and slapped his wet socks over the bed frame where he was chained. Then Gold untied her hair and brushed it out with her fingers. When she opened the stove to add kindling, her locks shone in the firelight like the copper on a jacketed bullet. Parson felt almost sad when she closed the grate and retied her hair. Then he reminded himself to look outside and not inside.

Parson's wrist throbbed as he kept watch. He wished he could see farther through the snow and fog, but not even NVGs could penetrate deep into that darkness. The murky shapes of mountains loomed like great ships convoying through an ocean of night, and it seemed to him that everything he'd ever feared lay just beyond the edge of visibility.

The mullah spoke again, several words enunciated clearly, as though he wanted to make sure Gold understood.

"What is it now?" Parson asked.

"He says this storm is the answer to his prayers."

"So he thinks he can conjure the weather?"

"There is such a thing as Islamic mysticism," Gold said, "but I couldn't tell you where he stands on that."

"Tell him I'm not superstitious."

Gold said nothing. After a time, her clothes dried and she redressed. She and Parson traded places again, and Parson stripped to his T-shirt and boxers, hung his clothes to dry. He added wood to the snapping fire, and at one point he looked at his watch and saw that he'd lost two hours while sleeping sitting up.

Parson found another empty ammo crate, and he began to take it apart with the ax, more carefully this time. He worked loose a slat, leaving it fairly intact. Then he held it by one end and split it with the ax blade, sheared off a stick about a foot and a half long. He chopped again and broke off another, then another. By repeating the effort, he sliced the box into a jumble of sticks, all roughly the same size.

"More kindling?" Gold asked.

"Nope."

Parson placed two sticks across each other and lashed them together with the cord he'd scrounged from the Russian tank. He added more sticks until he'd made a flat, crosshatched pattern.

"How long have you been an interpreter?" he asked as he tied a clove hitch.

"A long time," Gold said.

"Do you want to take a shower every time you talk to one of these guys?"

"Sometimes it's unnerving. Sometimes it's infuriating. And it's always sad."

"How can you stand it?"

"It's an education in human nature."

"You're not going to tell me we're all really alike, are you?"

"No. But they show us what people can turn into if they're taught a certain way."

Parson placed one of his boots on top of the stick frame, and he tied the boot to his creation.

"Ah," Gold said. "Snowshoes. I'm impressed, sir."

"Right out of the survival manual." Parson noticed the mullah watching him. "What is he looking at?"

"He thinks we're decadent sinners," Gold said. "He's probably surprised to see you coping."

Parson began to work on another improvised snowshoe. "So do these bastards really think they're going to heaven for suicide bombings and shit like that?" he asked.

"Some do," Gold said. "Some learned that stuff in madrassahs. Some are just confused kids. Some are criminals happy for an excuse to hurt people."

"What about him?"

"He's a true believer. Used to run the Ministry for Prevention of Vice and Promotion of Virtue."

"What's that?" Parson asked.

"You remember the religious police that beat up women for showing a lock of hair?" Gold said. "His boys."

"Very nice."

"His good eye is colder than his glass one."

Parson had a hard time imagining what motivated someone like the mullah. Or even someone like Gold, whose job was to understand these people. From the start of his career, nearly all his schooling had been technical. A degree in applied math. Training in aerodynamics, weather, physics. How to guide a plane from point A to point B. How to find your way with radio signals, satellite beams, or stars. How to make an airdrop hit the ground right where you want it. *Why* was up to the politicians.

Until now, Parson had not carried much anger as he'd flown his Afghanistan missions. It was just his job. But this felt like 9/11 all over again, only far more personal. And the man to blame was right in front of him.

He tried to think of something else, so he busied himself with his snowshoe project, made five and a half of them before running out of cord. He decided to take the half-finished one for himself.

When his clothes and flak vest had dried, he put them back on and took watch again. Gold stretched out on the floor by the stove and fell asleep immediately. The mullah snored. The noise irritated Parson, and he considered waking him to stop the snoring. But Parson let him rest so he'd have more strength when they had to walk again.

He stood the rifle on its stock and leaned his forehead against the hand guard. When his head drooped, he woke with a start, cursed himself for such carelessness. He had no idea how long he'd slept, but he saw that his breath had left a spray of frost on the M-4's receiver. White veins of rime decorated the gunmetal like fine engraving. In another time they'd have shot you for sleeping on watch, he told himself, and you'd have deserved it.

Parson turned on his goggles, looked carefully. He half expected to see a Taliban patrol he'd let sneak up on him. Maybe that wouldn't be so bad. To take a bullet in your sleep and not even know you'd left this world. How much worse could it be than this?

You have a job to do, he reminded himself. Whether God put you here for a reason, the Air Force sure as hell did.

He scanned again, watched the electro-green flickers of a war night. A swirl of fog around the trunks of the conifers seemed to hang there, and Parson watched what he thought must be his imagination. But the swirl remained still, then moved jerkily, then moved again like a solid object and like a man—a man walking, and the son of a bitch had an AK-47.

Three more figures emerged, and Parson felt his palms sweat. It will end for me here in this doorway, he thought. Stop it. Stop and think hard.

Two of the apparitions split from the other two and began circling around the clearing. Dear God, they're flanking me, Parson thought. They know where I am and I can't get them all. But they don't know I see them.

Parson realized all he could do was change the facts. I won't be where they think I am, he decided. He got up and prodded Gold.

"Listen," he whispered. "Four men are approaching from either side. I'm going out the back with your rifle. You take my sidearm. Anybody but me comes in the doorway, shoot them. I'll cough before I come back in."

Parson handed Gold his Beretta, and he slipped out the back door still in his bare feet. For the first few steps, the snow and ice stabbed like needles, then his feet went numb and felt nothing.

A wooded slope fell away from the back end of the shack, and Parson stumbled downhill in the first hint of gray dawn. At one point, he lost his footing and hooked his arm around a sapling, nearly dropped Gold's carbine. He feared that clumsy move had given him away. Then he thought, I'll know when they see me because they'll shoot. Parson circled around to the side of the clearing, climbed back up to where he had the campsite in full view. Then he took a knee, turned on his night-vision goggles.

There they were, two men creeping from the right toward the front of the shack. He could make out little detail in the NVGs, but their baggy clothes suggested insurgents rather than ANA. Beyond that he could tell little about what manner of enemy they were: Taliban or al Qaeda, Pashtun or Arab. He guessed they were of the same party he'd seen the first night, but even that was speculation. Nothing in their hands but their Kalashnikovs. Good. At least this pair didn't have night vision. They seemed intent on the shack, unaware of Parson watching them. He lowered the NVGs, tried to adjust his eyes to the dark shapes in what little natural light there was.

He placed his thumb on the M-4's safety and applied just enough pressure to feel the lever start to budge, easing the selector to the semiauto position without the usual click. Now the rifle would fire a round for each trigger pull, every shot an act of will. No sense wasting ammo by spray-and-pray.

Parson raised the weapon to his shoulder. The carbine had one of those new advanced optical sights. He watched the two figures through the scope, the dot reticle glowing red in the low light. Parson placed the dot of radioactive tritium across the first man's torso. He pressed the trigger.

The orange flash from the muzzle obscured his target momentarily, then the target was down. The shot scattered a flock of magpies from their roost. They squawked into the last of night, black rags twisting away through the trees. He swung the barrel onto the second man, fired two shots in quick succession, the recoil jolting his cheek. The insurgent dropped to the ground, moaning.

Shouts from the far side of the shack. Parson lay flat in the snow, waiting.

A man darted around the far corner of the shack and ran inside the front door before Parson could fire. Two shots exploded inside. Pistol rounds, he hoped. Please let that be Gold shooting.

Parson noticed movement in the corner of his eye. Someone approaching the shack's rear door. The guerrilla walked bent low, rifle held almost at arm's length. Long tunic with a military field jacket. British camo pattern. The insurgent swept his AK side to side in an arc as if it could illuminate all dangers.

Unseen, Parson had the luxury of a few seconds. He aimed through the M-4's sight and took his time placing the red dot directly on the man's forehead. The shot was so close he held a little low for bullet trajectory. Squeeze.

Red mist.

The guerrilla fell so hard and fast that Parson knew he'd made a clean head shot. Instant disconnect of the central nervous system. Parson shivered, yet a drop of sweat fell from the tip of his nose. In the dim light he saw his empty cartridge casings on top of the crusted snow, the hot brass melting little graves for themselves.

Wait, he told himself. Wait. You don't know there were just four. The world about him stood so silent that he heard his own pulse.

When Parson had satisfied himself that no one else lurked in the trees, he got up and brushed off the snow. He shivered, had trouble walking to the cabin because he had no sensation below his knees. He stumbled over to the insurgent in the British camo. Hate to imagine how he came by that field jacket, Parson thought. Dead eyes stared into the sky with no final expression. Death had

overtaken him with such velocity that his features never registered it. A small, round entry wound in the front and a mass of
hair, bone, brains, and blood on the other side.

Parson staggered through the back door. Gold swung the Beretta with both hands, wide-eyed. Parson felt a microsecond of
clarity, the recognition of an awful mistake. He tensed for the
bullet.

It did not come. He closed his eyes and let out a long breath.

"I'm sorry. I forgot to cough," he said.

"Thought you might."

"Why didn't you blow me away?"

"You said there were four," Gold replied. "I got one. I heard
you shoot at three."

"Good thing you're smarter than I am."

Parson sat by the stove and dried his feet with a desert scarf.
The prisoner sat on the floor, looking at the guerrilla Gold had
killed with pistol fire.

"Guess the cavalry didn't save you, huh?" Parson said.

"Inshallah."

"Somebody knows where we are," Gold said.

"Yeah, I hate like hell to leave a warm place, but we're lucky
we had it this long."

He handed the M-4 to Gold, took his pistol from her. He
holstered it in his survival vest, then gathered up the other sidearm
and magazines he'd taken from the airplane. Parson placed all his
gear in the backpack, now empty and damp. He filled the plastic
bottles with the water in the cook pot.

"Let's saddle up," he said.

Parson tied on his boots and took an experimental step with
the snowshoes. They felt clumsy on the bare floor, but the walking

seemed natural when he stepped outside in the snow. Fog now
obscured the trees across the clearing, mist advancing like smoke
from a wildfire. He went to the first two guerrillas he'd shot.

One lay motionless on his stomach. Pink slush spread from
under him. The other had fallen onto his back, one knee upbent.
The knee moved and Parson drew his pistol.

The man held his hands over wounds to his chest and abdomen. He wore a bandolier across his torso, the pouches filled with
magazines and brass cartridges, the odd jewelry of combat. Blood
channeled between his fingers, and he looked at Parson longingly.

"*Ash-hadu anla ilaha . . .*" breathed the guerrilla. "*Muham-
madan abduhu wa rasuluhu.*"

It was about all the Arabic that Parson understood. He'd heard
it in an intel briefing: *There is no God but God, and Muhammad
is His Messenger.* The Shahadah, the Muslim declaration of faith.
All Muslims usually recited it in Arabic, but this man's syllables
flowed like those of a native speaker.

The guerrilla whispered again. Barely audible, accented
English.

"Finish me," he said. "Finish me, Crusader."

Parson sighed long and hard. The man would not live without
immediate help. Parson could not take him along, and if he did
the Arab would die anyway. No morphine in the kit. No options
left but degrees of cruelty. Parson shot him in the head.

Gold bolted out with her rifle.

"It's all right," Parson said. He paused for a moment. I've
known ever since 9/11 we'd have to do things we'd rather not do,
he thought. Just didn't think I'd have to do them myself.

Parson picked up the man's AK. He pulled back the bolt just
far enough to check that the chamber contained a round. He

ejected the magazine, examined it, found it full. Then he rein-
serted it and took an extra magazine from the insurgent's vest.
Parson had never held an AK before, but the balance felt right, and
it gave him far more firepower than his sidearm.

"We should disable any rifle we don't take with us," Gold said.

"Good idea."

Gold disassembled the first guerrilla's weapon. She removed
the bolt and put it in her pocket. Then she went to the back of the
cabin and did the same to the rifle carried by the man with the
British jacket.

Parson looked down at the Arab at his feet. Sleet fell from the
sky and began collecting in the dead fighter's beard. White ice
pellets mingled with black whiskers and turned the beard gray, as
if in death the man aged years by the second. Parson wondered
what kind of fervor could have motivated this man to leave Yemen
or wherever to die on a mountain where it was nearly a hundred
degrees colder than his home.

There came a faint tearing sound, like someone ripping paper
at a distance. In the next instant, it seemed an invisible force of
biblical power slammed Parson to the ground. The blow to his
chest knocked the wind out of him. He fought to breathe. Dazed,
for a moment Parson thought lightning had hit him. But when
the next bullet kicked up snow beside his head, he realized what
was happening.

He crawled toward the cabin door, pain from cracked ribs like
stilettos in his lungs. He'd never heard the shots. He also knew his
flak jacket was designed to stop shrapnel, not rounds from a high-
powered rifle. The only reason the bullet hadn't gone right through
him and out the other side of the vest was that it had come from
a great distance.

Parson pulled himself inside as Gold came in the back door.

"What happened?" she asked as she kneeled beside him.

"Sniper," Parson said. He coughed and winced. "I'm all right; it hit my vest. We gotta move, but don't go out the front."

Gold unchained the mullah from the bed frame.

"Just tell him I fainted," Parson said. "Don't let him know his buds are still out there."

Parson struggled to his feet, used the AK for leverage. He shouldered his pack and inhaled deeply, still trying to catch his breath.

"There's a ravine that slopes away behind the cabin," he said. "Let's just get downhill as quick as we can."

Gold spoke to the mullah, who sat on the floor and did not move. She spoke again, and he shook his head. Parson drew his boot knife, soft clicks as the keepers in the sheath disengaged. He placed the point just under the prisoner's eye, and he traced a red scratch down toward the beard. The man jerked back his head and rose to his feet.

Parson looked at his knife, a smear of red on the point. Not a government-issue weapon but a gift from his father, the handmade tool belonged in a display case on a mantelpiece. Grip made of whitetail antler. Blade of old-fashioned Damascus steel, layer upon layer of alloy pattern-welded and hammered to form textured lines on top of each other. A double edge sharp as truth. Parson saw his own reflection distorted in the whorls of the shimmering metal.

Gold pulled the prisoner out the back door. The mullah looked down at the dead insurgent in the British coat and paused over the body. Parson pushed him forward, then slid down the embankment. Parson carried the AK slung across his back, and the rifle bounced against his neck. The mist closed in so thick he could see only a few yards in front and behind, as though time had swallowed both his past and his future. He felt grateful for it, though. If not for the fog, he supposed, another shot from that damned Dragunov would likely take off his head.

The wooded slope stopped abruptly at a small rill narrow enough to step over. Beyond the stream, Parson tromped into snow up to his knees. He found the walking difficult even with his snowshoes; without them only a few hundred yards would have exhausted him. Now he saw nothing but white, the snow and the fog intermingling so completely that his only sensory references were gravity and pain. He could not tell whether he trudged over road, open field, or frozen lake.

Parson continued ahead, each step a mission in itself.

CHAPTER FIVE

Parson led Gold and the prisoner across a surface that became mercifully flat. Big snowflakes like soap shavings descended silently through the fog. No terrain in the Hindu Kush should offer walking this easy, Parson figured, and out of curiosity he scraped through the snow with his snowshoe. The effort revealed black ice, the surface of a mountain lake. That concerned him a little, though he had not heard any creaking to suggest the ice giving way.

He drew his boot knife and chopped and probed the ice. He could not chip down to the water, and Parson remembered an old rhyme about the safety of frozen lakes: "Inches two, it'll hold you. Inches three, you and me. Inches four, put up a store." At least one break, then, in a place not known for kindness either to foreigners or natives. Even the name, "Hindu Kush," threatened. An intel officer once told him it meant "Slaughter of Hindus," in reference to some horror of antiquity.

Every breath seemed to pierce his chest. Pain from the cracked ribs made Parson think of the spikes of an iron maiden as it closed on a victim. Inhaling deeply brought a rattling sound.

"You going to make it, sir?" Gold asked.

"Yeah. We'll stop if we find a good place." Parson realized he had no idea what or where a good place might be.

He felt a sharp pain at one spot on his upper chest, bad enough that he kneeled in the middle of the lake to examine it. Parson took off his survival vest, unzipped his coat, fumbled with numb fingers on the buckles of his flak vest.

"What's wrong?" Gold asked.

"That slug might have gone farther than I thought."

Gold helped him pull away the front of the flak jacket, revealing a spot of blood reddening his butternut flight suit just above the Velcro patch for his name tag. Parson unzipped the suit enough to see that a bullet fragment had made it through the vest's Kevlar fibers and lodged under his skin. Wincing, he picked at the fragment with his knife and extracted it. He rolled the jagged shard of lead between his fingers, then dropped it into the snow.

The mullah watched with what seemed like professional interest. No smirk or taunt, only apparent curiosity, as if trying to learn what he could about American field medicine.

Parson found a Betadine pad in his first-aid kit. He had to remove his gloves to get enough grip to pull open the package. The gauze dripped with antiseptic the color of brandy, and it stained his fingers as he placed it over the wound. He taped the pad into place, then zipped, snapped, and buckled himself back together and started walking.

When he felt stones grinding under his snowshoes, he knew they'd come to the shore. What appeared as odd lumps in the snow turned out to be scrubby bushes drifted over. Not much other vegetation nearby. Parson knew they couldn't count on woods for cover all the time; he'd flown over enough of Afghanistan to see it had been largely deforested.

The mist lifted enough for Parson to realize they were deep in a valley. Walls of mountains rose into low clouds on either side. He saw variations of only two colors: the whites of snow and mist, and the grays of boulders and shale. So when he caught a glimpse of green up ahead, he crouched and rested a gloved finger against the trigger of the AK-47.

He motioned for Gold to stay put, and he advanced a little farther. He expected to find clothes drying on a line, a mud-brick hovel, some kind of habitation.

Parson plowed through dry, powdery snow, watching and listening. Listening to nothing. No village sounds, no bleat of sheep. Just his own ragged breathing.

He saw that the green fabric hung not from a clothesline but a pole. Four of them, in fact: four green flags with gold lettering he could not read, planted atop a mound in the snow. Parson signaled "okay" to Gold, and she and the prisoner joined him. The mullah sank to his knees in prayer.

Parson explored the mound with his foot, kicking away the snow, and he uncovered a pile of stones.

"What do you make of this?" he asked.

"The grave of a martyr," Gold said.

"Perfect. Friendly territory."

He looked up at the flags hanging in what he judged was a tribute to murder. "Let's get the hell out of here before he gets inspired or something," Parson said.

He led through the valley most of the morning, keeping to

the low hills within the pass. That course continued roughly in the direction of Bagram. He had neither the motivation nor the strength to head to either side of him, where the land rose so steeply an altimeter would be of greater use than a compass.

He wondered whether he'd ever flown through this valley on a low-level run to an airdrop. The terrain certainly made good cover for a tactical route. Parson had flown dozens of missions to drop supplies to troops, skimming the ground at nearly three hundred miles per hour, deep below the ridgetops. That's the way he wanted to cross this valley: chart in hand, stopwatch dangling from his neck, turbulence rocking the plane. The copilot's finger on a release switch, the whole crew waiting for Parson to call "green light."

He would have blasted through this valley in seconds, so low and so fast a jihadist could not have seen him in time to punch off a missile. Now they slogged through it for hours, exhausted and hungry like wandering penitents.

Eventually the valley seemed to widen, though the fog made it hard to tell. Parson guessed a stream nearby fed into the frozen lake behind him, but he saw only an expanse of snow. Its surface stretched before him unbroken by any tracks, a monochromatic world of white drifts and gray boulders.

He noticed a few brown twigs sticking up through the snow at regular intervals, the remains of some crop planted in rows. Parson brushed powder away from one of the dead plants, the brittle stems crackling in his fingers.

"Opium poppies," Gold said.

"I should have figured," Parson said. He knew most of the world's opium came from here.

The snowflakes had grown smaller and smaller until now they

fell like talcum, so fine they seemed just a slight thickening of the fog. Parson held out his hand and watched them collect on his glove. He wondered whether it was true that each flake had its own unique pattern, a geometry never appearing before and never seen again. Not in all the snow that surrounded him, not in all the snow that had ever fallen. He tromped on, thinking maybe lives weren't much different. Unique, never repeated quite the same way, one among billions, brief in the fullness of time.

But in the short moment we're here, he thought, one person can cause so much harm or good. Why would you dedicate your life to destruction and fly a plane into a building or blow yourself up in a crowded market? Parson thought about the jihadists he'd shot back at the shack. None looked more than thirty. Why couldn't they have been in a university learning something useful? Or raising a young family, or doing anything other than making it necessary for me to drag my ass through this fucking blizzard?

In the translucence of the snow and mist, the mountains that walled the valley hung blue in the distance. Ghosts of mountains. In the poor visibility Parson could not tell for certain, but he thought he saw some kind of large structure along one slope. He'd seen lots of villages from the air, mud-brick dwellings the exact color of the ground from which they'd been scraped, looking almost like a natural geological formation. But not this thing. As Parson drew nearer, he saw it was a single building, or more like a single ruin. Snow coated crumbling stone walls, and along the front wall Parson saw a wide gap, perhaps an opening for a wooden gate long since burned or rotted away. Some sort of fortress, maybe.

"You see that?" Parson asked.

"Yes, sir," Gold said. "I think it's an old caravansary."

"A what?"

"Caravansary. A place along a trade route where caravans could stop safely for rest. This used to be part of the old Silk Road."

Parson appreciated her professionalism, but he felt off balance that someone beneath him in rank had such commanding expertise of the language and culture while he knew nothing. His briefings on Afghanistan had been all about flying: approach corridors, tower frequencies, runway lengths, instrument procedures. We're in her element now, he thought. If we were flying, I'd have the knowledge and she'd be the dumb passenger.

From a distance, at least, the caravansary seemed abandoned. No movement, no goats, no smoke from a cooking fire. Parson wondered why any kind of sturdy structure would fall into disuse in such a poor country. But there it stood in silence, as if some dread disease had wiped out the population of a busy place. He considered whether to hole up there for a while. In survival school they'd taught him not to hide in an obvious spot. But his choices seemed so limited now.

"What do you think?" he asked.

"If the locals aren't using it, there's a reason," Gold said. "Maybe it's been a Taliban base. But it looks like nobody's home now."

"Let's check it out. That will at least get us out of the weather."

It took longer than he expected to reach the ruin's gate. The mullah walked slowly, staring at his feet. Parson fought the urge to grab the chain and jerk him along faster. The old man probably couldn't go much quicker.

The snow looked broken near the wall's opening. As they neared the structure, Parson pointed the AK forward, and his suspicion turned to fear when he saw that horses had churned up the snow. Several sets of hoofprints led into the courtyard, and hoofprints led out. Scattered piles of horse dung. Bootprints around the hoofprints. No other sign of life. Utter silence.

"What's up with this?" he asked.

"No idea," Gold said. "I can't see any reason for a bunch of riders to go in and out of here like that, especially in this storm."

"The fucking Twilight Zone."

"Do you want to take shelter here?"

"Maybe. What do you think?" Parson asked.

"I don't get a good feeling, but I'm not sure why."

"Let's just watch the place for a while. Make sure his gag is secure."

Parson kneeled behind a jumble of stones, the remains of a wall that had crumbled to the ground. He watched Gold pull the prisoner into a room off a central courtyard. When she settled in, Parson saw only the barrel of her rifle. He checked his watch. Eighteen past the hour. We'll watch until at least the top of the hour, he told himself. In that time, any bad guys around here should make some noise or show themselves.

He watched mist from his breath rise above the rocks. Their snowshoe prints mingled with the tracks left earlier, so nothing but his exhalations gave away their position. His fingers hurt now, and he pulled off his gloves and breathed into his cupped hands. He wished he'd brought different gloves. Nomex was designed for fire protection, not cold, and the chill air soaked right through. Parson shivered a little, but at least he wasn't wet like that first night when they'd splashed through the creek after the shootdown. Back home, he had wanted a bigger house and a nicer car, but now wealth was simply to be dry and not hungry.

Peering from behind the pile of stones, holding a rifle, reminded him of countless hours in deer stands, waiting for his prey. Centering the crosshairs just behind the animal's shoulder where the bullet would strike heart and lungs. Telling himself not to pull the trigger unless he had a good shot; you owe that to the animal. Exhale, hold breath, squeeze. The shove of recoil. The deer down where it stood.

But now he felt more the prey than the predator. Something he had not experienced before, except a taste of it during the escape-and-evasion exercise at survival school. And Parson had approached the training with the same attitude as everyone: This will not happen to me.

While he watched and waited, he inventoried the tools in his survival vest, things he'd never expected to need. He felt the pouch containing his first-aid kit; he'd already broken the seal. The kit included fishing hooks and line, which struck Parson as wildly optimistic. GPS and radio. He had all his electronics turned off now to conserve batteries. Knife, compass, signal mirror, flares. God, to pop smoke and summon a helicopter. But this storm made it nearly impossible to walk, let alone fly. Planes had crashed by flying into Afghanistan's cumulogranite clouds.

Parson found a compact of camo face paint in light green, dark green, and black. Useless in this winter expanse. Magnesium fire starter. Water-purification tablets. Multitool with pliers and screwdrivers. His Beretta, of course, and extra magazines. He'd added the magazines on his own. He knew Army troops who'd survived extended firefights; they said their lesson learned was you could never have too much water or ammunition.

Taken together, these things in his vest hinted of desperation. To need them, Parson thought, meant you were in about as much trouble as you'd ever encounter. It couldn't get much worse. Down to nothing to lose. And now the world itself gone but mountains and snow and the enemy.

He looked across the courtyard and examined the ruin. A series of rooms, some open to the sky, gave off from the courtyard on three sides. The larger ones, with wide doorways, he guessed to have been stables for horses or camels. So you could bring your load of silk or silver or whatever in here, Parson thought, and rest your animals while hiding from the bandits outside. This country had always been dangerous for every soul in it.

When the minute hand on his watch reached the top of the hour, he stood painfully, placed his hands on his knees. Still no sign of anyone else. At Gold's hiding spot, he saw little beyond the doorway. He clicked on his flashlight as Gold and the mullah stood. The room contained nothing but scattered straw.

"Let's see if we can find anything useful," Parson said.

Gold nodded and pulled the prisoner down the walkway and into the next room. She unlocked the cuff from around her wrist and held the chain in her hand, rubbed her wrist.

This time Parson's flashlight revealed a wooden table, with no other furniture in sight. A wicker basket sat atop the table. Parson shined his flashlight into the basket. It was filled with dried fruit. He picked up one, held it to his nose. It smelled faintly sweet.

"What are these?" he asked.

"Dried mulberries, I'd guess," Gold said.

Parson raked his fingers through them, looking for signs of mold. Seeing none, he picked up another mulberry, sniffed it and bit off part of it, rolled the fruit around on his tongue.

"Not bad," he said. "Wonder why somebody left these?"

"Maybe because they left in a hurry."

Parson didn't like the sound of that, but he was too tired and cold to ponder the mystery of hoofprints and food left behind. He dug into the basket, gathered a fistful of berries, and handed them to Gold.

"Might as well take off his gag and let him eat some of these," Parson said. "I don't have any more MREs."

"If they're bad, at least we'll all get food poisoning together," Gold said, chewing. She untied the gag and gave the mullah some fruit. He ate in silence.

"Keep an eye on him," Parson said. "I'm going to look around."

Back out on the walkway, he found it snowing harder. He noticed a lump in the snow on the stone path. He nudged the mass with his foot. The white powder fell away to reveal empty plastic packaging with English lettering: "Sony InfoLithium Camcorder Battery."

Now he didn't know what to think. Had GIs just been here? He knew Special Forces teams sometimes used horses in Afghanistan. What damned awful luck to miss them. He put his hand on his radio, thinking to ask AWACS about nearby friendlies, but he decided to explore first.

When he stepped into the next room, it smelled different, not the same mildew odor as the first two. A little foul, not strong. He played his light across the room. What he saw brought him to his knees.

Black blood covered most of the stone floor. Amid the pool of drying blood, a body. In an American flight suit. Headless.

Parson leaned forward and retched. He vomited what little he had in his stomach, bile and masticated fruit. He blinked his watering eyes and looked again. So much blood. He dropped his flashlight, and it clattered on the stones. Spittle drooled from his chin.

"Gold, get in here," he called. The phlegm in his throat gave a rattle to his words. He spat and closed his eyes. Gold led the mullah down the walkway.

"What's wrong?" she asked.

"You better sit down," he said. She kneeled beside him. He picked up his flashlight. "Look."

Parson heard her inhale deeply and stifle a sob. He felt her hand on his back.

"I'm so sorry," she said.

The mullah began speaking.

"What's he saying?" Parson asked.

"It doesn't matter."

"What is that motherfucker saying?"

Gold sighed. "He says the soldiers of God have struck a blow for justice."

"I'm going to strike a fucking blow," Parson said. He jerked the chain from Gold's hand and grabbed the mullah, dragged him outside, slammed him against the wall. The prisoner jabbered, grinning.

"He says if you shoot him, your CIA cannot question him," Gold said.

Parson swung the back of his fist against the mullah's face. Blood ran from the man's nose, streamed into his beard.

"Tell him don't worry. I won't shoot him."

Parson punched him in the stomach. The prisoner doubled over.

"Stop," Gold said.

"Like I said, I won't shoot him. That's too good for this piece of shit."

Parson opened a pocket on his survival vest, dug out a signal flare. He pulled off the plastic cap. He felt the raised rings on one end, a MK-124 night flare.

"What are you doing?" Gold asked.

Parson slid out the trigger tab at the end of the flare, arming it. He held the flare with his thumb on the slide lever. Pressed hard. The trigger made a loud crack, followed by the whoosh of igniting chemicals. A dagger of flame more than a foot long leaped from the flare, sparks arcing to the ground. Phosphorous drippings burned holes in the cobblestone. The flame so hot and white it hurt Parson's eyes.

He took the mullah by the throat.

"I'm going to send you to hell in style," he said.

Parson felt Gold's rifle stock slam the side of his face. The blow knocked him to the ground. The flare skittered away, spinning in circles like a wayward comet. It burned for several more seconds, blackened stones, melted a swath in the snow. The flare finally sputtered out, smoke curling from its burned tip.

Parson felt his cheek and glared at Gold. He fought the urge to hit her back. The mullah stared wide-eyed, breathing hard, trembling. Gold locked the chain around her wrist again.

"You shouldn't have stopped me," Parson said.

"You know our mission, sir."

Parson knew he'd let emotion overcome his reason, but he was too angry to admit it out loud. It felt as if a primal fury hidden dormant within him, something ancient, had been awakened by these murdering camel jockeys and their religion of blood. If they got to him so much that he lost his professionalism, then he'd lost everything. He looked into the distance and watched the snow shower, rubbed his bruised face. He felt as if he'd failed some test.

Or that Gold had kept him from failing it. But he hadn't asked for any of this.

He rose up on his knees. His flak jacket and survival vest felt heavier than ever. Parson leaned forward, placed a hand on the wall to steady himself, then raised himself to his feet and reentered the room.

The sight brought bile to his throat again. He saw no identifying patches or name tag on the flight suit, only Velcro where patches would normally go. That was standard procedure; crews usually sanitized their uniforms before combat missions.

Parson stepped inside slowly, and he felt congealed blood sticking to his snowshoes. Despite the lack of insignia, he thought he knew who this was. He tried to pick up the body's right wrist, but rigor mortis had frozen it in place.

He pushed back the sleeve and aimed his light onto the forearm. The tattoo read: "La Vida Loca." Parson closed his eyes and squeezed the lifeless wrist.

"I should have stayed with you guys," he whispered.

He let go of the wrist and smoothed down the sleeve, then backed out of the room. He sat on the cobblestones, cradled the AK-47.

The mullah kneeled on the walkway. Wiped sweat from his face with his sleeve. Looked away when Parson met his eyes. So I wiped that smirk off your face, thought Parson. You feel fear just like the rest of us.

Parson opened a pouch on his survival vest and took out his GPS receiver. He pressed the ON button with a trembling, gloved thumb, then waited for the receiver to initialize. The device found its artificial stars and displayed the caravansary's latitude and longitude.

He placed the GPS on the stones beside him and opened another vest pocket to get to his radio. He put the PRC-90 on his lap, pulled off his gloves. Parson rolled the rotary switch on the radio. A click, but no static. He pressed the TRANSMIT button. Nothing.

He drew his knees to his chest, folded his arms, and put his head down. What else could go wrong? He looked up again and exhaled hard, once, twice, three times.

"Radio dead?" Gold asked.

"Leave me alone."

Parson tugged off his gloves, dropped them beside him. He patted his vest pockets until he found his spare battery. He unscrewed the radio's battery compartment, removed the dead battery, and threw it as hard as he could. The metal cylinder flipped end over end as it sailed over the courtyard and dropped into the snow with a *whump*. Parson slid the fresh battery into the radio and screwed the cap back into place. He rolled the switch again and the radio hummed to life.

"Bookshelf, Flash Two-Four Charlie," he called.

"Flash Two-Four Charlie, Bookshelf. Good to hear from you, buddy. You doing all right down there?"

"Negative. Stand by to copy some information."

The radio hissed for a moment. "Flash Two-Four Charlie, go ahead."

"Bookshelf, Flash Two-Four Echo is dead. I found him in an old ruin. They cut off his head. The location of the body is as follows."

Parson transmitted the coordinates, offset by a classified reference point.

Before the acknowledgment could come, a loud squeal blasted

over the radio, the sound of one transmitter blocking another. Then foreign chatter. A taunting tone. Parson made out the word "Amrikan," but nothing else except the sneer in the voice.

"I bet that's Nunez's radio," Parson said to Gold. "What are they saying?"

"I don't know."

"What do you mean, you don't know?"

"It's not Pashto. It's Arabic."

Then not Taliban, but al Qaeda, thought Parson. "Do you think they understood what I just told AWACS?"

"Maybe. They do have English speakers."

"We better move," Parson said. "Now." He cursed himself for blabbering so much information in the clear. The coordinates were coded, but if the bastards on the radio were the same ones who slaughtered Nunez, they knew exactly where he was talking about. It seemed to Parson things kept happening faster than his chilled and pain-racked brain could process.

"Do you think they're close?" Gold asked.

"These radios are line of sight."

He wondered if it was any use to run. If the enemy had horses, they could follow tracks in the snow and chase him down quickly. When the blizzard first started, he'd counted on falling snow to cover his tracks, but now the snow was too deep for that. He thought about the problem for a minute, looked down at his feet.

"Let's backtrack over our own trail coming in," Parson said. "With these half-ass snowshoes, they can't see which way the tracks go. We'll veer off when I find a good place."

Parson led the way out of the caravansary. The snow squeaked under his boots, and the makeshift snowshoes left wafflelike imprints. The tracks going in looked just like the tracks going out.

The sky hung low, gray as steel. In the quiet, with the enemy nearby, every sound seemed too loud—the crunch of snow, the clink of buckles and zippers, the rub of rifle slings. Parson listened closely for hoofbeats; he expected horsemen to thunder out of the fog at any moment and strike him down. He carried the AK at port arms. The faster I can get this rifle to my shoulder, he thought, the more of them I can take with me. What kind of war is this that I'm on the ground worried about the raghead cavalry?

Flakes fell large and thick, spiraled down like dying mayflies. The mullah's breath came in labored wheezing, and the pack grew heavy across Parson's shoulders. Parson glanced at Gold, who wore an aggrieved expression. She had more than enough reason to look frightened or worried, but this was something else. More like deep sorrow or profound disappointment.

Well, I gave her reason to be disappointed in me, Parson thought. She kept looking back at the mullah. Was she disappointed in him, too? What the hell did she expect?

A squadron of cliff swallows darted by, five or six little brown birds crisscrossing each other, their rapid wingbeats taking them away through the storm. Parson wished he could take flight and join their formation. But he could only place one foot in front of the other, in an old track if possible, wandering like a pilgrim on a quest for enlightenment, carrying the burden of all his sins.

CHAPTER SIX

They stood in open country now, the heavy fog their only cover. Parson had hoped for a stream to provide a good place to veer off their old trail, but he'd found nothing. So about two miles back they had started into unbroken snow, hoping to find a village, preferably abandoned. Parson hated the thought of another night in a snow cave.

The hands on his watch showed just after five in the afternoon. Not much daylight left. His expensive flier's chronometer did him little good now, with its stopwatch function and digital window set to Zulu time. Hardly need a watch at all, Parson thought, when you've had an airplane blown out from under you.

He froze at the bleat of a goat.

"You hear that?" he whispered.

"Yeah," Gold said.

"What do you think?"

"Maybe I can get a villager to take us in."

"Should we chance it?" Parson asked.

Gold shrugged. "Pashtunwali," she said.

"What?"

"Tribal law. In their culture, if they take in travelers they have to protect them."

"Even us?"

Gold turned her palms upward and raised her eyebrows. Not the answer Parson wanted, but he didn't have a lot of options.

Parson clicked off his rifle's safety, placed his finger directly on the trigger. If somebody came to my door looking like us, he thought, I sure as hell wouldn't take them in, let alone feel any obligation. I do not understand these people.

He crept forward until he came to a stone wall about chest high. Beyond it, two goats fed from a trough, their fur a dirty cream color and matted. Their hooves had churned the ground to a foul slush of mud and manure. The smell reminded Parson of horse stables, but worse.

Beyond the goat paddock were three mud-brick dwellings adjoining each other. Not even a village, Parson guessed, but the compound of a single extended family that had probably scratched a living from this valley for generations. He remembered flying over many such compounds, sending sheep and goats scurrying and the women running inside. Parson always wondered why the women ran. In fear of bombs? To get a rocket launcher? Sometimes shoulder-fired missiles came up from these compounds, setting off the aircraft's missile warning system and forcing the pilots to bank hard in evasive maneuvers.

"If they let us in," Gold whispered, "lower your rifle, sir, and enter with your right foot first."

Parson nodded and let Gold through the compound's gate ahead of him. When he was sure the mullah wasn't looking, he took a strobe light from his survival vest. He snapped the infra-red lens into place and turned it on. With the naked eye, Parson did not see the IR strobe flashing, but the soft, steady clicks confirmed it was working. He placed the strobe on top of the rock wall, concealed by snow except for the lens. Insurance, Parson thought, or at least a grave marker.

He followed Gold and the prisoner to the door of the first hut, stepped carefully around goat dung. Smoke rose from somewhere in the back of the dwelling, but Parson found no chimney or stovepipe. He unzipped a thigh pocket on his flight suit and pulled out his blood chit. The cloth chit, about the size of a handkerchief, bore a U.S. flag, along with a message in several languages: *I am an American flier. Misfortune forces me to seek your assistance. . . .* A serial number adorned each corner of the chit. He handed it to Gold.

"Show them this if you think it will help," he whispered.

"It might," she said.

Gold knocked on a decaying, wooden door. A rope held it closed, looped through a hole where the knob might have been. The rope had rubbed smooth the edges of the hole, and lines of grain stood out in the planks, the softer wood between the grains beaten out by years of sleet and rain.

No answer. Gold knocked again. Parson moved back a half step to give himself plenty of room to bring up his weapon.

An eye appeared at a crack in the door. A male voice spoke from the inside, and Gold answered in Pashto. Parson listened to the conversation flowing back and forth. The way Gold held her M-4, he figured it wasn't going well. It couldn't help that she was a woman. But the rope slackened through the hole in the door, and the door opened a crack. Gold offered the blood chit, dangling it from two fingers. Something snatched it inside as if a rush of air had sucked it in.

A long pause. Then the rope came to life, running through the hole in the door like a cobra until the knotted end smacked against the wood.

The corners of Gold's lips turned up almost imperceptibly. She shook her head and whispered, "I'll be darned." It was the nearest Parson had ever seen her come to smiling, swearing, or looking surprised.

"What?" Parson asked.

"They're not Pashtuns. They're Hazaras."

"Is that good?"

"That's very good."

About damn time we had some luck, thought Parson. I don't understand what's going on here, but if she likes it, I like it.

The door groaned open, and a weathered, wrinkled man appeared before them. He stood about shoulder high to Parson, and he could have been forty or sixty. In his right hand he held an ancient bolt-action rifle. Parson recognized it as a British .303 Lee-Enfield. The man made a sweeping motion with his other hand, bade them to come in. He glared hard at the mullah and the mullah glared back. Parson didn't need translation to decipher the hate.

As Parson's eyes adjusted to the dark, he saw two other people in the room. A woman, presumably the wife, tended her cooking over a fireplace. The smoke had no vent but a narrow window. The wife wore a multicolored shawl over her head, not like any burka or abaya Parson had ever seen. She made no effort to cover her face.

In one corner, a teenage boy sat with a metal plate in his lap.

He was breaking a piece of flat naan bread and feeding the crumbs to a mynah bird perched on the back of his chair.

This is damned weird, thought Parson. Even if they're friendly, I'm glad I left that strobe outside. Wish Sergeant Gold would tell me what this is all about.

Gold and the man of the house continued talking. Parson didn't understand it, but he did notice that Gold kept repeating herself and slowing down. So he understands Pashto, thought Parson, but it's not his first language. No wonder that conversation through the door took so long and almost came to gunfire.

The boy held out his finger and the mynah hopped onto it. The teenager disappeared into an adjoining room. He came back with an armful of embroidered blankets and spread them across plank platforms along the wall. Except for the boards where he'd placed the blankets, the floor was dirt.

The boy gestured toward the blankets. Parson unslung his rifle and sat down near the fire.

"Thank you," he said.

Gold and the prisoner also sat. Parson looked around for something to chain him to, but he saw nothing big and heavy enough. Guess we'll have to keep him hitched either to Gold or me, he thought.

"So who are these people?" Parson asked.

"They're Shia Muslims," Gold explained. "The Hazaras had it pretty rough under the Taliban, who are Sunni, so there's an awful lot of bad blood."

"So these guys must like us."

"Maybe."

"Works for me." If these people think we're not their worst enemy, thought Parson, that's all I need to know.

The wife brought Gold and Parson steaming cups of chai. Parson inhaled deeply; he thought he'd never smelled anything finer. When the woman gave him his clay cup, she said something he didn't understand, but he did get the soothing tone. Unlike every other woman he'd seen in this part of the world, she looked directly into his eyes. Her own eyes were blue-gray, and she had high Mongolian cheekbones and straight hair. Her rounded face seemed friendly even when she wasn't smiling.

Parson sipped the chai, and as it went down it seemed to warm his very soul.

"They don't even look Afghan," he said.

"Some people think they're descended from Genghis Khan."

"Wow," Parson said. "Tell him to bring me the blood chit."

Gold translated.

"He wants to keep it," she said.

"I'm going to let him keep the part that might do him some good," Parson said.

More halting Pashto. The man handed Parson the piece of cloth, and Parson drew his boot knife. He cut off one corner, making sure to sever the entire serial number.

"Tell him to take this to Kabul when he gets a chance," Parson said. "Explain to the American embassy or any U.S. officer that he took us in. Tell him we can't promise anything, but our government might pay him for helping us."

"He might not go to Kabul all his life," Gold said, "but I'll tell him."

While she spoke, Parson unzipped his survival vest and worked himself out of it, one arm at a time. He grimaced as the movements pulled at his injuries, especially the cracked ribs. He unbuckled the fasteners on his flak vest and repeated the effort. That hurt even worse, because the stiff flak jacket was harder to take off. The wife watched him. He noticed her staring at the blood spot on his flight suit from the bullet fragment. She began puttering at a collection of jars and bottles.

"Hey, Gold," Parson said. "Make sure these people understand the chances they're taking."

"I already did."

Parson looked at Gold for a moment. In that case, he thought, you're making decisions above your pay grade. He decided not to make an issue of it. When he'd lost his temper and almost torched the prisoner, he figured, he'd stopped functioning as an officer. For today, at least, he'd lost any right to upbraid Sergeant Gold.

The wife placed a leg of lamb in a boiling pot, shook in salt and pepper. She added something else Parson didn't recognize, but it smelled good. Saffron, maybe. Parson's mouth watered. Finally, some decent luck and some decent food.

The woman ground a mixture with a mortar and pestle. She brought it over to Gold and Parson, and she began speaking. Gold shook her head, then nodded, responded in Pashto.

"She has something for your pain," Gold said.

"What is it?"

"Tobacco mixed with opium."

"You gotta be kidding me," Parson said.

"It's up to you, sir. She's the nearest thing to a doctor you're going to get."

"You won't rat me out?"

"I have bigger things on my mind, sir. And if you were back at base, the flight surgeon might give you codeine. Guess what that's made of."

"All right, I'll try it. Don't let me do anything stupid."

"I won't."

No, you won't, thought Parson. I got the bruise to prove it.

The woman set down a cup of the mixture on the blankets beside Parson. He took a pinch and placed it inside his lower lip, noticed only the earthy taste of tobacco. But eventually a warmth infused his whole body, along with a sense of well-being entirely unjustified by his situation. He still felt his pain, but it seemed somehow distant.

He closed his eyes, let the drug do its work. Parson dozed off, and he woke as the woman unzipped his flight suit enough to examine his chest injury. He guessed he'd slept for less than an hour. He smelled the lamb now, and the opium still kept the pain somewhere off to the side. The wife handed him an empty cup, and he spit tobacco juice into it.

She cut away part of his bloody T-shirt and peeled off the Betadine patch. The blood had mixed into the gauze with the antiseptic. The woman sponged the wound and began patting some kind of poultice onto it. To Parson, the poultice's aroma seemed more like food than medicine. He figured that was just his hunger and the opium talking.

Parson raised his right arm, and he saw that someone had rebandaged and splinted his wrist while he slept. The wife had Parson's first-aid kit out of his pack. She tore off some bandage material and taped it over the poultice.

Behind her, Parson saw the boy and the husband setting a low table. The family chatted in their own language. The man nodded to Gold and Parson, and he motioned toward the table.

Parson spat out the tobacco wad into his cup, and with his fingertip he dabbed at the flecks remaining on his tongue. He blinked his eyes and stumbled his way to sit cross-legged at a table set for five. The mullah sat tied to a chair.

"They won't let him eat at their table," Gold said. "I'll feed him after we're done."

Parson leaned to one side, then pushed himself upright with his right hand. He became aware of a burning in his wrist. Dumb, he thought. If I weren't stoned, that would hurt like hell.

The wife ladled rice and mutton onto Parson's plate. He forced himself to wait until everyone sat, and then he began spooning the food, slurping. Parson thought he'd never tasted anything better than that lightly seasoned lamb. He had no utensil other than the spoon, but he didn't need a knife. The meat fell apart at a touch. If I live through this, he thought, I'll never take hot food for granted again. He ate so quickly that juice ran down his chin onto his whiskers.

"Sorry," he said, wiping his face with his flight suit sleeve. "Tell them I don't know how to thank them."

Gold spoke in Pashto, and the husband smiled and answered. More chatter back and forth.

"They want to know what we were doing before we got shot down," Gold said.

"The less they know, the safer they are," Parson said.

"That's what I told them."

"So what's their story? You say these people had it rough?"

"I'm not sure how much I should ask them, but I'll see."

Long conversation, Gold nodding gravely.

"He says his wife came from a village the Taliban wiped out," Gold said. "He also says he fought against them after the Russians left."

"What did he do in the war?"

"He says the less we know, the safer they are."

"Fair enough," Parson said.

"He did say the Taliban killed his uncle and three cousins."

"How?"

"Stoning."

"No wonder he hates those fuckers."

Parson rose to his feet carefully, this time steadying himself with his good hand. When he found his pack, he rummaged through it, examined night-vision goggles, pistol, first-aid kit. He wanted to find something he could spare that would do the family some good. The pack had belonged to the flight engineer, and Parson unzipped the outside pockets to see what Sergeant Luke might have put there.

"Ask them if their boy goes to school," Parson said.

"He does sometimes," Gold said. "They already told me he can read."

Parson found what he wanted in a side pouch. Luke's calculator. A grease pencil and a Cross pen. He put them on the table.

"School supplies," Parson said. "Show them how that calculator works. Tell them when the battery dies, just use it in sunlight."

When Gold finished talking, the husband took Parson's good hand in both of his own, shaking, smiling, speaking what was gibberish to Parson. The boy also spoke, and he saluted Parson in the old British style, palm out. Parson smiled weakly, returned the salute. Then he pulled his radio and GPS receiver out of the survival vest and kneeled by the open window. He plugged in the earpiece, placed it in his ear.

"Bookshelf," he called, "Flash Two-Four Charlie."

Nothing but hiss.

"Any station, Flash Two-Four Charlie on guard."

"Flash Two-Four Charlie," came the reply, "Fever Six-Two has you weak but readable."

Fever call sign, thought Parson. Who are they? The pilot's voice, unmistakably New York. Oh yeah, he recalled, rescue Herks, an HC-130 out of that Air National Guard unit on Long Island.

"Fever Six-Two," he said, "stand by to copy my position." More offset coordinates.

"Fever Six-Two copies all. We're briefed on your status. Expect an aircraft on station overhead your vicinity until they can get you a helicopter ride."

"That's good to hear," Parson said. "What kind of weather data can you give me?"

"Not good. I'll give you details as soon as my copilot gives me back my weather sheet. We also got some information on friendlies—"

Loud squeal and crackles. Behind it: *"Allah-hu akbar, Allah-hu akbar!"*

Parson cursed and took out the earpiece. He clicked off the radio. He watched Gold remove the mullah's gag so the prisoner could eat.

"Rice and bread," Parson said. "Don't give him any of their lamb."

CHAPTER SEVEN

Parson heard the galloping before he saw the horsemen. They came at a dead run through the early-morning mist, their coats flowing in the swirling snow.

The opium had worn off, and he'd slept well when not keeping watch at the window. For the first time in days, hunger and cold did not slow his mind and reflexes. He felt like an officer again. Or not even that. Long practice kicked in, and his eyes, muscles, and nerves melded into a targeting system.

He brought the Kalashnikov to his shoulder, aimed at the first rider. The AK lacked a scope, but iron sights were good enough now. He focused on the front sight post. The man's torso went blurry behind it. Parson fired. The guerrilla fell backward as if he'd hit a wall.

The second rider came at an angle, a crossing shot. His ammunition belts and rocket launcher bounced around him as he gripped the reins. Parson led him ever so slightly. The bullet caught the man in the chest. He collapsed from his mount and lay in a motionless heap while his horse wheeled, turned, and slowed to a trot as if it knew its master had already entered the next world.

The remaining two neared the house. One raised his AK and brought it to bear. Parson had no time for precision now, so he fired a burst, cut down both insurgents.

Parson did not become aware of any other guerrillas until an explosion opened the wall behind him. The rocket-propelled grenade stunned him and he fell to his side. He sensed dull pain at the back of his head, a rush of cold air. He thought he heard screams, far off. Gunshots like dull thumps. Every sound strangely muffled. Dust from the exploded wall stung his eyes.

A boot caught him in the chest. The blow knocked the breath from him, and pain from his already cracked ribs coursed through him like an electric shock. He could not make himself inhale; thought he would suffocate. Reached for his rifle. Through the dust he saw a boot kick it away.

Another foot pinned his arm to the floor. Hands grabbed him by his clothing, pulled him to his feet. Eyes glared through balaclavas. A punch to the stomach stopped his breathing again. He fought for air as another blow hit him in the cheek. Yammering in Pashto and Arabic. Gunshots and shouts. Someone slammed him against a wall. The black-clad face in front of him went out of focus as he lost consciousness.

WHEN PARSON CAME TO, he found himself tied to a chair, hands behind him. His right wrist burned, and someone had removed the splint. He saw no sign of the Hazara family.

Gold sat tied to a chair a few feet from him. A black hijab

covered her hair. Her eyes were closed, and she looked almost serene but for the track of one tear. Realization crushed Parson like dungeon walls closing in. Nunez. A beheading on video. He began breathing heavily, hyperventilating. He remembered news coverage of a contractor's murder by militants in Iraq. The television networks cut away when the knife came out, but radio newscasts let the sound play on. Three distinct screams, an eternity of twenty seconds. An audio feed from hell.

He panted hard and still could not catch his breath. A panic attack, he knew. So this is what happened to Nunez. That contractor. That reporter in Pakistan. Now us.

Parson struggled against his ropes and let out a long animal sound, more growl than scream. Gold opened her eyes and looked at him. Control, thought Parson. Try to be an officer. Don't let her down again. You got nothing left but dignity.

A man wearing foreign military fatigues came in from the next room. He leaned his Dragunov rifle against the wall. So it's you, thought Parson.

"There is no call for shouting," the guerrilla said. Perfect English, British accent. Olive complexion. Black hair, shorter than that of the other insurgents. Also in contrast with the others, the man's teeth were clean and straight. Dark eyes that regarded Parson as if drinking information from his clothing and injuries.

"I'm just doing my job," Parson said. "You should know that."

"I do. And I am doing mine."

"Who are you?"

"You may call me Marwan," the guerrilla said. "And who are you?"

Name, rank, service number, thought Parson. "Major Michael Parson, United States Air Force."

"And how did an Air Force officer come to be walking through the wilderness of Afghanistan?"

"I think you know that."

"I do," Marwan said. "But you will tell me more."

Parson closed his eyes. Felt out of breath again.

"What was your initial destination?"

Parson struggled for air. Rapid breaths. He cursed himself for letting his fear show.

"What was your initial destination?"

"The weather was bad," Parson said. "We didn't know where we'd end up."

"You insult my intelligence."

"That's all I know."

"Shaheen," Marwan called. Chatter in Arabic. Parson looked at Gold.

"People depend on us, sir," she said.

"Quiet, woman!" Marwan shouted. He slapped her face. A drop of blood slid from her nose. "You and I have much to discuss," he said, "but the men are talking now."

Another insurgent stood behind Parson's chair.

"Your destination, Major Parson?"

"They didn't tell me."

"That would make it hard for a flier to do his job, now, wouldn't it?"

Marwan nodded, and the man behind Parson grabbed his right hand and twisted. Flames shot from Parson's wrist throughout his body. He didn't know nerve endings could transmit that much pain. Parson cried out, a high-pitched wail. Arched against the ropes.

"Memory getting any better?"

Parson tried to think and reason. Fear and pain overwhelmed every word of every thought. "Seeb," he said. "Seeb International in Muscat."

"I doubt that very much," Marwan said. "That is a civilian airport. Your leaders are decadent, but not stupid. Neither am I."

Marwan unsheathed a bayonet and pressed the tip to Gold's cheek. Her eyes widened, but she made no sound.

"When I'm done with this harlot, she will want to cover her face as women should," Marwan said.

Now Parson had nothing left. Maybe he could handle a blade through his own flesh, but not through hers. "Masirah Island," he said. "Off Oman."

"Recalling that flight plan a little better, are we? And from Masirah to some secret prison, I presume. So those Ibadhi fish-mongers in Oman continue to cooperate with infidels. Why does that not surprise me?"

My God, this guy knows a lot, thought Parson. And he didn't learn to speak English like that in some raghead madrassah.

Marwan put away the bayonet and gave orders in Pashto and Arabic. "Now," he said, "you are going to get your fifteen minutes of fame."

Parson sweated despite the cold, struggled to control his bladder. Insurgents, all with faces covered by balaclavas or scarves, took their places behind Parson and Gold. Each terrorist brandished an AK or a grenade launcher. One tacked a black flag with gold lettering on the wall behind them. Parson nearly broke down, but then he saw that Marwan's bayonet remained sheathed. Enough of Parson's reason still functioned for him to realize they would make at least two videos. They would not kill him in this one. First, they'd make an impossible demand. Then they'd kill him when his government didn't meet the demand. The recordings would show up on Al Jazeera and on radical Web sites, downloaded, burned onto DVDs, and passed around the jihadist world like snuff porn.

On the other hand, Parson thought, they might as well make both videos at once. That's probably what happened to Nunez. Parson shivered from sick fear, knowing his fate lay entirely in the hands of people who thought killing him bought a ticket to heaven.

Marwan stood between Gold and Parson, held a Koran in his right hand. A guerrilla with a video camera aimed it and pressed a button.

"In the name of God, the Merciful, the Compassionate, this is a message to the White House from the defense ministry of the Islamic Emirate of Afghanistan, its true government, the Taliban," Marwan said. "You attempted to transport one of our top spiritual leaders to one of your torture centers. But you failed.

"The soldiers of God struck the plane from the sky. God Himself sent a mighty blizzard to prevent a helicopter rescue. And now we have recovered our mullah and captured the crew. They will be punished for their treatment of our cleric, the Commander of the Faithful, peace be upon him. But they will be executed outright if you do not release all Muslim warriors from your CIA detention centers. You have two weeks to meet this demand, or you will witness the slaughter of these two infidels at my side.

"Your only hope of peace is to return to Islam. I say 'return' deliberately. All are born Muslim, and some turn away. You must return to the one true faith, your Capitol becoming your Grand Mosque."

Is he that crazy? Parson wondered. Can you reason with someone like this?

"If you fail to do this," Marwan continued, "I warn you a storm is coming. A blizzard like you have never seen on your soil. One greater than the storm that has grounded your aircraft in Afghanistan. One greater than the storm you witnessed that day in September.

"In the name of God and His fearsome justice, I caution you to consider my words carefully."

The video operator lowered his camera. Parson let out a long breath. So they would not kill him now. But two weeks? They'd kill him eventually, and the waiting would be horrible. If they'd killed him during the first taping, it would be over by now. Twenty seconds or so.

All of the Taliban fighters filed out of the room except Marwan.

Parson tried to remember his training. Establish a bond. Make them see you as human. Not that it had ever worked with jihadists before.

"Where did you learn such good English?" Parson asked. He wanted to sound in control, but his voice quavered.

"England."

"Is that where you're from?"

"You are a good soldier," Marwan said, "albeit an enemy of God. You are using what you've been taught. Excellent. But it will not benefit you and this harlot. I think we all know how this ends."

Parson felt his bladder start to let go, and he clenched his muscles to stop it. The warm liquid soaked into the seat of his flight suit. His heart raced. So did his mind.

He tried to think. How can this motherfucker read my thoughts? What the hell was he doing in Britain? It doesn't matter, Parson decided. No use. This all leads to that bayonet, agony, gouts of blood.

He tried hard, but he lost it. Parson inhaled with a sob, then bit his lip to keep his breakdown silent at least. Tears ran down his face and dripped onto his clothing. Gold looked away, her shoulders heaving.

"Phase One," Marwan said. "Despair."

"Go to hell," Parson said.

"Not likely. You will certainly see it ahead of me. But before you go, we will talk more." Marwan left Parson and Gold alone, joining his men in the next room.

Parson had always felt that his most important prayers had gone unanswered, so he'd given up talking to God. What was the point? But he prayed now. To wake up from the nightmare. For deliverance. For a bullet instead of a blade. He closed his eyes hard and repeated all of it silently, nodding his head all the while.

His wrist hurt so much that he would have cried from pain alone had the pain not been overtaken by dread. My lot in life, he thought. Pain and now failure. Because I can't fucking think and move fast enough, a horrible death. And as far as the mission goes, defeat snatched from the jaws of victory. The mullah should be under interrogation by now. Instead, Parson thought, that raghead gets honored as a returning hero, his stature magnified.

Parson could tell the sun was going down only because the light went grayer. He saw no shadows lengthening; the snow and fog allowed for none. Just an insidious gloom that eventually took over completely. Chant of Muslim prayers next door. Growl of turboprops overhead. The HC-130 was looking for him, surely calling for him on the radio.

Parson remembered that he'd reported his position, but he dared not pin hopes on that. Ceiling remained damn near zero. Aircraft could orbit over his position all day long and do him no good. In this weather, no one could see the strobe he'd left outside except from the ground.

He considered the life he might have had, a future ripped away like leaves in a hurricane. Parson hadn't ever given much thought to his own death, and he'd certainly never pictured anything like this. He'd heard of the stages people go through: denial, anger, bargaining, acceptance. That must happen in more normal settings, he thought, because he felt it all at once. One moment shaking with fear, the next moment unable to comprehend it, the next in a rage.

After a time, two of the insurgents came back in. One held an AK on Parson while another tried to feed him rice. In the flickering of an oil lamp, Parson watched the dirty spoon approach his mouth. He had no appetite, and he forced down only a few bites. That went against his training for this situation. Eat when they feed you, he'd been taught, because you don't know when you'll get food again. But he just could not make himself. Gold didn't eat, either.

When they were alone again, Parson said, "So they plan to keep us alive for a while."

"Not for long," Gold said.

Parson stared at the floor. "What happened to the family?" he asked.

"I'm pretty sure they killed them. I heard shots."

I brought this on them, Parson thought. Might as well have shot them myself.

Footsteps interrupted his mourning. Marwan entered the room, carrying one of the family's wooden chairs. He placed it on the floor and sat in it with his legs crossed as if he were about to take tea. No bayonet, Parson saw. Not yet, then.

Marwan took a notepad from the pocket of his field jacket and began scribbling.

"You're doing well," Marwan said as he wrote.

"What?" Parson asked.

"Your composure. I've seen people in your situation reduced to incoherence."

"Does that disappoint you?"

"Not at all," Marwan said. "In fact, I have come to believe your faculties make you too valuable to behead. That's why I'm here to offer you a proposal."

"What are you talking about?"

"If you do two things for me," Marwan said, looking over his reading glasses, "I promise you and the harlot a quick and painless exit from this world."

"What are they?"

"First of all," Marwan said, "it is my distinct honor to be your speechwriter. You will make a statement for my camera confessing your indiscriminate bombing of Muslim villages."

Marwan held his pad so Parson could see the page. In precise, flowing script, it began: "My mission was to take as many Muslim lives as possible. These aerial murders came as part of a larger campaign to crush Islam in a new Crusade. I must now ask the forgiveness of God and His people, the faithful of Islam."

"I fly cargo," Parson said.

"Come now, Major. Surely you understand psychological operations."

"That's why I won't do it."

"Oh, I think you will. I don't enjoy using the blade, but I have done it in service of Allah. Some of my men, however, relish it, and they know how to do it slowly."

Parson looked at Gold, who stared out into the dark through a window of oiled paper. No cues from her at all.

"The other thing I need you to do is to make a radio call," Marwan said. "When the weather clears, bring in your helicopter. I will video its destruction at close range. Psychological operations, you understand."

"Forget it."

"I thought you'd say that at first. I will give you until the morning to take a decision. At that time, we will shoot a video of one kind or another."

"Fuck you."

Marwan folded his notepad and picked up his chair.

"Choose well, Major," he said.

CHAPTER EIGHT

Parson sat awake all night. He watched Gold stare at the floor. Sleep deprivation gummed his thoughts; he could not concentrate on any line of logic. He still heard aircraft engines thrumming overhead from time to time, but the plane might as well have flown in another dimension. Parson saw no way it could help him now. Nothing registered clearly in his mind except fear and resolve, in that order.

"What are you going to tell him?" Gold asked finally.

"That I won't do it."

"Good." Gold looked squarely into his eyes. "Good."

"I've gotten enough people killed already."

"You didn't kill them."

"Still. I won't give him a helicopter crew," Parson said. "Fucking raghead."

"At least we'll go out doing the right thing," Gold said.

"No one will ever know it."

"Doesn't matter."

"Do you believe in heaven, Sergeant Gold?"

"Yes, I do."

She didn't even have to think about that one, Parson realized.

The window went from black to dark gray, the only indication of daybreak. Large snowflakes struck the oilpaper pane and disintegrated, piling on the sill like ground glass. Parson knew he would never see the sun again.

Footsteps. Parson felt a droplet of sweat fall from his armpit down his side.

Marwan entered, again carrying his chair and notepad. He placed the chair next to Parson and stood with one foot on its seat. Marwan studied his notepad, resting it on his knee. Parson noticed the guerrilla leader's hands. Ropy veins. Some kind of class ring. A Breitling watch. What the hell kind of terrorist was this?

"Have you taken a decision, Major?" Marwan asked. "I have crafted quite a statement for you."

"I can't help you."

Marwan peered over his glasses at Parson. The look turned Parson's blood to ice.

"Really?" Marwan said. He closed the notepad. "That is indeed a pity. I did not wish to hear your screams today."

Marwan kicked his chair, and it clattered against the wall.

"Shaheen!" he called, striding out of the room.

It will be over soon, thought Parson. It will be over soon.

He felt weak and frail. In his career he had seen what metal, either sharp-edged or high-velocity, could do to the human body. During an Iraq deployment he had helped transport the remains of civilians killed by a terrorist raid in Kirkuk. Black, dripping bags in the cargo compartment. All hopes, dreams, intellect, and talent gone, leaving nothing but slack and torn flesh. Decades to build, moments to destroy.

Parson felt sweat roll down his back. His legs began to shake. I'm gone already, he thought. None of this matters, because I'm already dead. I'm not even here.

Strange sounds came from outside the room. A snapping or cracking sound. Someone exhaled hard, with a grunting moan as if punched in the gut. Thuds, like someone falling. Something smacked against a wall, like a rock thrown hard. Another crack. Snap.

"Get on the floor," Gold said. She jerked to the side and fell over in her chair.

Parson looked at her, puzzled. Had she lost her mind in fear?

"Muhammed?" a voice called.

Whack. Thud.

"Get down!" Gold shouted.

Parson jerked to his left and fell. His head banged the hard dirt floor. Automatic-weapons fire crackled all around him.

The window burst open. Dust fell from a row of evenly spaced pockmarks that appeared in the wall. Another rip of automatic fire. Screams. Shouts in about three languages, including English.

A metal object sailed through the torn window and bounced across the floor. Parson grimaced, waited for the shrapnel.

The explosion knocked him dizzy. Dust choked him. When he opened his eyes, a trickle of blood dripped from his nose onto the floor. No other injury. But the flash-bang grenade had deafened him. Parson coughed and squinted, tried to make sense of what was happening. Bound to his overturned chair, he could not even roll over.

A guerrilla ran into the room. He grabbed Gold by the back of her chair. She struggled to kick and bite. The ropes kept her from doing any damage. The man dragged her from the room and out a rear door. Parson spun himself around with his legs, tried to keep sight of Gold. She was gone.

Another insurgent stood over Parson, leveled a pistol, shouted silent words.

The guerrilla's head erupted in a spray of blood and brains. The man fell beside Parson, decapitated except for his lower jaw.

A soldier stood in the doorway, holding a shotgun. In what seemed like slow motion, he pumped the Benelli. A twelve-gauge hull ejected, spun to the floor. The man wore the fatigues of the Afghan National Army, with a snow camo overcoat. He turned to his left, fired again. Recoil jolted the Afghan's cheek and shoulder. Parson did not see the target. He did not hear the shot, either, only the ringing in his ears from the flash-bang.

The man motioned for Parson to stay down, then disappeared. Parson saw boots and legs run by the doorway. He heard what seemed like far-off drumming of rifle fire.

Another man appeared in the doorway. "Are you hurt, sir?" the man yelled. Parson barely heard him.

Still stunned, Parson looked at the man's uniform. Subdued U.S. flag patch. ISAF patch on the other arm. Bars of a captain. The officer carried an M-4 rifle painted in three-color desert pattern.

"There's another American," Parson yelled. "A woman. They took her out the back."

The captain turned and ran to the rear door, dropped to one knee, fired two shots on semiauto. Fired once again.

"Clear," shouted someone outside the room.

"Clear." Another American.

"Clear!" Afghan accent.

"Clear, bullshit!" Parson shouted. "The woman. Where is she?"

The captain came back into the room. He drew a Yarborough knife and cut the ropes that bound Parson. Two quick strokes. Parson rolled away from the chair, onto his back.

"Did you get her?" he asked. His limbs tingled as the blood returned. Parson turned onto his side, rose up on his knees.

"They put her across a horse," the captain said. "I think I hit the horse, but it kept going. Couldn't risk another shot when they got too far away."

Parson struggled to his feet. Why was this bastard just standing here talking?

"They'll kill her," he shouted. Parson felt his chest throbbing, animal panic. "Let's go now! We have to follow them."

"We'll never run down bad guys on horseback, sir," the captain said. "And they'll want to keep their hostage alive at least for a while."

"Who are you?"

"My name's Cantrell. Special Forces."

"Captain Cantrell," Parson said, "I'm giving you a direct order."

"Listen to me, sir," Cantrell said. "We'll do all we can. They have wounded, and some of their horses are wounded. They won't go far."

Parson realized Cantrell was right. All his instincts told him to try to rescue Gold now, but a mad dash might just get her killed. When you wounded a dangerous animal, you didn't immediately tear into the brush looking for it. You gave it some time for its injuries to bleed and stiffen. Then you went after it.

And sometimes it still got away.

"I can't lose her, too," Parson said, palms out to his sides. Sweat began clouding his vision. He stumbled backward against the wall. Could not seem to find his balance. His limbs were numb from the hours he'd spent tied to the chair. He slid back down to a sitting position. He put his head in his hands, elbows on his knees. Rocked as if in a zealot's prayer. "My crew is all dead," he said. "Everybody on my plane but her. Her and that raghead."

"What raghead?" Cantrell asked. "Sir, you're not making sense."

Parson stared at the commando. Bearded face, desert camo baseball cap turned backward. A patch of duct tape on Cantrell's shoulder bore hand lettering in black marker: "O+ POS." A stranger, Parson thought. Not an enemy, but not a friend. All my friends are gone.

The shotgun-toting Afghan came back into the room. Same guy who'd blown the insurgent's head off a few minutes ago.

"Just this one?" the man asked.

"Yes," Cantrell said. "They carried a woman hostage with them. We take any alive?"

"Negative."

"There was an old man," Parson said. Function. Try to think. "A high-ranking mullah. We were flying him to Masirah."

"Gone," the Afghan said. "I believe he is wounded."

"One of those knuckleheads was picking up a camcorder when I nailed him," Cantrell said.

"Where did you come from?" Parson asked.

"We were on patrol, and we'd holed up because of the storm," Cantrell said. "We got word about you on the satphone. We headed toward your last known position and saw the strobe."

The only thing I did right, thought Parson. He tried to stand, felt light-headed, lowered himself to one knee. He held his wrist and grimaced. Exhaustion and stress closed over him like waves over a drowning man. Nothing to breathe but guilt and despair. All dead but me, and I have failed. Parson looked at the floor. He could not make his eyes focus. Everything turning dark.

HE WOKE TO FIND his feet up on someone's pack as if he'd been treated for shock. He looked at his watch, but he had no idea what time it had been when he lost consciousness.

"How long was I out?" Parson asked. He struggled to get up, but he felt currents in his stomach that shouldn't have been there.

"Just a few minutes, sir," Cantrell said. The captain lifted Parson's head and offered him a canteen. Parson took it, hand shaking, sipped. The water tasted like purification tablets.

A Green Beret medic gave him a shot of morphine. It burned a little going in, then spread warmth through his bloodstream like the opium chew from the Hazara woman, only stronger. He felt detached from his pain, as if it belonged to someone else. But the anguish was still all his.

The medic splinted Parson's wrist, then uncapped another needle.

"Antibiotic," the medic said.

Parson shrugged. He felt the cold steel, but no sting.

"We have to get Sergeant Gold back one way or another," he said. "I don't want to think about what they'll do to her."

"We will follow them at the proper time," the Afghan said.

"That's Captain Najib," Cantrell said. "My guys are supporting his unit."

Parson didn't know what to make of that. The Muslim was in charge? Najib nodded to Parson. The man looked a lot like Marwan, only younger. His black beard was trimmed closely. Najib's English was as good as Marwan's, but he spoke it with his own native accent. His choice of weapon, that inexpensive Italian shotgun loaded with buckshot, suggested to Parson a soldier who wanted to get close to the enemy and do a lot of harm. Had to give him credit for guts, at least.

Parson rose to his feet, steadying himself against the wall with his good hand. His vision turned gray, as if he were hypoxic. He remembered the feeling from altitude chamber training, colors fading with lack of oxygen. But the hues came back as his circulation returned. Not that there was much color to see. Splatter of blood on the floor and wall. Brass ammunition.

As he limped into the main room, he found the rest of the Afghan-American team searching the clothing of the dead insurgents. One U.S. soldier carried a scoped rifle tipped with a noise suppressor. Parson did not see Marwan among the bodies.

He looked about for his gear and found only part of it. His survival vest hung from the back of a broken chair, its pistol holster empty, radio gone. He discovered his pack, robbed of the first-aid kits, night-vision goggles, and extra handgun, and his flak vest had disappeared entirely. Parson hunted through the pack and felt the GPS receiver in a side pocket. At least they hadn't taken that. And they had never found his boot knife. They hadn't seen it under the zippered leg cuff of his flight suit. So he still had what his father had given him, and he still had the means to navigate. Signals from the stars and a sharp piece of steel.

He found his parka and put it on. He felt cold and clammy; sweat had soaked most of his flight suit. It seemed every moment brought another kind of discomfort. But he breathed more steadily now. I have to find a way to handle this, he told himself. Got to function. What happens to me does not matter. Not likely I'll live through this, anyway. What matters is Gold. What does she need from me? What would she have me do? She'd probably tell me to focus. If you must have anger, control it and use it. Don't let it control you. All right, Sergeant, I'll try.

Cantrell examined one of the insurgents' bodies. The guerrilla sat slumped against the wall, eyes open, shot through the head. One lifeless hand remained on his video camera as if he'd carefully placed it on the floor. Cantrell found two memory cards in the dead man's cargo pockets. He took the cards and put the camcorder in his pack.

"Boys, let's police up anything of intel value," he said. "Time to move."

Najib gave an order in Pashto, and his own men checked their weapons and inserted fresh magazines. Parson followed them outside. Some wore white anoraks dappled with brown and black, causing the troops nearly to disappear into the wintry landscape. Others wore American-issue N-3B parkas, hoods lined with fur. The snowshoes Parson had crafted had gotten lost. As soon as he stepped into the drifts he knew the hiking would come hard.

The bodies of the Hazara family lay sprawled in the snow behind their homestead. Light flakes floated like thistledown, obscuring the frozen faces in a translucent shroud. The boy's mynah bird hopped and pecked in the snow, left delicate prints.

The guilt hit Parson almost physically, a cold fist crushing his heart. If he'd taken a different path, they'd still be alive. He supposed these Hazaras had been the nearest thing to a happy family one could find in Afghanistan. When he'd entered their home, he'd opened their door to a war not of their making, and it had rushed in like poisoned air filling a vacuum. He remembered when he'd sliced off a corner of his blood chit and handed it to the husband. The serial number on that scrap of cloth was supposed to bring reward, perhaps even asylum. Instead it became a bad draw in some lethal lottery. Parson felt as if he'd killed them himself.

Najib kneeled by the bodies and said something so low that Parson could not hear. A prayer, he guessed. Parson wondered if he should do the same thing, and if he should have done that for Nunez. But he could think of no words. Nothing spoken in any language would bring them back. Can't change it now, he thought. Concentrate on what you *can* change.

Najib's sergeant major walked point, guiding the team of two dozen men away from the compound. Close behind, Najib gave hand signals to his men, nodded at one of them.

So he's leading from the front, thought Parson. A good sign, perhaps, but Parson still wasn't sure how much trust to place in Najib and the other Afghan troops.

Several sets of horse tracks led away into the fog. When Parson could no longer see the compound, the group came upon a wounded horse writhing in the snow. The animal raised its head, looked at the team through widened, black eyes. Blood from gunshot wounds slicked its flanks.

"What a shame we had to do that," Najib said. "This beast has done no wrong."

"I got it," Cantrell said.

He pointed his rifle at the horse's head, the muzzle just inches from the brown fur. When he pressed the trigger, the shot reverberated through the mountains. The echo seemed to loop back on itself until the bang extended into a roar that finally died away. The horse went limp.

"The animal was not the only thing bleeding," Najib said. He pointed to a blood trail that extended beyond the horse. It took Parson a moment to see it. The droplets had sunk into the powdery snow, left tiny holes tinged with pink. Only where the blood had fallen into a bootprint did Parson see a burgundy smear. To his hunter's eye, that meant a slow dripping of dark venous blood, not bright red arterial spurts. Somebody was hurt, but maybe not badly.

Najib took out a topographical map and studied it with Cantrell and the sergeant major. It didn't look much like an aeronautical chart, but Parson knew enough to realize the tightly clustered contour lines meant steep terrain.

"What's the plan?" Parson asked.

"I know this area," Najib said. "There are only one or two places they can go. When they stop, we will strike them again."

Najib took a compass bearing and spoke to his men in Pashto. The team followed Najib into the fog and light snow, and just as Parson had predicted from the map, the walk turned into a climb. Parson braced himself against gray boulders topped with crests of snow and ice. The scree crumbled beneath his feet, sent pebbles bouncing downhill until they vanished into drifts. Rotten ground.

He wished he had an ice ax, some line, and a few carabiners. And he felt naked without a weapon and a flak vest. Oh well, he thought. People in hell want ice water. Or maybe people in hell want an ice ax and some line. And some night-vision goggles and a rifle. I want to get Gold back. God, I don't want to lose somebody else.

As they gained elevation, the fog began to clear, swept away by a breeze speckled with large flakes. Parson saw to his disappointment that the cloud ceiling remained at the treetops. He'd hoped the weather would open up enough for another assault force to go after Gold in a helicopter. A Black Hawk could sure as hell outrun their damned horses. He trudged on under a gun-metal sky.

The team entered a stand of creaking timber, evergreens with spines of snow along their trunks. Parson watched Najib approach the gnarled root mass of a toppled tree, shotgun ready, safety off. If I were lying in wait, Parson thought, that's where I'd be. But no threat emerged, and Najib checked his compass, moved on.

Near the end of the day, they stopped among thicker woods beneath the ridgetop. Some men dropped their packs and began to set up four-man cold-weather tents. Parson watched as they tied off lines and spread the white rainflies. At least we won't freeze our asses off, he thought. Several of the troops set up a perimeter and scanned the terrain through binoculars and rifle scopes.

Inside a tent, Cantrell offered an MRE to Parson. Parson ate applesauce from the MRE pouch, scooping with a brown plastic spoon. He did not feel like eating and he did not taste the food. Najib entered the tent, and Parson guessed the two officers wanted to ask him more questions, but they waited while he ate. He noticed again the strip of duct tape on Cantrell's uniform. It struck Parson as a matter-of-fact, by-the-book statement: This is my blood type. If I'm bleeding out, you know what to do. Parson had seen other American troops wearing similar markers.

Najib wore no such tape. It was as if he believed in fate or predestination: I'll get seriously wounded or I won't, and it's not as if there's a blood bank behind the next tree.

Orders and regs versus the natural order. Both had their place, but command and control seemed a long way off right now, and living and dying so very close.

The pain in Parson's wrist was still just a dull ache thanks to the morphine, but the narcotic caused itching on his nose and the backs of his hands. He pulled off his gloves and scratched as the soldiers questioned him.

"He said his name was Marwan," Parson said.

Najib and Cantrell looked at each other.

"Spoke English better than I do," Parson continued. "Expensive watch. Expensive education, too, I bet."

"The devil is a gentleman," Cantrell said.

"I've never seen an Afghan like him," Parson said.

"He is not Afghan," Najib said.

"He's not?" Parson asked.

"Marwan was a lieutenant colonel in the Pakistani army and an officer in their Inter-Services Intelligence agency, the ISI," Najib explained. "Many Indian commanders have fallen to his rifle. That you met him and lived makes you fortunate, indeed."

"We have orders to capture or kill him if we get a chance," Cantrell said. "With that damned rifle of his, we'll probably have to shoot him to get near him."

"Anyway, this Marwan knows way too damn much," Parson said. "He knew something about my training. He seemed to know what bases we're using."

"He would be quite familiar with coalition forces," Najib said. "He attended Sandhurst on an exchange program. He trained with the British SAS." Najib sounded almost envious of Marwan's schooling.

"Oh, hell," Parson said. He'd always thought of terrorists as rabid dogs. Mindless malevolence. But a thinking enemy, especially one with that much on the ball, meant a higher order of foe altogether. Parson felt as if the rules of the game had changed around him and everyone playing it knew more than he did.

"Did he say anything else?" Najib asked.

"In the video, he said he'd kill us if the U.S. didn't release all the prisoners. He also said a storm is coming. Something about 9/11."

"Let us look at that video," Najib said. He picked up the camcorder Cantrell had taken from the dead insurgent. Cantrell handed him the memory cards, and Najib placed one in the camera and extended the rectangular screen. Najib pressed function buttons until he figured out the device. Finally, he said, "This is the statement with Major Parson and Sergeant Gold." He held up the camera for Cantrell to see. Parson shuddered as he listened to Marwan's crisp English accent.

In the tiny screen, he saw himself sitting beside Gold. She looked more frightened than he remembered. And she's still with them, he thought. Sweat trickled down his torso. He thought he would be sick, but he kept his stomach under control.

Najib scrolled until he found another file on the camcorder. Parson looked over Najib's shoulder. He saw Nunez at the caravansary, seated and bound. Marwan and his men stood behind him, one terrorist holding a machete.

"I don't need to see this," Parson said, turning away.

"Sorry, sir," Cantrell said. "No need for you to."

Parson looked outside, still fighting nausea. He heard Marwan chattering in Arabic.

"So this one is for a different audience," Najib said.

"Would have been," Cantrell said.

"My Arabic is not good," Najib said. "Captain Cantrell?"

"Let me get my pad," Cantrell said. He pulled a pen from the front of his body armor and retrieved paper from a leg pocket.

Parson heard Marwan's voice rise, and then he heard all the others begin to mumble, *"Allah-hu akbar."*

"Turn that shit off," Cantrell said. "All right, play it back. Please."

Cantrell took the camera and played the statement again, pausing the machine every few seconds and taking notes. "Pretty damned weird," he said.

"What does it say?" Parson asked.

"The mighty hand of Allah has drawn the curtain," Cantrell said, frowning at his pad. "Only Allah may see the work of the faithful. Seasons turn as Allah wills, and the lions of jihad stir from their dens. The martyrs await their orders."

"I am sure such abstract thoughts mean something specific to someone," Najib said.

"What did that other video say?" Cantrell asked. "Something about a blizzard never seen before in America?"

"Yes," Najib said.

Cantrell looked out through the tent flap. He pulled off his gloves with his teeth. Balled up the gloves in one fist. His fingers curled around his rifle barrel. Knuckles white. Scar along the back of his hand like a knife slash, with dots of needle scars alongside it, as if the wound had been sutured in the field and in a hurry. "Marwan is talking about a Pakistani nuclear bomb," Cantrell said.

Najib nodded.

"Oh, God," Parson said. "But the Pakistani government—"

"Is not even in control of itself," Najib said. "The ISI almost openly backs fundamentalists."

Parson had never heard of the ISI's divided loyalties. His own intel briefings had focused on the needs of fliers: threat areas, recent antiaircraft missile launches, brevity codes. But he'd read enough about Afghanistan to know the fighting usually stops in winter. The passes freeze over and everybody sits around reloading.

But the bad guys sure as hell weren't sitting around now. And they had recovered their mullah in a way that might very well have killed the old man in the shootdown. So they'd rather have him dead than questioned. Parson had no idea what to think. He wondered what Gold would say. Parson stared through the trees, watched snow fall like ash.

CHAPTER NINE

Parson lay awake in the tent. Najib and Cantrell seemed to sleep soundly, but Parson could not. He listened to the whisper of the wind and the breathing of his tentmates.

He wondered about Sergeant Gold. Was she in pain? Could she manage to escape? Was she even alive now? Maybe they shot her on the run. And maybe that was the best thing to hope for, given the other possibilities.

Parson dozed a short time, woke up alone. Still dark. Instinctively he felt for his sidearm and then remembered he no longer had one. He heard Cantrell on the satphone outside.

"Yes, sir, we'll proceed as briefed," Cantrell whispered. "Sir? You there, sir? Damn it."

Parson opened the tent flap. He pulled the zipper tab with his right hand and the pain made him grit his teeth.

"What's wrong?" he asked.

"Call dropped out," Cantrell said. "Battery's about gone."

"Spare battery?" Parson asked.

"That's what I'm using," Cantrell said.

"What you got for radios?"

"Just MBITRs," Cantrell said.

Cantrell pronounced the acronym "embitters." Parson had seen those sets before. Multiband Intrateam Radios. Too short-range to call the Air Operations Center at Bagram.

"We're also low on ammo and food," Cantrell said. "What's the old saying? 'When you're running out of everything but the enemy, you're in combat.'"

"What kind of resupply do you guys have set up?" Parson asked.

"There are planes on standby at Kandahar," Cantrell said, "but they're grounded now. Task Force is working on getting a drop from somewhere else."

"Maybe I can help with that," Parson said. Finally, something in his field of expertise. Perhaps he could coordinate a precision drop with a steerable chute guided by GPS. The airplane could be high and miles from the drop zone when it released the load.

"If you can talk to somebody and speed things up, that would be great," Cantrell said. "Get what we need to shoot, move, and communicate."

"If everything in Afghanistan is socked in," Parson said, "the plane would have to come from Manas or Al Udeid. Unless it's a model that can refuel in the air, it would have to land someplace like Jacobabad."

"Let's go for it," Cantrell said. "Let this phone battery rest a little. Then you can call your AOC. You won't have long to talk before the battery dies. The worst they can say is no." Cantrell removed the battery and placed it under his body armor, inside his shirt.

The chance of doing something useful made Parson feel stronger. He was a gear in a machine, a cog snapped back into place and turning. Maybe if he helped these guys, he was helping Gold. My whole crew is dead now, he thought. She's all that's left. Keep your shit together and help her. What can I do while I wait for that battery? he asked himself. Find a drop zone.

The eastern sky began to turn gray, backdropping the trees like a black-and-white photo slowly developing. Parson knew he didn't want to put the airdrop load here. If it floated down too far back in the direction they'd just come from, it would tumble down the hill. They might find the equipment damaged, assuming they could recover it at all. If it landed on target it would come through the trees. The pallet would probably weigh enough to break branches and reach the ground even if the chute fouled in the pines, but you never knew. Parson looked up at the dark limbs above him clattering in the breeze like dry bones. It would be a pain in the ass to climb one of those trees to cut parachute risers.

Parson saw one of Najib's men spread a tarp on the snow. Najib joined his troops and unsnapped a canteen from his web belt. He unscrewed the cap and poured water into the men's cupped hands and onto a towel. They washed their hands, then scrubbed their faces. Took off their boots and socks, took more water, washed their feet. Najib opened his compass and turned to the southwest. He and his soldiers bowed until their palms reached their knees. They stood straight, then kneeled and bowed until their foreheads touched the tarp.

Parson stepped back to give them distance. He shuddered as he listened to the same Arabic he'd heard while waiting for his execution; the only difference was that these men whispered. They saved my life, he reminded himself. Why are you guys here? he wondered. You pray to the same God as the terrorists. There are more Muslims than anyone else in this campsite. You could have killed all of us in the night if you'd wanted.

He wondered what they could be praying for. Well, what would I pray for? I'd pray for Gold. I'd ask for skill and alertness. Wits. Please, don't let me screw up. I don't want to let anyone else down.

Parson told Cantrell what he was about to do, that he wouldn't wander far. He saw that the forest continued along the ridgetop, and because of the trees it didn't take him long to lose sight of the camp. Now Parson felt even more exposed when he considered he no longer wore a flak vest.

The ridgeline came to an abrupt end and the ground sloped downhill sharply. The evergreens gave way to scrubby brush enveloped in snow, so that in the distance the vegetation appeared only as white lumps.

Parson kneeled under the last tree on the ridge, looked down into the ravine. No drop zone here. Across the ravine, another ridge sloped so sharply you could almost call it a cliff. Parson figured a creek must flow through the bottom. It would have taken fast-moving water to cut such a gap. Not that he saw any water. Though the ridge was in the early, dark stages of dawn, full night remained down in the ravine. A primitive man standing here, Parson thought, might have imagined this as some portal to Hades, the way darkness ponded like floodwater. True daylight would not come to this place until noon.

He emerged from the tree line and walked downhill to the nearest mound in the snow. Up close, the bush looked a lot like the mesquite in the southwest United States. He stopped beside it for what little cover it provided, and surveyed his surroundings. Perfect quiet, no tracks. Yet he felt he was being watched. From where, he could not say. Just your nerves, he told himself. If the Taliban saw you out here, you'd know it. Just keep it together a little longer.

Irregular drifts and knolls appeared on the incline below him like a rock-strewn moonscape blanketed by snow. As Parson advanced, he found that some were indeed boulders instead of brush. He leaned beside one skirted by wiry grass gone brown with winter.

Parson still felt eyes on him. He couldn't shake that feeling no matter how far he looked without seeing anyone. As he moved forward toward the next rock, his boots sank deeper into the snow with each step downhill. Old snow, he realized. This ravine gets so little direct light, there's not much melting. I'm stepping through snow dropped in this blizzard and the one before that, Parson thought, and maybe the one before that. Some drifts came up to his hips, making quick movement impossible.

In the dim light, he discerned the black ribbon of the stream at the bottom of the cut, a faint gurgling rising from the water. Across the creek he saw the same landscape through which he'd just descended: icy rocks the size of Humvees, brush swaddled in white, trees up above.

Parson believed he saw movement behind one of the boulders, and he froze. Now you've done it, he thought. Some raghead is going to cap your ass, and the rest of the team will have to abandon their mission to find you. Then there's no hope for Gold.

He expected to see the end of a rifle barrel, perhaps the distinctive post of an AK-47's front sight. Nothing. But there it was again. Not black metal. A bit of clothing, perhaps. Then it flicked above the rock again, a swatch of dirty yellow fur.

A paw of the same color appeared from behind the base of the rock. Parson realized he'd seen the tip of some animal's tail. Then the paws appeared on top of the boulder, and the creature raised its head to stare at Parson with orange eyes the size of half dollars.

A snow leopard.

For an instant, Parson forgot the war and marveled at the big cat, its mouth parted slightly, pink tongue between white teeth. Its tail, mottled with black spots and nearly as long as its body, twitched left and right as if the animal were devising a plan. Perhaps trying to decide whether Parson was prey.

He reached down and unclipped his boot knife, just in case. He'd fight back if he had to.

The leopard made a chuffing sound and glided onto the boulder. A powdering of snow dusted its whiskers and back. Then the animal ascended toward the trees, its movements like butterscotch flowing among the rocks.

So I'm a little too big for a snack, thought Parson. He would have enjoyed seeing the leopard if he didn't have so much on his mind. Something good in this god-awful place. Parson felt for the cat, a hunter too often hunted.

When the cat melted away, Parson stepped across the cascading water, found it only a few inches deep. In the riffles, overlapping layers of ice curled around smooth stones like braided steel. He followed the animal's tracks uphill, stopped to admire its paw prints atop the rock where it had stood. The leopard had disappeared into a copse of birches, and Parson kneeled and waited. He didn't want to crowd the cat, but he did want to see what kind of terrain lay beyond that copse. The mist made it hard to tell, but Parson thought the ridge flattened into a plateau. If it ran like that for long enough, he could put the airdrop there. Not a good place to drop paratroopers anywhere near here. Even in the level spots, these rocks would break legs and ankles. But it might do for one pallet of supplies.

Parson watched and listened for a few minutes, then rose and brushed powder from the knees of his flight suit. He climbed slowly, and it took him maybe twenty minutes to reach the stand of birch trees. When he got next to them, their white bark looked like peeling parchment etched with frost script. The leopard had vanished as if dissolved. Parson could not even find its tracks. But he did find level ground that stretched several hundred yards before yielding to the next rise. No trees, just an open field of undulating drifts, granules so fine and dry that Parson thought of walking through sifted flour.

He pulled his GPS receiver from his coat pocket and turned it on. His flight glove now showed so much wear that the leather thumb pad had pulled away from the cloth. When the receiver initialized and displayed coordinates for present position, Parson did not need to remove his glove to press STORE with a bare thumb.

Good a spot as any, he decided. The navigator who couldn't hit this field with a precision rig probably couldn't hit Afghanistan. If this weren't an emergency and I had time to write a proper mission plan, Parson thought, I'd name the drop zone DZ Leopard. Parson felt like himself for the first time since the shootdown. He was out of place among these Special Forces snake-eaters; his job made him more technician than tactician. But he knew special operators fought smart as well as hard, and they'd welcome any know-how he could provide.

When Parson returned to the camp, he found Cantrell rolling

the satphone battery between his bare hands. Najib sat writing on a notepad.

"Find a good place?" Cantrell asked.

"It'll work," Parson said. He gave Cantrell the drop zone's coordinates. Cantrell snapped the battery into the satphone and handed the phone to Parson.

Najib gave Parson the notepad. Parson paused, took the pad. He thought of Marwan, writing a war crimes confession for him.

"We are making a list of things we need," Najib said. "Can you think of anything else?"

Parson skimmed the list. MREs, water, an M-4 carbine and ammo. Night-vision goggles, snow camo parkas. Pistol and some rounds. Winter sleeping bags. Medical kit. A Hook-112 radio and several kinds of batteries.

"That's good," Parson said, "but I'm also going to ask for a weapon that will reach out and touch someone."

"All right," Cantrell said. "If you can't dazzle them with brilliance, riddle them with bullets."

"Exactly," Parson said. He wanted to hurt someone.

Parson turned on the satphone and punched in the number for the Air Operations Center.

"Bagram AOC," answered a duty officer.

"This is Major Michael Parson. Flash Two-Four Charlie. Do you understand?"

"Parson?" the officer said. "Yes! Thank God. Where are you?"

"This phone is going to die any minute. Get a pen and paper and take notes. You ready?"

"Go."

"I'm with a Special Forces ODA. I no longer have my cargo and passenger Gold, but I believe they are still alive. I have a priority Alpha request. Emergency airdrop. The zone's a little narrow, and you're going to need a Firefly rig."

Parson gave the coordinates for his DZ Leopard, and he read the list of supplies.

"I also need a rifle," he said. "An M-40 or an M-25 maybe. Anything with a scope. But don't delay the drop for any one item."

"Got it," the duty officer said. "There are some serious-looking civilians here who say to give you whatever you need."

"We've lost some of our comm gear," Parson said, "and what we do have is low on batteries. I may not be able to give drop clearance when the aircraft gets overhead. They're just going to have to drop anyway. When can we expect it?"

Parson heard discussion in the AOC, then the duty officer came back and said, "Twenty-four hours."

"Can you do it sooner?" Parson asked. A beeping interrupted him. Parson took the phone from his ear and looked at the screen. A flashing message read: LOW BATT.

CHAPTER TEN

Parson huddled in a snowdrift at the drop zone, burrowed in for concealment and a little warmth. Najib and Cantrell lay nearby, also hidden. Beyond them, some of the Special Forces troops ringed the DZ for security. Parson did not see any of them, but he felt better knowing they were there.

He listened for the sound of an airplane, but he heard only the thump of his pulse. That, and a faint electronic hiss from the earpiece in his left ear. Cantrell had loaned him an MBITR, and Parson kept it tuned to 243.0. He knew no other frequency to monitor, because the satphone had died before he could discuss details with the Air Operations Center. The emergency channel would have to do, and he hoped the flight crew would make the same guess. And he hoped they'd received the word to drop without clearance, because Parson thought the radio's hiss was growing fainter as its battery drained.

Assuming there was a flight crew and a plane

at all. The drop was late. Every passing minute made it seem more likely this operation was a fool's errand. Too much had to go right.

Parson thought about an old joke he'd heard about complicated missions: There's always one more idiot than you planned for. Sure as hell wasn't funny now. And without resupply, Parson thought, Gold is dead.

He saw Cantrell whisper into his own radio, but Parson couldn't hear it. He knew Cantrell transmitted on a different frequency, remaining in touch with his men out on the perimeter. Maybe this was normal ops for these snake-eaters. On the back side of the world, out of food and almost beyond the reach of command.

Parson heard what sounded like warble in the static from the radio. He turned up the volume and heard nothing. Probably just interference, Parson thought, sunspots or atmospheric disturbances or bleedthrough from Radio Uzbekistan. Just in case, he turned the volume up to the stop. He barely made out the words.

"Flash Two-Four Charlie, Reach Six-Eight-Three."

Parson pressed the talk button so hard the radio shook. "Reach Six-Eight-Three," he called, "Flash Two-Four Charlie. You are cleared to drop. Winds light and variable at the surface."

More hiss. Then: "Flash Two-Four Charlie, Reach Six-Eight-Three. Do you read?"

Parson answered again, heard nothing back. He called once more. Nothing.

He gripped a fistful of snow. The tools he needed to do this thing, to recover Sergeant Gold, to carry out his aircraft commander's last order, were up there somewhere. Without them, he saw little chance of survival, let alone success.

He heard the faint thrum of turboprops. Way up. Cantrell looked at him with raised eyebrows.

"They sound high," Cantrell whispered.

The engine noise faded to silence. Cantrell frowned.

"Are they gone?" he asked.

Parson placed his index finger to his lips and strained to listen. Overhead, he heard the shushing ripple of nylon in the wind.

"No," Parson said.

A metal cylinder like a coffee can with an antenna on one end dropped from the clouds, trailing a small drag chute. Despite the chute, the object punched through the snow and hit the ground hard enough for Parson to hear the impact.

"What is that device?" Najib whispered.

"Windsonde," Parson said. He told Najib how it transmitted wind data as it fell through the column of air. The data would be fed to the aircraft as the navigator set up a release point.

That navigator better be as good as me, Parson thought.

The sky grew silent again. Parson heard only a bird's single chirp. Najib and Cantrell looked at him. He circled his thumb and forefinger in an "okay" sign. Just wait, he thought. Give them time to start their run-in. Hope they got wind modeling data for these mountains.

The airplane noise returned. Faint. Growing louder. Parson pursed his lips and nodded, imagined himself on board. Preslow-down checks, complete, navigator. Slowdown, slowdown now. Five, four, three, two, one. Green light.

The engine thrum began fading. Now or not at all, then.

More nylon ripple, along with clicks and whirs. Parson knew that meant inertial reels pulling on parachute risers, making minute adjustments in course.

The chute appeared from the murk overhead as if the clouds themselves had formed it. Beneath the billowing rectangle of cloth, a pallet hung from the risers, several boxes covered in cargo netting.

Parson heard the *whump* when the load hit the ground. The chute collapsed and settled like a blanket.

"It's down," Cantrell radioed. "Hold your positions." Cantrell looked over the barrel of his rifle.

They waited to see if the airdrop had drawn the attention of bad guys. That wasn't likely. The clouds hung so low that the chute would have been visible for only three or four seconds before it landed.

Cantrell gave Parson a thumbs-up. Parson, Najib, and Cantrell trotted over to the pallet. Parson scanned the tree line even though he knew the troops had the perimeter. For a change, he was glad the weather sucked. If it can't be good enough for a chopper landing, he thought, let it be bad enough to cover us while we break down this pallet.

Parson gathered up the folds of the parachute and placed the chute beside the load. He tried to detach the cargo netting. His hands were so cold he fumbled with the clips, so he gave up on working the hardware. Instead, he drew his boot knife and cut away the netting.

"Let's get this stuff into the trees," Parson said.

The supplies had come in black Pelican cases, except the ammunition in wooden crates and food in cardboard cartons. With his good hand, Parson took the handle of a long box—a rifle, he hoped. He picked up another case with his right hand, but that hurt too much and he put it back down. He carried the long box into the woods. Najib and Cantrell brought the rest.

Parson opened the case. On the black foam padding inside, he found an M-40 rifle with a Schmidt & Bender scope. Noise suppressor at the end of the barrel. The weapon, a military version of the Remington 700, smelled of gun oil. Parson lifted the rifle and felt its familiar heft. He had once owned a 700, though not of this caliber. His own Remington chambered for .243 had taken its share of deer. But for the work ahead of him, he was glad for the heavier 7.62-millimeter. The case also contained a handwritten note: *This rifle is zeroed to five hundred yards. USMC Precision Weapons Section. Semper Fi.*

All right, thought Parson. Somebody has my back. Actually, a lot of people do for this drop to have happened.

The load included a laser range-finder, night-vision goggles, and a Hook-112 survival radio. Batteries for everything. Two parkas in winter camo. Snowshoes. Not the traditional type with wooden frames and rawhide decking, but modern ones of stainless steel and Nytex.

"You must have been good this year," Cantrell said.

"Can't believe they pulled this together so fast," Parson said.

The snow fell in tiny motes, settled like sediment. Parson put some of the gear in his pack. He and Cantrell handed out food, ammunition, and batteries to the American and ANA soldiers. Parson placed the radio in an empty pocket of his survival vest. He buckled on a set of snowshoes and gave the other pairs to the troops. Then he took off his filthy desert parka and donned a snow camo coat. He laced a cold-weather sleeping bag to his pack.

Parson opened another box and found a handgun. Not the usual Air Force nine-millimeter, but a .45 Colt. The model 1911 issued to his father and about three generations of GIs. The weapon felt substantial in his hand, solid as a bar of lead.

He picked up a magazine. Cartridges nearly the size of the end joint of his thumb. He placed the magazine into the Colt's grip, slammed it home with the heel of his good hand. Racked the slide to chamber a round. That hurt and felt good at the same time. Parson put the sidearm in the empty holster on his survival vest, and he picked up the rifle by the sling. With one fluid motion, he let the M-40 ride over his arm to rest across his shoulders.

"All right," Parson said. "Let's go get her."

Najib led the team into some evergreens at the far end of the drop zone. The trees were too sparse to provide much cover. Soon they gave way to scrub and boulders, all with a white coating. Mist floated through the clearing, and through its translucence Parson saw an incline close to vertical.

"Have you the strength for a climb?" Najib whispered.

"Yeah," Parson said. Don't ask me if I feel like it, he thought. For God's sake let's keep moving. Will we get there one minute after they cut her head off?

"There is a village on the opposite slope," Najib said. "I know it from childhood. Men on horseback would have approached it through the far valley."

"So you have us coming from a different direction," Parson said.

"Precisely," Najib said. "This Marwan is a cobra. Cold-blooded and deadly. We must become shrewd like the mongoose."

Parson liked the mongoose comparison. A scrappy creature, all teeth and claws. Permanently pissed off. Mad enough to ignore fangs and venom. Let's get our mongoose asses up this mountain, thought Parson.

The morphine had worn off and his wrist hurt like hell, but it felt good to be moving with some kind of plan. The slope offered no cover at all, just low brush and big rocks. Stalking across such exposed terrain went against everything Parson had learned in survival school. But now he wasn't just evading; he was pursuing. And for the moment, the mist provided what the landscape did not. He guessed the visibility at a matter of yards.

The unbroken snow lay flawless across the mountainside, not marred by so much as a goat's hoof. Even with the snowshoes, the powder came up nearly to Parson's knees, making it impossible to see the smaller stones on the rough ground. He placed his feet carefully, trying not to fall. Eventually the incline grew so steep the snowshoes hindered more than helped. Parson untied them and stowed them across his pack. He struggled to keep up with the soldiers, and twice they stopped to wait for him.

Najib handled the navigation, and Parson noticed that the Afghan no longer checked his compass as he led. So he really did grow up around here, thought Parson. Maybe he walked these mountains as a hunter like me. If Najib knows the terrain the way Gold knows the culture, no wonder they hooked him up with Special Forces.

Parson twisted the cap from a bottle of water delivered in the airdrop. He drank in gulps, grateful for water that didn't need chemicals to kill germs. It tasted clean and pure, but he couldn't really enjoy it. He knew how much Gold probably needed water by now. Parson had three other bottles. He decided to save them for her. He kept the empty bottle, stuffed it with snow, capped it. He placed the bottle in the pocket of his parka.

The light began to fade, and Parson shivered with the drop in temperature. His new coat had a tiny thermometer dangling from the zipper tab. Eighteen degrees Fahrenheit. He made fists inside his gloves to warm his fingers. Snow spat intermittently, and a

subtle shift of breeze touched his cheek. For a moment Parson
thought the snow might stop. Then the wind rose and a snow
squall enveloped the mountain. The whiteout cut visibility so fast
it made Parson think of flying into a cloud bank at three hundred
knots. Curtains of snow lashed his face so hard that he had to turn
his head to breathe.

Najib, now a barely visible wraith, stopped and held up his
hand, palm toward the men. The team halted. Najib found a ledge
broad enough to pause for rest, and the troops set up their low-
slung tents. A few of the soldiers stayed outside. They put on
goggles, pulled white ponchos over themselves, and set up security
in a triangle formation. The men seemed to vanish except for the
thicket of M-4 barrels pointing outward into the gray and white
nothingness.

Parson knew little of infantry tactics. He marveled at how the
team could stop and, as if a single organism, form itself wordlessly
into a stationary strongpoint, lethal and damn near invisible.

He followed Cantrell into one of the shelters. Cantrell snapped
a new battery into his satphone and made a call. Parson listened to
him report position and situation. When Cantrell finished, Parson
took the phone and called Bagram AOC.

"I'm still among the living," he told the duty officer, "Flash
Two-Four Charlie." Parson gave his coordinates and said the airdrop had worked.

"We got all kinds of pararescue guys standing by to pick you
up," said the duty officer. "Choppers on alert. We just need a break
in the weather."

"How's the forecast?" Parson asked.

"No better. The weather shop is calling this a hundred-year
blizzard. They expect at least four more days of this."

Parson pressed thumb and forefinger to the bridge of his nose, closed his eyes.

"What's your altimeter setting now?" he asked.

"Uh, two-seven-five-six."

Parson had never seen barometric pressure that low. No wonder this squall hit like a fucking train. He wanted to ask to speak with the weather shop for more details, but he decided to end the call. No point using up batteries over what couldn't be helped.

He unrolled his sleeping bag inside Cantrell's tent. Kept on his boots and survival vest. He placed his pack at the foot of the sleeping bag and leaned his rifle across it. Unholstered the .45 and placed it beside him. He fell asleep immediately with his hand on the Colt.

PARSON WOKE TO A shove at his shoulder. He came to consciousness like rising from a frozen lake to crack through ice. His thoughts tumbled and he felt for the pistol.

"Easy, cowboy," Cantrell said. "We're moving out."

"Good."

Still dark, still snowing, though not so hard now. Maybe five more inches of powder had accumulated. Parson rolled up his sleeping bag, crawled outside, hoisted his rifle and pack. Took a drink of snow water from the bottle in his pocket. Swished the water in his mouth, spat it out.

The land around Parson lay in perfect blackness. No lamp, no sign of habitation. Like the first night on Earth, or maybe the last.

The team struck tents in silence. Najib and his sergeant major led again, and the men followed them uphill in a staggered column. Parson switched on his night-vision goggles. The falling snow glowed and swirled as if it were energized, minute shavings of a pulsar disintegrated and scattered to the ground.

Parson's wrist hurt some, though not as bad as yesterday. His chest ached, from both the cracked ribs and the frigid air chilling his lungs. The cold seemed to overtake him from the inside out. His cheeks had no feeling. He held his hand over his face and exhaled, but his breath hardly warmed his skin at all.

As he climbed, he thought how the war and the storm had brought him to some primitive state. His multimillion-dollar airplane a pile of scrap. Satellite signals, laser beams, and microwave transmissions reporting his situation around the world, doing him damn little good. Injured and angry, wanting to kill the other tribe. Stripped to my core, he thought, maybe this is just how it is.

The slope grew steeper, and Parson had to pull himself up by the branches of scrub bushes that somehow clung to life on this god-awful rise. He dug through the snow for handholds, an effort that slowed him down and covered his arms in powder. When he grabbed the stems of a brushy evergreen, he noticed a sickening odor. Parson frowned and wiped his gloves on his coat.

"You have found a lipad," Najib said. "Some of my people believe the plant keeps away evil spirits."

"I'll take all the help I can get," Parson said.

To the east, a smudge of gray lightened the deep black. The grayness spread until Parson didn't need NVGs to see the snow falling. The cloud ceiling still seemed so low he could touch it. But underneath, visibility had improved a bit overnight.

Up ahead, Najib crouched. Signaled by pressing his open hand toward the ground. The men flattened themselves into the snow. At first Parson wondered if Najib had seen the enemy, but the Afghan didn't look alarmed. Parson realized they had reached the spine of the ridge. The troops didn't want to be silhouetted atop the crest.

Parson crept forward and looked down the mountain. He saw only more mountain, more snow and boulders. But Najib seemed to focus on something. Parson pulled out binoculars and glassed the slope.

Perhaps a mile away, a stalk of smoke rose to join the clouds. If not for the smoke, Parson might have missed the village altogether. But on close inspection he made out what looked like facets in the distant snowfield. Flat surfaces of roofs, blanketed. No movement. No animals. Pallid mud walls. The place apparently drained of life and color, as if the village itself had bled to death.

CHAPTER ELEVEN

The team watched the village for the better part of an hour. Nothing changed except that the smoke grew fainter until Parson could no longer distinguish it from the snow and mist, the fire having consumed whatever had fed it. He wondered if he'd find Gold, or what was left of Gold, in one of those dwellings.

Najib and Cantrell split the team into squads. They began approaching the village from four directions. Parson followed Najib's squad as they doubled back down the slope for concealment. Then they crossed the ridgetop south of the village and stopped to watch again.

Nothing new from this angle. Najib walked along wearing the headset from his MBITR, with its tiny microphone suspended in front of his lips. Parson saw him whisper, "Negative."

Snow continued to fall on snow. The flakes fell diagonally in such a way that Parson lost his sense of horizon. The effect left him a little dizzy, as if his internal gyros had failed. He stumbled, went down on one knee.

"Are you all right?" Najib whispered.

Parson nodded. Najib offered a hand and helped pull him back to his feet. Scabs of packed snow stuck to the leg of his flight suit, then fell off.

As the team converged on the village, Parson saw nothing of the other three squads. Najib paused and told him, "Wait here." Parson lay prone in the snow and scanned through his rifle scope.

Najib's squad crept forward, and Parson finally saw two of the other elements take positions on either side of the mud-brick homes. Overwatch and security, Parson guessed, while the remaining squads entered the village. He thumbed his safety to the FIRE position, trained his scope on a door here, an alleyway there.

He saw Najib kneel under a small, wood-frame window, pull the pin on a grenade. Najib did not throw it, just seemed to listen. A soldier kicked in a door and tore in, pointing his rifle. Two other men right behind him, barrels aimed at opposite corners.

Parson waited for the sputter of gunfire. It never came. The team kicked in more doors, rushed more rooms. Not one shot. Najib put the pin back in the grenade.

Cantrell appeared from behind a building, conferred with Najib, pointed. He pulled out a digital camera and took photos of something on the ground. Parson wondered what they could have found of intel value. His next thought made him grip the rifle so hard that it hurt his wrist. Was that Gold?

Najib motioned for him to move up. Parson rose from the

snow and headed into the village at a jog, holding his weapon across his chest. The way the soldiers were standing, Parson knew that whatever had happened here was over. He trotted up to the troops, breathing hard.

At Cantrell's feet lay four bodies nearly covered by snow. Najib kneeled and brushed the powder away from their faces. All Afghans. Eyes open. Blood drying and freezing. With a touch of his fingers, Najib closed each set of eyes.

"The Prophet said when the soul departs, the eyesight follows," Najib said. He leaned on his shotgun, its stock to the ground. "May God curse the blasphemers who did this." A shotgun shell dropped from his bandolier, and he rolled the shell in his fingers.

"Did you know them?" Parson asked.

"Distant relations."

"There's more," Cantrell said.

Six bodies lay in a row outside one dwelling. They included a teenage girl. Other bodies in groups. Parson counted nineteen. Two dead men found alone at separate spots. Maybe those guys had gone down fighting, but the others had been executed. A horse, dead of multiple wounds spaced evenly across its body, apparently from a burst on full auto. No sign of an American woman.

"Looks like they killed the whole fucking village," Cantrell said.

"What the hell for?" Parson asked. Cantrell shook his head.

Parson caught an odor of smoke and maybe kerosene. He discovered what looked like a muddy, black slag pile, the remains of a bonfire. In the ashes he found a charred blanket, blackened and wet like a discarded pelt. An unburned corner of a cardboard box. Plastic vials misshapen by heat or burned away to nothing but a fire-stained cap. A foil pouch with browned lettering, still readable: "Bacitracin Zinc Ointment EXP DEC11." An Army-issue parka, eaten by flames and now sodden. Gray stains down-wind where ash had mingled with snow.

He nudged the mess with his boot, felt something solid. Parson scraped soggy ash away from the hard thing and recognized it as a steel pallet. Stenciling on the edge: USAF PROPERTY.

Relief supplies. Parson had dropped several loads of them himself. Food, clothing, and medicine to help remote villages get through a winter of war. Those motherfuckers had torched it all.

"What do you make of this?" asked Parson.

"The Taliban forbids outside help," Najib said. "I have seen them destroy supplies before. But it would take something more for them to murder the entire town."

Cantrell took his pistol in one hand and a SureFire light in the other. "Search everything," he called. "Watch for booby traps."

The men entered the houses one by one. Parson heard thumps and crashes, but nothing to cause alarm. He checked out the tracks and hoofprints on the ground, wondering what story he could infer. It was mainly a jumble, snow churned and stomped into frozen ground, or mixed with mud and blood near the fire in a slurry that was starting to refreeze.

Cantrell emerged from a narrow cellar. "Captain Najib," he called. "I think you better see this."

Parson followed Najib down the steps. Cantrell trained his light into a corner. The beam revealed a boy about twelve years old, trembling, mouth open. Parson thought the child looked like a trapped animal, unable to fight or flee, waiting to be finished off.

"I found him under a tarp," Cantrell said.

"Meh wirigah," Najib said. He repeated the phrase, offered his hand. The boy took it and followed Najib up the stairs. The child blinked and stared at the soldiers.

"Check him out," Cantrell called to his medic. "Open an MRE and see if he'll eat anything."

One of the soldiers produced a green blanket and draped it over the child's shoulders. Black lettering across one of the blanket's folds read: "U.S." The men steered the boy through a doorway, out of sight from the carnage outside. The medic shined a light into his eyes, prodded his limbs and abdomen.

"Ask him if this hurts," the medic said. Najib translated and the boy shook his head, though tears rolled down his cheeks.

"Tsok?" Najib asked. *"Kelah?"*

The boy began speaking quickly, stopped and cried, spoke quickly again.

A soldier sliced open a pouch of carrot cake. The boy took one bite and swallowed, then held the pouch and cried. Crumbs on his tongue and his face. Najib spoke what sounded like soothing words, but Parson wondered what balm words could offer now.

"He says Taliban came with an English woman soldier," Najib said. "The village elders did not want them. You see the result."

"Ask him if the woman was hurt," Parson said.

"He says she was alive when they took her away. He says some of the Taliban left with her."

"You mean they split up?" Cantrell asked.

Najib questioned the boy again.

"He says there was a holy man on a horse, and most of the men left with him."

"What about Marwan?" Parson asked.

"I am quite sure Marwan would remain with the mullah," Najib said.

"Why would they separate Sergeant Gold?"

"Perhaps to move faster," Najib said. "To make our job harder. Why matters little. They did it."

"At least they haven't killed her yet," Cantrell said. "Maybe they want her for propaganda or ransom. Or worse."

Parson stepped outside, started to slam the door. He caught himself. Don't scare the boy, fool. He's probably fucked up for life as it is. Parson held on to the top of the door, ran his other hand along his rifle sling. Seethed.

He walked out into the snow, examined the ground again. The torn-up snow through the village told him nothing. But beyond the fire he saw several sets of boot marks and one set of hoofprints leading off into the distance. That he saw the tracks at all meant they'd been made after the squall blew through. But lighter snow had begun to fill them so that they looked like puncture wounds starting to heal. He found fresh tracks where Cantrell's squad had come in. Then another set going out, slightly obscured by new snow. Three, no four. Four people. No horse. One line of smaller tracks. Good. Whatever they'd done to her, she could still walk.

Parson showed the tracks to Cantrell. "Trail's getting fainter by the minute," Parson said. "If we get to her, maybe another team can track down the rest when the weather clears."

Cantrell called to his comm sergeant, "Set up the Shadowfire. I need to talk to Task Force."

The sergeant took off his pack. He unloaded a black metal frame and extended its legs and four antenna panels so that it resembled a giant spider. Connected a coaxial cable.

If they're using all this secret squirrel comm gear, Parson figured, they must be serious about what they think Marwan is up to.

Cantrell lifted a handset. "Bayonet," he called, "Razor One-Six." After a pause, he said, "Sir, we got a decision to make." Cantrell described the massacre, the boy's account, the two trails in the snow. "I understand, sir."

Parson studied Cantrell's face for hints. Cantrell nodded as he listened, glanced at Parson, looked out into the snowfall.

"We will, sir," Cantrell said. He gripped the handset's cord, closed his eyes as if hit with a migraine. "I'm sure it's a hard call. We'll keep you informed. Razor One-Six out."

"Well?" Parson asked.

"They have crews on alert at Bagram to get Sergeant Gold as soon as the storm ends," Cantrell said. "But the Task Force commander wants us to stay on Marwan and your detainee."

"When the storm ends?" Parson said. "That could be days."

"I don't like it either, sir. But if those guys do what we think they're trying to do, we could lose a lot of civilians."

"So you're saying Gold is expendable."

Cantrell sighed, looked past Parson. "I wasn't going to say it, sir, but that's the word the colonel used."

So they were just going to give her up. Parson had hoped it wouldn't come to this, but part of him was not surprised, given the stakes. In his military courses, he had learned about a set of regulations rarely used, or even read. In the clinical language of the Pentagon, they established a category of missions for which recovery of personnel is not a consideration. Well, he'd still consider it.

"Call 'em back," Parson said. "I want to talk to that colonel."

"There's no point in that, Major," Cantrell said.

Najib came outside. Cantrell told him about the Task Force's instructions. Najib placed his hand on Parson's shoulder.

"You have done everything you could," Najib said. "You are a good soldier."

"So is she."

"We have all lost someone," Najib said. "We will lose more before this is over."

Yeah, thought Parson. Not if I can help it. He kneeled by Gold's tracks, eyed where they vanished into the teeming snow. "I'm going after Sergeant Gold," he said.

"You're nuts," Cantrell said. "And we have our orders."

"*You* have orders," Parson said. "You guys are a unit with a mission. I'm just a downed airman. I can do whatever the hell I want."

"If you don't stay with us," Cantrell said, "you will die. Period."

"I understand," Najib said. "You love your comrades more than you hate your enemies."

"I don't know about that," Parson said.

"Don't encourage him," Cantrell said.

"I do not encourage," Najib said. "I merely understand. Too many of my own friends are dead."

That's why you understand, thought Parson. Good. You get it.

Parson strode into one of the houses, swung off his pack, and dropped it on a table. He dug through the pack, taking inventory. Najib and Cantrell joined him inside.

"Can you give me one or two MREs?" he asked.

Najib pulled a meal pouch from his own pack, laid it in front of Parson. Cantrell shook his head.

"I got more double-A batteries than I need," Parson said. "Take some of these." Clunked them onto the table.

"Your rifle needs camouflage," Najib said. He found a roll of white tape in one of his pockets. Picked up Parson's M-40 and began spiraling the tape around the barrel, forend, and stock. When he finished, the tape did not cover the weapon entirely, but it broke up the outline so thoroughly that the rifle seemed to disappear against Najib's snow camo anorak.

"Oh, fuck it," Cantrell said. "Listen to me. I can't make you into an infantryman right now. Even if I could, this would still be insane. But remember you got nothing but stealth. Everything runs to your disadvantage except that." Cantrell pointed at Parson, ignoring rank now, lecturing a trainee. "If you do make contact, do not get in a hurry. Take your time. Your only hope is a far ambush. At least you got the weapon for that."

Parson checked his magazines. All full, plenty of ammo. An extra battery for the Hook-112. Cantrell examined the radio. "Let's stay in touch on 243," he said.

"You got it," Parson said. "But the bad guys have at least one of our survival radios. We have to assume they hear us."

"Really?" Cantrell tapped his finger along the side of the radio. "We can use that. Tactical deception."

"How?"

"I don't know. We'll think of something."

"Too bad we can't talk secure," Parson said.

"We can do the next best thing," Cantrell said. "Start every call on 243. But if one of us says the word 'delta,' we'll switch to 282.8."

"Slick," Parson said. "They've been fucking with me over these radios. Good to get a little payback."

Cantrell spread out a topographical map. "You clear on where you're starting from?" he asked.

Parson examined the topo chart. It wasn't marked in familiar lat/longs. Instead it used the Army's military grid reference system. It took him a minute to do the math, but he found the valley that cradled this newly extinct village. He knew he couldn't mark the map with a pen. That could give the bad guys information to use if he was captured. But he creased the chart with his thumbnail.

"About here," he said.

"Close enough," Cantrell said. "Take this map with you. We got others."

Parson leaned on the edge of the table and buckled on his snowshoes. Took his M-40 from Najib.

"Thanks for what you did for me," he said. "It would have been a bad morning if you hadn't come along when you did."

Snow began to blow in through the open doorway. Settling on the floor, fine as dust. Parson took that as a bad omen. He'd heard old-time outdoorsmen say big flakes meant the snow would stop soon; tiny ones meant more accumulation. He'd never thought to ask the meteorology guys if there was any truth to that.

Some of Najib's men came inside. Parson guessed they had

figured out what he was doing and they wanted a last look at the crazy infidel flyboy about to get himself killed.

"God go with you," Najib said.

Parson hoisted his pack, tightened the straps, and headed out into the storm.

CHAPTER TWELVE

Parson followed the tracks through welts of drifted snow. The footprints wended up a slight rise where birch trees stood with white trunks like the bleached ribs of some giant dead thing. He came to a spot where the tracks narrowed close together, three sets of large prints around a set of small ones. Snow tossed and stomped. No blood. Some minor struggle, Parson guessed. Maybe she kicked one of them in the balls.

The tracks continued more or less straight across a cut where mist seemed to have rolled down the mountains and collected. Visibility dropped to near zero. The fog and fine snowflakes filtered the daylight so that it seemed late dusk, though Parson's watch read just after two in the afternoon. He had reset his watch from Greenwich Mean Time to local Afghanistan time. The luminous dial glowed like a distant moon until he covered it again with his parka sleeve.

Parson stopped and looked around. The mist hid all terrain features. He saw nothing but snow at his feet and the swirling ice fog. The village and the special ops team were about four miles behind him now.

A chill came over him and he trembled slightly, more shudder than shiver. He thought how he'd never get more alone than this. Never farther from home. At least he knew what to do. Better to lose comfort than purpose.

He opened his lensatic compass and took a bearing. The tracks were leading roughly two-three-zero, though he could see only about four steps ahead. Why southwest? Parson wondered where they were taking her. Were they fleeing aimlessly? Probably not. He hoped not. It would do no good to find them all frozen to death.

Parson followed the trail one step at a time, wanting better visibility, not getting it. He saw what looked like a heavy bank of mist ahead of him. As he took more steps, the thing grew solid. The wall of a mud-brick hut.

Parson froze. Waited for a shot.

You stupid motherfucker, he thought. At least they can't see through this shit any better than you can.

He wanted to drop to the ground. But now movement could give him away. He held his breath, held his rifle. Thumbed the safety and the click sounded like a thunderclap.

No noise, no movement ahead. Maybe if he saw the enemy he could make a snap shot. Bring up the M-40 like shouldering a shotgun to take a pheasant on the rise. And you better make it good, he thought. If you miss and have to chamber another round with this bolt action, those bastards will be on full auto. Mow your ass right down.

He waited eternal seconds, minutes. No sign of bad guys except the footprints. Parson eased himself down on one knee. No sign of anybody. He slung the rifle over his shoulder, drew the

Colt. He pulled back the hammer and held the .45 in both hands, ignoring the pain in his wrist. Then he moved up to the wall.

The tracks diverged there, some going left around the house, some going right. Parson listened closely, heard nothing. He went to the left, poised to fire.

The tracks continued along that side of the mud-brick home. Or that side of the ruin, actually. Parson saw that the roof had been blown off, along with chunks of the wall. Snow covered the rubble inside.

The footprints led to an adjoining house. It, too, had been blown open. One wall leaned as if it were about to fall. Parson aimed the pistol through a doorway, swept the room with the barrel. He had enough daylight to see because that roof was gone, too. Nothing inside.

In all there were five destroyed dwellings, long abandoned. The footprints came together on the other side and continued along the rise. He supposed the insurgents had hoped for something intact enough to provide shelter, and they'd found the place wanting.

He took cover behind a collapsed doorway, just in case. He surveyed his surroundings and saw his breath condense and float away into the mist. So what did these poor folks do to deserve the Taliban blowing them away? he wondered. Bastards. Parson guessed that whatever horror had happened here, it was a while ago. He found no bodies, no animals, no object of value.

He noticed three holes in one wall. A partial roof sheltered that wall from snow, so he saw the punctures clearly, each about the size of his fist, and angled as if the rounds came from above.

It took a moment for Parson to realign his thinking. So this wasn't their doing but ours. An air strike. Those holes looked about right for the thirty-millimeter nose cannon on an A-10. It fired rounds made of depleted uranium, designed to punch through a tank. Likely wiped out whatever and whoever was here.

So maybe this was a Taliban hideout as far back as 2001. Or maybe not. Parson knew of close-air-support missions that had saved coalition troops and ripped up terrorists, but he also knew of some god-awful fuckups that had blown away civilians. The fighter jocks liked to brag that they could thread a needle with their precision targeting, but that didn't help if you threaded the wrong needle.

Parson took out the topographical map the snake-eaters had given him. He made a fold where he thought he was, though the chart showed no village. He didn't expect the map to include every grouping of hovels. The newest American charts had terrain data gathered from space by radar, but not even NASA could track life at ground level in Afghanistan.

He decided to check in with Cantrell. Parson tried to plug the earpiece into the Hook-112, but his fingers were so cold he missed the receptacle twice. He finally connected it and turned on the radio.

"Razor One-Six," he whispered. "Flash Two-Four Charlie, radio check."

"Flash Two-Four Charlie, Razor One-Six has you five by five. How me?"

"Loud and clear. Flash Two-Four Charlie out."

So at least this much of the plan is working, he thought, but now those guys are just a source of information and maybe a relay for communications, at best. They had a mission, and they weren't coming to get him if he screwed up. Parson switched off the radio and stood up.

He followed the tracks downhill a while, then across an open plain where the snow got deeper. Each step an effort. Now and then he stopped, listened, watched. He didn't want to repeat the mistake of blundering right up on something in the low visibility.

The trail led downhill again. The grade eventually became steeper, and Parson began slipping. One of his snowshoes caught on a rock and he lost his balance. The heavy pack pulled him down, and he hit the ground rolling on his side, instinctively guarding the injured wrist. He found himself facedown in the snow. Now his chest hurt again from the ribs cracked days before by Marwan's bullet.

Sonofafuckingbitch, he thought. He picked himself up, at least grateful he hadn't worsened the wrist injury. He checked the rifle. No apparent damage, scope lens still intact. He felt the cold powder inside his parka, inside his gloves. He shook out most of the snow, brushed himself off. Even colder now. Gotta keep moving, he thought, and that will warm you up.

The tracks led back into sparse woods, a thin stand of larch. Parson examined the footprints for any hint of how Gold was doing, any suggestion of further struggle or resistance. He found nothing but one boot track in front of another.

When he halted to listen again, he could not stop shivering. Could not feel his fingers. Parson kneeled and, with some effort, pulled off his gloves. Wet gloves. He hadn't removed all the snow from when he'd fallen, and it had melted inside the flight gloves. No fucking wonder. He blew into his cupped hands, and when his fingers touched his lips it was like kissing ice.

All right, he thought, gotta get these dry. I don't have time for this shit. Gotta get to Gold. But what did Cantrell tell you? Take your time. She's either dead or she's not, and you will be soon if you make a mistake. Like getting frostbite.

No choice now but to make a fire. At least the fog still hung low and thick enough to hide smoke. Parson had precious little options for fuel. He wished he'd thought of taking rags or something from the village before he parted ways with the Special Forces team.

Parson broke a branch from one of the birch trees, cracked it again across his knee. Hurt his wrist some. Then he drew his boot knife and used it to peel birch bark. He decided to try making a Dakota fire hole, the stealthiest fire technique he knew. He would normally dig into the soil for that, but he had neither the tools nor the strength right now for digging into frozen earth. I'll just have to try it in snow, he thought. If it melts and collapses, it melts and collapses.

He dug a hole by a tree, using his hands. He hoped the tree branches overhead would help disperse any smoke that didn't disappear into the fog. When he'd made a hole in the snow about two feet across, he put three hand-sized rocks at the bottom and piled the bark, then the twigs and branches. He dug another hole off to the side and connected it with the fire hole at an angle to create a vent.

The cold-saturated twigs and branches gave him little confidence, so he decided to add something. He fumbled through his survival vest for a magnesium fire starter, a silver rectangle about the size of a cigarette lighter. He started to use his boot knife again, but decided he didn't want to dull it. Instead he opened the blade on a multitool from his vest. He began to scrape shavings from the block of magnesium. His hands shook so violently he nearly cut himself. Any doubts he might have had about taking the time to build a fire left him now, because he was going into honest-to-God hypothermia.

Parson scattered the shavings all over the tinder, then made a concentrated pile of magnesium in the middle. Struck the sparking rod once, twice, three times. The shavings caught and flared up as intensely as a welding arc. Parson squinted and looked away.

The flash from the magnesium ignited the birch bark like paper. Feathers of flame billowed up from the tinder. Occasionally a stray shard of magnesium would light off like a tracer round in a burning city. A firefight in a tiny holocaust.

The wood smoke smelled good, but he worried how far the scent carried. He glanced above him. The smoke seemed to disappear into the branches and mist. The flames remained below the surface of the snow, invisible to anyone just yards away. Snowmelt trickled to the bottom of the fire hole and puddled and hissed around the rocks.

He peeled off the soggy gloves and draped them on sticks over the fire. He held his hands in the heat, clenched and unclenched his fists. Parson's fingers ached as the circulation returned. He checked them for waxy whiteness, the first sign of frostbite that would eventually turn black and dead. So far so good. They were all red and they hurt.

A calculated risk occurred to him, and he decided to go ahead. He sat down, removed the snowshoes, unlaced his boots. Pulled off his boots and felt his socks, which were damp. Rolled off the black socks and hung them with the gloves. Pushed the empty boots near the fire.

He cocked the .45 and placed it on his pack. Peered at his toes, and they looked all right. They ached, too, as they warmed.

Parson ate some MRE crackers as he waited for the gloves and socks to dry. He grew sleepy and shook his head to fight it off.

When everything had dried, he pulled on the stiff gloves and socks. The warmth felt good, but it reminded him of all the comforts denied him now. Parson laced up his boots and put on the snowshoes.

He decided to check in with Cantrell again. Turned on the radio and inserted the earpiece.

"Razor One-Six," he called. "Flash Two-Four Charlie."

"Go ahead, Flash Two-Four Charlie."

"Just checking in. I'm proceeding as briefed."

"Copy that," Cantrell said. A pause. "Change of plans for you. We are all to proceed to the LZ for extraction. A chopper will get us out of here when the weather clears. Proceed to landing zone Delta. Repeat, landing zone Delta."

What the hell is he talking about? Parson wondered. Then he remembered. He changed frequencies.

"Flash Two-Four Charlie, you up on this freq?" Cantrell called.

"Got you loud and clear," Parson whispered. "Go ahead."

"We're proceeding as briefed, too. If they heard that, maybe they'll think we're leaving. And if they stop running, we won't have to chase those motherfuckers all over these mountains."

"Roger that," Parson said. "Understood."

Smart son of a bitch, thought Parson. He pocketed the radio, lowered the hammer on his Colt, and holstered the weapon. He kicked snow into the fire hole until it smothered the embers. He pushed in more snow to hide the ashes. Closed up his pack and settled it across his shoulders. Picked up the rifle and moved on.

The trail was getting harder to follow now. The snowfall continued filling in the tracks, and they were beginning to look more like depressions in the snow than bootprints. The tracks led across an open plateau smothered in mist. Parson crossed it slowly. Watching, listening. Fatigue and sleep deprivation started to set in again. Once when he stopped, kneeled, and closed his eyes to listen, he caught himself nodding off.

Parson wanted to rest, but he feared he'd lose the trail altogether if he didn't keep going. A few years ago he had tracked a wounded deer through freezing rain. As he followed the red drops and smears, he became tired and chilled, and he wished he'd never taken the shot. But he felt he owed it to the animal to finish it off. He'd pushed on as rain diluted the blood spoor. He found the buck, dead and cold, in the middle of a clearing.

But I didn't know from tired back then, he thought. I didn't know cold or pain, either.

The minute crystals came down hard and steady now, ticking against his parka. Parson wondered how this storm system could have gathered so much moisture. Apparently it had picked up half the Arabian Sea, frozen it, and dumped it on Afghanistan. With no upper air currents to move it anywhere except right on top of my ass, he thought.

It felt strange to be so completely on his own. Like any other U.S. serviceman, Parson was used to having huge technical advantages over the enemy. Even though a helicopter couldn't get to him, he might normally have had other resources at his disposal. He thought about what an unmanned drone might do for him. Maybe he could get a radio patch for some kind of Conference Skyhook, and a Predator driver sitting in Nevada could tell him exactly where the bad guys were. Better yet, if it were an armed drone like a Reaper, the aircraft could make the bad guys go away.

Just a black puff on a video screen. But this damnable blizzard negated all that. Except for his GPS, about the only difference between him and the Brits who got routed here in the 1840s was that his rifle loaded at the breech and not the muzzle.

He plodded on under a slate sky. The mantle of snow lay unbroken around him except for the fading line of little white sinkholes. The first wash of dusk caused him a hint of panic. If I don't find them today and the snow doesn't stop, he thought, I'll never find her. If they don't kill her outright, they'll take her across the border. And then we won't recover so much as a dog tag. Gold's name on MIA bracelets forever. To hell with that.

As the light started to die, the tracks became nearly impossible to see. Parson dropped his pack, hunted for his night-vision goggles. He turned them on, looked through them, and got nothing but blank green. Still too much skyglow. He'd have to wait for black night to get any use out of them, and he realized, My God, that won't be long.

He glanced down at the trail again and saw nothing. Too dark now for the naked eye. And the goggles might not have enough resolution to pick out tracks. He took a mental bearing of the direction the bootprints had led. No help from a compass or a satellite now, navigator, he said to himself. Just a vector based on instinct. Maybe even a prayer, if there's anybody listening. Guide me tonight unless You want her dead.

Maybe this is another test, he thought, like the one he'd botched when he almost torched the mullah. He wanted to do better this time. He had to, for Gold's sake. It seemed this blizzard, this whole damned predicament, was probing him down to the core of his soul.

Parson trudged straight ahead, blindly. He felt the terrain rise, and he saw the dim outlines of trees. Other than that, he could make out nothing. He struggled uphill, and he stopped when he sensed that he had reached the crest. Beyond it pure, undistilled blackness. As if his oldest predecessors had been right and he'd sailed to the edge of the earth and looked out into the void.

Damned NVGs ought to work now, he thought. He switched them on again and saw that he overlooked a valley. It appeared empty, just another fold of snow and rocks in the Hindu Kush. Parson had flown over many like it, as rugged and unpopulated as the day they were formed. He scanned with the goggles, and he made out only the slope below him. The NVGs could penetrate mist for a short distance, but when Parson tried to focus on things farther out, he got little but sparkle and backscatter. The goggles worked by extreme amplification of any light source, but there was just nothing out there. Until he moved his head to the left. A bright green dot glowed like a smudge of phosphorus on the black surface of a night ocean.

Gotcha, thought Parson. There you are. There you are. That has to be an oil lamp or a flashlight. And it has to be them. There's no one else here.

Parson judged the light at better than a mile away, but he knew that was just a rough guess. Night-vision goggles gave poor depth perception even in clear weather, let alone with fog and snow in the way.

He fought the urge to plunge ahead toward the light. He couldn't use the M-40 at long range in the dark, anyway. The optic was not any kind of thermal nightscope. And they've obviously stopped for now, he thought. They aren't going anywhere, and you better think of some plan other than just shooting until one of them shoots you. And her.

In a deep drift windward of a boulder, he dug a snow cave, taking care with his sleeves so powder didn't get inside his gloves again. He stretched out inside and raised the NVGs to look at the light again. Still there.

Parson took the bottle of snow water from his pocket and drank it all. He filled the bottle with snow and, when it melted inside his coat, drank it all again. He didn't feel that thirsty, but he wanted the water for an alarm clock. He'd wake up to piss before dawn. An old trapper's trick.

He leaned the rifle on the end of his pack to keep the barrel out of the snow. Then he unrolled the sleeping bag, slid into it, and zipped it up. Held the Colt in his left hand, outside the sleeping bag, his thumb on the hammer.

We'll settle this thing tomorrow, he thought, to the satisfaction of one party or the other. He remembered Cantrell's admonition to take his time, and Najib's line about being shrewd like the mongoose. Parson liked that comparison. Because, he thought, a mongoose has one thing in mind: I'm gonna fuck up that snake.

CHAPTER THIRTEEN

Parson's bladder woke him as planned. He checked his watch and saw he'd slept about four hours. When he switched on his night-vision goggles, the light was still there. He crawled out of the snow cave, unzipped, and urinated. Then he rolled up the sleeping bag, put on the snowshoes, and gathered up his gear. Kicked in the snow cave. Slung the rifle over his shoulder, Colt in one hand, NVGs in the other. Hell of a way to start your last day, he thought.

The snow fell steady and even, skittering against Parson's coat like blown grit. He trekked along the ridgetop toward the light, stopping every few steps to look through the goggles. The ground fog had cleared somewhat. Parson saw that the light came from inside a little collection of mud-brick hovels, much like the bombed-out compound he'd seen yesterday. He couldn't tell much else from this distance.

Parson stalked through sparse alders and what looked like ash trees. The valley below was treeless, so Parson knew he'd have no cover if he tried to approach all the way to the compound. But he didn't intend to, at least not at first. As Cantrell had told him, a distant ambush was about the only way to take on a larger force. Inflict harm from afar.

He picked his way through knee-deep snow until the mud huts lay down the hill directly beneath him. The ridgeline provided an elevated position above his target, as close to ideal as he was likely to find. He placed his pack on the ground and brushed away snow around it. Then he lowered himself into prone and looked over the pack through his NVGs.

In the emerald glow, he saw that the insurgents had chosen the only intact dwelling from what had been a group of four. The roofs on the others had been blown away, along with part of the walls. No livestock pens. Probably another long-dead village. He saw no light from this angle, but he knew no one had left the house since he'd awakened.

Parson leaned his rifle across the pack. Checked the chamber for a round. Pressed the pack down in the snow until the weapon aimed naturally toward the village. Now he could use the pack as a bench rest, steadying the rifle and sparing fatigue on his arms.

For once, he felt he had all the tools he needed for the task at hand. He took the laser range-finder from his coat pocket and placed it on the pack beside the NVGs. Then he watched for movement. Waited for light.

When the first hint of dawn allowed him to make out the shape of the huts without the NVGs, he looked at the village through the range-finder and pressed the range button. The LCD readout told him 532 yards. The note from the armorer had said the rifle was sighted in to 500 yards. Close enough for government work. No need to adjust the bullet drop compensator.

Parson knew the limits of his own marksmanship. A real sniper would have put thousands of rounds through this weapon, would know its nuances well enough to place a bullet squarely through the head of any target. Though Parson was a good shot, he couldn't pull off a feat like that with a rifle he'd never fired before. He'd just have to aim for center mass and leave the rest to a jacketed slug moving at better than two thousand feet per second.

It was still too dark to use the scope. Parson could barely distinguish the crosshairs. He turned an adjustment turret to switch on the illuminated reticle. Now he saw the crosshairs but little else. The German scope was one of the best daylight optics money could buy, but it needed at least a little ambient light. That's okay, thought Parson. I got all day.

A gossamer strand of gray smoke began to rise from the hut. It climbed straight up until it melded with the low cloud ceiling. "Thoughtful of you," Parson whispered to himself. They'd given him a wind drift indicator. Now he knew he didn't have to move the windage dial.

He began to shiver. He hated to move around any more, but better now than later. Parson sat up, untied his sleeping bag. Unrolled it and slid his legs inside. He turned over onto his belly and lay prone again. Felt himself warming some. At least now he could hold the weapon steady.

Parson tried to tally the odds. He considered the four sets of bootprints. So there was Gold and three insurgents, best case. That's assuming they didn't meet anybody down there. Unlikely but not impossible. So were they just stopping for a night's rest or stopping for good? That might depend on whether they had heard Cantrell's little trick over the radio. No way to know that.

It doesn't matter, dumbass, he told himself. You know where they are now, and this is the only chance you're going to get. Damned lucky you got this one.

He looked through the scope again. Better now. He discerned the village structures behind the mil-dot reticle. The magnification confirmed what he'd thought: The place was abandoned except for the one hut. Even that dwelling had suffered damage. One wall had a hole big enough for a man to walk through.

Somebody come out and say hello, thought Parson. At least they won't be expecting me. Full daylight, dimmed by thick clouds, came before he saw any movement. Finally a door swung open. Parson was looking over the rifle when he saw it. He placed his cheek to the stock and looked through the scope. Bigger door now, bisected by crosshairs. Still nothing else. Safety off. Finger pad on the trigger. Wrist throbbing. Calm down now, he thought. No time for buck fever.

A man stepped from behind the door and tromped out into the snow. Parson followed him through the optic. The man wore an olive-green anorak, and his head and face were covered by a gray shemagh. Parson had seen that kind of headgear in Iraq, Kuwait, and Saudi Arabia. You got no more business on the ground here than I do, he thought. Should have kept your ass at home. Parson closed his left eye.

The insurgent shuffled around in the snow, perhaps looking for something to burn. He bent over to examine an object on the ground. When he stood up, Parson centered the cruciform reticle on the man's torso. Adjusted his aim point slightly. Released air from his lungs. Pressed the trigger.

The silenced weapon made little noise, just a *pffft* like a soda can opening, then a crack as the bullet broke the sound barrier. The guerrilla dropped as if a trapdoor had opened beneath him, felled behind a drift.

Parson ejected the spent cartridge. The finely machined bolt moved as if lubricated with butter, and the empty brass tumbled into the snow. He closed the chamber on a live round. Watched through the scope. Blinked once.

No movement but smoke rising. No sound from the man he'd shot. Parson waited, waited. Cold now, but not shivering. The tick of his watch.

He heard faint voices inside the dwelling. Voices not alarmed, but annoyed. Bitching, Parson guessed. What the hell is taking him so long? Where did he go? Well, come on out and see.

The door opened again, and another man came out. Black overcoat, flat-topped hat. The insurgent stopped, apparently saw his comrade on the ground. Called a name. Walked upright toward the body.

That's right, thought Parson. You didn't hear shit, did you?

The man stopped again, perhaps when he saw the blood. He whirled, looked around, maybe realized his mistake. His last one. Parson fired.

Not as good a shot this time. The man fell, writhed. Parson judged from the exit wound's spray that he'd caught him in the abdomen.

The man let out a sound between a growl and a scream: *"Ash-haduuuuuuuu!"* Garbled syllables. Parson wondered if he was trying to recite the Shahadah. The wounded man couldn't quite seem to get through it.

Now some other kind of words. *"Mamannnnnnn . . ."* Is he calling for his buddy? Parson thought. His mother? Wet coughs.

Parson almost felt pity. I should have nailed him a little higher, he thought. Die, for God's sake. He chambered a fresh round, listened to the moans. Damn, I wish I hadn't done that to him. Better a clean kill.

Focus, Parson told himself. He settled his cheek back onto the stock, scanned through the scope. Get ready in case the third one is totally fucking stupid.

The wounded man lay on his back now, raised one quivering hand to the sky. His fingers and arm were covered in dark blood. Through the scope, Parson noticed red droplets fall from the man's fingertips. Parson thought about finishing him off, but he couldn't see the head. Didn't make tactical sense, either. Maybe the screams would eventually draw out another target.

The insurgent made a gurgling noise, tried to speak again: *"Il-allahhhhh . . ."* The words trailed off, stopped with a spasm of coughs.

Parson felt nauseated. Shut the fuck up and die already. No, don't. Call for help. Call for your buddy.

No buddy came out. So he's not a complete idiot, thought Parson. Too bad.

The barrel of an AK-47 appeared through the hole in the wall. The man holding the weapon shouted in accented English. All Parson understood was "Infidels!"

The man fired a long burst. The line of bullets whipped into the snow like a lash, nowhere near Parson.

What the hell do you think you're shooting at? Parson thought. He tried to settle his crosshairs on the gunman. So you're going to make this easy after all. The man disappeared inside. Shit. Okay, so you're not.

The wounded guerrilla cried out again, a guttural howl that

rose to a high keen before trailing off. Shut the hell up, thought Parson. I'm trying to concentrate. Parson turned the rifle to look at the man again through the scope. He saw the legs, part of the torso. Everything bloody. He still could not see the head.

Parson considered firing again anyway. Not even a terrorist deserves to die like that, he thought. Maybe another round into him anywhere would hasten his exit. And possibly give away your position. And yes, he does deserve to die like that.

You better pay attention to business, Parson told himself. Put that scope on the one who can still hurt you. He centered the crosshairs over the hole in the wall. Nobody there.

Parson worried that the man inside would shoot Gold. If he's ever going to do it, he'll do it now. Please God, don't let me hear a shot from in there. Maybe they had instructions to keep her alive until they could make another video. If so, I hope he's more afraid of his boss than he is of me.

Snow still steady. Flakes that touched the rifle barrel melted instantly and beaded up, the steel warm from two shots. Parson watched. Nothing.

So this is turning into a contest to see who's more patient, Parson thought. I got all the time in the world, motherfucker. I have no role in life but to lie here and wait to put a round through you. I am a weapons system.

Another moan from down the hill. Weaker now. So you're still with us, Parson thought. That's a long time to suffer that kind of pain. He put the scope on the wounded man. One of the insurgent's feet dug at the snow, the heel scraping back and forth.

Parson placed his finger on the trigger. No, no, no. The bastard inside doesn't know where you are, he told himself. Don't give away your only advantage. Mercy has its place, but not here. What kind of mercy did they show Nunez? And I didn't want this. I should be in Masirah by now, sipping a beer. But everybody I would have been drinking with is dead.

I'll soon join them if I don't pay attention, Parson thought. Crosshairs on the hut again. No change. What is that son of a bitch up to?

All right, so he has orders to keep her alive, Parson guessed. Otherwise he'd have shot her by now. But the more freaked out he gets, the less discipline he'll have. What if he decides his boss didn't anticipate this situation, so the instructions no longer apply? Do these people think like that, anyway? Maybe time's not on my side.

The wounded man cried out again. A full-throated scream this time. Parson shuddered, panned with the crosshairs until they stopped on the heaving chest. Damn it, damn it, damn it. Will you please stop breathing? Parson pressed the trigger, felt the recoil. The torso jerked, lay still and silent.

Parson cursed himself for the impulse. Fucking idiot. Just another chance for the guy inside to figure out where you are. He ejected the spent brass and chambered another round.

No sign whether the terrorist in the hut had heard the rifle's faint report. But it's quiet out here, Parson thought. Quiet as outdoors ever gets.

Hell, this isn't working anymore, he decided. That guy in there is warm, and he won't come out now unless he completely loses his mind. And he'll likely shoot her if he goes that crazy.

Parson studied the hut through the scope. He wanted mainly to know if the insurgent was looking at him. No one at the hole in the wall. No one visible anywhere.

He slid the sleeping bag off his legs and rose up on his hands and knees. Then he eased backward, rifle over his arm. Kept his eyes on the hut until it disappeared behind the ridge. Snow powder covered him now.

Parson left the sleeping bag and pack. He could move better and present a smaller profile without them. If he succeeded, he could come back for them. If he failed, he wouldn't need them.

He stumbled downhill to keep the ridgetop between him and the little village, and he worked his way along the shoulder of the mountain to get past the village. He wanted to get far enough away from the dwellings to move into the valley unobserved.

The snow fell straight down as if sifted. The cloud layer hung low, so dark it seemed night had not gone completely but hovered just overhead. Parson snowshoed along for about half an hour, then hiked uphill to look over the ridge again.

He was disappointed to see he hadn't put as much distance between himself and the village as he'd thought. Parson wanted to get well west of it, then descend into the valley and approach from the side where the destroyed huts were. He doubted the bad guy inside could see him come from that direction as long as the man remained indoors. He looked through the binoculars. A wisp of wood smoke. Nothing else.

Parson retreated to the back side of the ridgeline and forged ahead through ice-glazed trees. He topped the ridge again and scanned the dead village once more. Now it lay farther to his right, small even in the binoculars and veiled by descending snow. He hoped that same veil would conceal his next move.

He started down the slope above the huts, headed into the valley. A few steps took him out of the timber and onto the exposed face of the mountain. Parson walked fully upright; there was nothing for cover now except distance and snowfall. He thought if the remaining insurgent ever spotted him, it would happen during this part of the stalk. But maybe the winter camo parka and the white tape over the rifle would help him disappear into the frozen landscape. If it doesn't work, he thought, I'll know it when the bullet hits me.

When he reached the bottom of the slope, he lost sight of the village. That encouraged him. Parson had the lay of the land; he still knew where the dwellings were. But if he couldn't see the village, the village couldn't see him. Yet. When he judged himself in the bed of the valley, he turned east toward the huts.

After several minutes of hiking, he took a knee and glassed the expanse ahead of him. There was the village again, mainly rubble from this angle. Parson wondered if an air strike had done the damage here, too. He imagined the Warthogs coming in from this same direction, low and fast, spitting fire and steel at such a rate that their guns sounded like chain saws. He watched for a few moments, then stood and advanced.

When he came within a couple thousand yards of the huts, he stopped again. He went down on one knee. Then he lay prone in the snow. Parson put away the binoculars and scanned through the rifle scope. If he's within range for me, Parson thought, I'm within range for him if he's good enough. But the optic revealed nothing except snow-topped walls, blasted open some time ago.

Back on his feet, he trudged forward for several minutes. Stopped. Lay in the snow and scanned. The crosshairs still found no sign of life. Parson repeated that process twice until the mudbrick ruins were only two hundred yards away. Then he removed his snowshoes, left them behind, and stayed on his belly. Low-crawled through the downlike powder.

The snow got inside his clothes, but he ignored it. If I pull this off, he thought, I'll have time to get dry inside. If I don't, something else will get me long before hypothermia. He listened closely but heard no sound. Parson feared hoofbeats. He wondered whether his enemy had a radio to call for help.

Parson crept forward, eyes on the ruins. He heard no noise, saw no motion. Just smoke still rising. When he reached the outermost wall, or what was left of it, he left his rifle against a pile of stones. Too close for that weapon now. Parson drew the Colt and pulled back the hammer. Held it with his right hand. Pain there, but bearable. Picked up a fist-size rock with his left hand.

He walked in a low crouch along a wall that connected all the huts. That part of the structure remained pretty much intact. He peered along the wall and saw no one. Heard nothing. Parson placed each step straight down into snow that came above his knees. Tried to stay out of the rubble. He was within a few yards of his enemy now, and he wanted to make as little noise as possible.

Near the end of the wall, he came to the hole where the guerrilla inside had fired his panic burst from the AK-47. Parson flattened his back against the mud bricks, facing outside. Held his breath, listened. He hurled the rock backward over the hut and heard it clatter.

The AK opened up. Parson did not see where.

He ran forward. Crouched at the opening in the wall. Aimed the pistol inside with both hands.

A man at the door, firing out. The man turned, brought around the weapon. It took him half a second to move up the barrel to clear the doorjamb. That was all the time Parson needed. He fired twice.

Blood spurted from the man's arm. He dropped the AK, fell.

Parson fired again. The man jerked. In the corner of Parson's eye, he saw a woman tied to a chair.

He charged through the opening, over crumbled stones. Crossed the room in three strides. Stood over the downed terrorist. The man looked only stunned. His eyes were still moving.

The man kicked with both legs just as Parson fired again. Knocked Parson off his aim. The bullet gouged the mud wall. One heel caught Parson's shin. The other boot hooked the back of his knee. He fell against the man and felt the body armor.

The man grabbed Parson's Colt by the barrel, using his good arm. Parson held the weapon with his injured hand. Placed his other hand over his enemy's. The man raised his wounded arm. Struggled to place his finger inside the trigger guard. The weapon shook as four hands fought for it. Parson ground his teeth from the pain in his wrist.

Wide eyes, orbs of hate. Parson watched the pistol barrel turn despite all his strength and will. Saw the rifling grooves inside the barrel. He clawed at the safety. Useless. He tried to push back the slide so the weapon couldn't fire. The man's grip was too strong. Now the muzzle pointed at Parson's left eye. Two inches away. A bead of sweat dropped from Parson's nose onto the gunmetal. The man tried to push his thumb toward the trigger. Parson heard noise behind him. Something falling.

Two feet, boots tied together, came down on the man's face. The man let go of the pistol. Parson rolled to his side, held the .45 with his left hand. The insurgent sat up, reached for the AK.

Parson fired. So close the blood spattered into his face. The warm flecks stung his eyes. When he blinked, he saw brain matter on the door. The man slumped against Parson's shoulder. He pushed off the body, using the heel of his hand and the butt of the pistol. The dead insurgent smelled like some kind of livestock, and Parson wondered if his own body was as rank.

Gold lay on her back, hands tied behind her. Feet bound together. Gag tied around her mouth. A vein pulsed at her temple, just underneath the hairline.

An empty .45 casing rested on the floor between them. A feather of smoke curled from it, vanished. Parson saw where the firing pin had punched into the primer. His hands were shaking. He safed his pistol.

CHAPTER FOURTEEN

Parson pulled his boot knife and kneeled beside Gold where she lay on the floor of the hut. A hijab cut from rough cloth covered her hair.

"Just the three of them?" he asked.

She nodded.

He untied the gag, sawed the ropes around her boots and legs. She got up on her knees, turned her back to him so he could free her hands. He cut the nylon cords with the Damascus blade. He noticed raw, red flesh at the ends of her fingers. Gold had no fingernails.

Parson moved in front of her and picked up her hands, squeezed one of her wrists just barely. "Did they—" he started. Stopped himself. Didn't know how much he should ask.

"That's all," Gold said.

Like that's not enough, Parson thought. Shouldn't have asked anything. "You need a medic," he said.

Gold pulled the hijab from her head and dropped it. She sat cross-legged on the floor and hugged herself tightly, rocking, head down. Then she cupped one hand inside the other, and both hands trembled. She examined her fingers. She looked around and asked, "Where's the team?"

"There is no team. Just me," Parson said. "The guys who raided the house after we got captured were Special Forces. They went after Marwan and the mullah."

Gold stared out where her former captors lay dead. He tried to imagine what she was thinking. We all know the mission comes first, Parson thought. We all know we're expendable. But nobody really believes it.

"I left my pack up the hill. There's a first-aid kit in it," Parson said. "Are you going to be able to travel?"

"This will hurt whether I'm walking or not."

"I wish I had some morphine or something, but all I have in that kit is antiseptic and bandages."

"I'll manage," Gold said.

"Are you going to be all right?"

Gold nodded slowly, as if she were trying to convince herself of something she didn't quite believe. Parson wasn't sure he believed it, either, but he knew they had little choice. Cope or die.

A low fire burned in a hearth made from creek stones. Parson could not see where the guerrillas had located firewood. Whatever they'd found must have been wet and green; the fire popped and hissed and gave poor heat. Still, Parson spread his coat and gloves to dry. His fingers nearly touched the flame before he sensed any warmth.

Parson couldn't decide what he should say or feel. He thought he should have some sense of accomplishment. Gold rescued and the enemy dead. But he felt sick. Gold might have been spared all this if he'd made better decisions to begin with.

"These people were Arabs?" he asked.

"One was. And an Afghan and a Chechen."

"Did they get off a radio call?"

She nodded. "I didn't hear it well."

No wonder, Parson thought. Probably hard to concentrate when you've had all ten fingernails ripped out.

That radio call meant he and Gold needed to move, but his coat was still wet. Though he didn't want to hang around the mud hut, he knew wet would kill him now as surely as a bullet. He felt the front of his flight suit. It was damp, too. He took off his boots. Then he unzipped the flight suit and pulled it off, stripped down to T-shirt and thermal underwear.

He held the flight suit by the fire and shivered. The firelight glowed against the Nomex cloth and brought out the bloodstains. Some from Parson and some from his crew. He found the hole from Marwan's bullet. The rip from the razor wire at the old Russian camp. The major's oak leaves on the shoulders. Where I've been, what I've done, and what I have to do, he thought. He wanted to mend the holes, but he had no thread.

As he stood by the hearth, he wondered how close any more bad guys might be. It would be a hell of a note to get shot half-undressed while your clothes hung by a fire. Gold did not speak or make eye contact. She spread out her hands. Parson wanted to comfort her, but he wasn't sure which lines not to cross. Maybe someone who's been tortured doesn't need anyone touching them in any way.

He finally decided it was all right as long as he made it about the job. He pulled on his flight suit, which had dried before anything else because it was so thin. Then he kneeled beside her and put both hands on her shoulders.

"Sergeant Gold," he said, "you are a credit to your Army."

"Thank you, sir," she said. Her voice tensed like a flier straining to talk through a purging oxygen mask. It gave Parson some idea what the pain must be like.

When the rest of his things dried, he laced on his boots, now stiff and warm. He pulled on his coat and gloves. Parson stepped over the dead guerrilla and looked out the doorway. A thin layer of snow now frosted over the two bodies outside. The red slush was already fading. They all had it coming, he thought. Of course they did. He thought of something he'd heard from infantry troops: You don't gotta like it; you just gotta do it.

He decided to take the body armor off the insurgent he'd shot inside the hut, but that was harder than he expected. The man had worn a coat over the flak vest. Parson rolled the corpse over, tried to slide the arms out of the sleeves. Nothing heavier than a dead body. The open eyes seemed to mock him. Entrance wound in the forehead.

Parson finally got the man's wounded arm out of the coat. Parson's pistol bullet had broken the upper bone. The dead arm slipped from the sleeve and dropped to the floor like slaughterhouse meat. Parson looked up at Gold, who watched without expression. He started to ask her to help but didn't. He rolled the body again and freed the other arm. Unclipped the snaps on the vest. He knew how because it was an American flak jacket. He pushed the shoulders and hips and turned over the corpse once more. Now he was sweating. He loosened the vest's straps, pulled off the vest; it came free except for one strap still under the guerrilla's chest. Parson yanked the vest, kicked the cadaver. Held up the flak jacket.

"Put this on," he said.

Gold shook her head.

"Why not?"

She turned away. He took off his parka and donned the vest. Blood down the front, not all of it fresh. He zipped up his parka over it. Then he picked up the AK-47 from the floor. Handed the rifle to Gold. She took it without looking at him.

"I left some things outside," Parson said. "Wait here till I get them."

"No. I need to get out of here." Gold pulled gloves from one of her pockets. She winced as she put them on.

Gold looked toward the corpses outside, started to say something. Parson waited, but she did not speak. He peered through the hole in the wall. Parson went out through the breach and led Gold along the ruins until they came to where he'd left his rifle. He lifted the M-40 and carried it across his chest. Gold looked at the weapon with a puzzled expression.

"Long story," Parson said. "I had some things air-dropped." She didn't ask him how.

Parson followed his own tracks away from the village. He looked back at Gold. She walked unsteadily, nearly lost her balance once. When he found his snowshoes, he handed them to her.

She kneeled in the snow and began to put on the shoes. She stopped after she had donned the first one, closed her eyes. Placed both hands on her thigh, fingers outstretched. Took a deep breath and pulled on the second snowshoe. Parson stooped and helped her with the bindings.

He glassed the valley and the ridges above it with the binoculars. No sign of approaching enemy. The job wasn't over; he still had to be careful. He wished Gold would move faster; more insurgents could be anywhere. But he didn't want to push her too hard. A stratum of low cloud rolled overhead, shades of gray from the color of pond ice to cold iron.

He retraced his steps, leading the way out of the valley and back up onto the ridgeline. As they climbed, Gold stopped and leaned on an evergreen. Her hair hung loose, the bun half untied. Snowflakes settled in the blond strands that hung over her cheeks. She did not brush the hair aside, and the flakes turned to rivulets against her face. Parson took her wrist, careful not to touch her fingers. He pulled her uphill for a couple of paces. She regained her footing and pressed on.

When they came to where Parson had left his pack and sleeping bag, he brushed the snow from the pack and dug inside for one of the water bottles he'd saved. He twisted off the cap and handed it to Gold. She drank half the water without pause, then reached the bottle back to Parson. He waved it off, and she finished it. He opened another bottle and she drank all of it. Gold looked down the mountain at the village where she'd been held.

Parson opened a first-aid kit and fished out a Betadine vial. "Let me see your hands," he said. Gold paused, then pulled gently at the fingers of her left glove. She shut her eyes hard, and Parson wondered whether what little medical help he could provide was worth the pain it caused her. She loosened the glove slowly, repeated the process with the other glove. She kneeled, placed the AK across her leg, and spread her fingers across the flat of its stock.

The sight made Parson shudder. The ends of Gold's fingers resembled something you might see while dressing game, a hoof or paw with the skin pulled off. Several bled from lacerations. He guessed that to be the work of a knife blade twisted with the sharp edge down. He wondered whether the insurgents had wanted in-

formation or just sick entertainment. If they'd sought information, Parson imagined, they must have had a hard time getting it.
Otherwise they wouldn't have taken all ten fingernails.

He unscrewed the vial of antiseptic and pulled out the ap-
plicator brush attached to the cap. Parson dabbed the liquid onto
Gold's fingers, staining a yellow tint over the blood and torn tissue. Gold flinched but made no sound. He tore off a length of
white medical tape with his teeth. He cut it into shorter lengths
and taped gauze around each of Gold's fingertips.

When he finished working on her right hand and started on
her left, she picked up some snow and let the powder rest on her
palm. The white snow and five white bandages. The gesture made
Parson think of a child from a hot climate seeing snow for the first
time. Light breeze lifted some of the dry snow from her hand.

"You're the only one I could save," he said. "You're my crew
now." Parson cut open an MRE.

"I don't think I can eat," Gold said.

"Can you try some crackers?"

"Maybe."

Parson opened one of the wafers, nearly as wide as his hand.
The big crackers always made him think of Civil War hardtack, but
they tasted all right. Just not enough salt. He broke one in half and
handed both pieces to Gold. She ate while Parson dug his radio
out of the pack. He wanted to check in with Cantrell again.

Parson pulled off his gloves and blew into his hands to warm
them, but it didn't help. He put the gloves back on, turned on the
112, and inserted the earpiece. Snowflakes settled on the radio
and did not melt.

"Razor One-Six," he called, "Flash Two-Four Charlie." No
answer. He repeated, "Razor One-Six, Flash Two-Four Charlie."

A long pause. And then Parson had to listen closely, because Cantrell whispered when he said, "Flash Two-Four Charlie, go ahead."

"I'm waiting at LZ Delta," Parson said. He changed frequencies and listened for the callback.

"Have you found her?" Cantrell asked.

"Yeah, she's still with us. Where are you?"

Several seconds of nothing but hiss. Parson guessed Cantrell couldn't believe he'd done it.

"We followed those bastards to a cave complex," Cantrell said when he finally spoke. He gave Parson coordinates. Parson pulled off his gloves and uncapped a pen. It was a hotel pen he'd picked up in his room during a mission months ago, and the lettering read: "Regency Marriott, Kuwait City." A place of warmth, luxury, and lots of food. He put the cold tip of the pen in his mouth. Spat, then wrote the numbers on the heel of his left hand. It hurt to write.

"Flash Two-Four Charlie copies all," Parson said. He signed off with Cantrell. Then he said to Gold, "Maybe we should head in their direction." As far as he knew, Cantrell and his men were the nearest coalition forces. The nearest safety. Parson wanted to get space between him and the village ruins. The radio call Gold said the insurgents had made might have been a call for reinforcements.

Parson stared at the numbers on his hand, black marks on shivering flesh. He unfolded his map and traced a grid line with his thumbnail. Then he placed the map on a flat spot in the snow. Opened his compass and placed its edge along the grid line. Oriented the map to north, took a bearing. For a moment, the calculations settled his mind. Navigation came down to mathematical sureties: radials and vectors, the angle of wind drift, the declination of Polaris. Numbers worked the same everywhere, a mental lodestar for him.

He found a ham slice in the MRE he'd opened for Gold. Slung the pack over his shoulder. Ate the ham in four bites and wiped his hands on his parka.

"Heading one-five-zero," he said. "Just over five miles."

Parson rolled up his sleeping bag and tied it to the pack. Then he lifted his rifle. At first he led the way down a narrow vale, but he knew the easy walking wouldn't last. Through the snowfall and mist, the next ridge loomed ahead like a wall. He wondered what kind of endurance Gold would have. She seemed willing to keep going, but only so fast.

They stumbled down the escarpment, sliding rather than walking. Their progress through the deep snow left what looked more like a trench than a line of tracks. Parson knew pursuers would have no problem trailing them now, but the bad guys would have to cross the mountains under these same arctic conditions.

At the bottom of the ravine, the snow came up to Parson's thighs. Gold forged on, staying within a few paces of him. Parson opened the last of the water bottles he'd saved and handed it to her. She drank part of it and handed it back. He finished it, filled it with snow, capped it, returned it to his pocket.

"You all right?" he asked.

She shrugged.

"We still have a chance," he said. Didn't know if he should have said anything.

Parson took out his binoculars and surveyed the peaks. No evidence of any other human life. The ridges loomed like cathedral spires. Juniper branches drooped with their burden of snow, some near to breaking. The air smelled like the purest water Parson had ever tasted. He heard no sound but his heartbeat thumping fast from exertion. Who would have thought hell could be so beautiful? He adjusted his pack straps. Put one foot before the other. Felt himself sweating underneath his flight suit, though his hands stayed numb with cold.

The ascent up the opposite slope came hard. In all the equipment from the airdrop, he'd not asked for climbing gear. He hadn't planned on summiting mountains, so he lacked ropes and tackle. He and Gold could only climb slowly, feeling for footholds. Parson used a low branch to pull himself and got showered with crystals for his effort. Snow grains in his eyes. When Gold became stuck where she found no leverage or handhold, Parson unhooked his rifle sling, dangled it to her, hauled her up. He used both hands, and it made his right wrist burn again.

A sound like a pistol shot cracked somewhere to the left. Parson whirled with his rifle to see a tree limb tumble to the ground in a shower of white. The broken end jutted from the snow like a compound fracture. Parson slung his weapon across his shoulder and moved on.

It took more than three hours to reach the crest. The land dropped away beyond it, but not with the same punishing grade. That side of the mountain sloped more gently, and Parson saw it had once held terraced fields. The land did not look to have been tended in at least a couple of seasons. No dried stalks of crops, just dead weeds sticking up through the snow. Whatever had grown in these fields, war had put an end to it.

Parson glassed the disused farmland with his binoculars. He found this side of the mountain as unpopulated as the other. Small, barren trees stood along one side of the field, a dead orchard. He rolled a focus knob and brought the trees into sharp view, each twig overlaid with flakes delicate as crushed feathers. From his briefings about food sources, he guessed these were walnut and maybe pistachio trees, unable to do him any good now. Gold stooped with her hands on her thighs, catching her breath.

As they paused, snow swept across the mountainside in swaths. A column of white bore down on them and cut visibility to yards. When it passed, Parson watched it recede across the landscape, hanging from gray clouds like tattered strips of muslin.

They slogged downhill into the first field. As they labored across it, they came to four small hillocks in the snow. The rises stood out in an expanse of white that otherwise stretched over the field as if smoothed by a trowel. Parson placed his foot near the end of one of them. The snow crunched and crackled, and he felt loose rocks turn under his boot. He kicked away the layers of powder to reveal a stone barrow about five feet long.

"Graves," Gold said. Her voice almost startled Parson. She picked up a stone, a tile of shale, crumbling and stratified. She pulled off her glove and held the rock in her cupped hand, kept her white fingertips off it.

"What do you think happened to them?" Parson asked.

She shook her head. Tossed the shale. It disappeared into the snow, leaving only a narrow shaft to mark its passage.

Most of a family dead of something, Parson guessed. Disease if not violence. And now gone. Gone forever, like his crew. Concentrating on Gold's rescue had taken his mind off his crewmates for a time. But the graves made him think of them. They were not on another mission. They would not land soon back at base. They were not waiting for him at the club. They were dead. They would soon rest in their own graves, and they would be there for a long, long time.

The thought of his crew reminded him of how his father had lived and how he had died. His dad had been a selectee for full bird colonel in the Air National Guard when Desert Storm kicked off. On one of the first nights of the war, he was flying the back seat of an F-4G Wild Weasel. Parson had seen news video from that night that showed triple-A filling the sky over Baghdad like a swarm of exploding fireflies. His father and the front-seater had flown right through it to put a HARM missile into an air defense radar site.

Coming off the target, a burst of shrapnel peppered the canopy and wounded the pilot, so his dad took control of the jet. He could have ejected, but that would have put the incapacitated pilot on the ground in enemy territory, in the dark, without medical help. So his dad flew the damaged aircraft back to Prince Sultan Air Base. The gear collapsed on landing, and the jet veered off the runway in a shower of sparks. When it hit that soft, powdery sand, it cartwheeled and blew up.

Parson was surprised by the touch of Gold's hand on his arm. He looked up to see her beside him, a blurred vision through his brimming eyes.

I'm supposed to be taking care of you now, thought Parson. Not the other way around. Do your damned job, he told himself.

Gold said nothing. She just seemed to want to remind him she was there. Parson appreciated the gesture. And the silence. She watched him in a way that made him wonder what she was thinking. Whatever it was, she didn't seem to be judging him.

Then she appeared to look into the distance. With what she's been through, Parson thought, she doesn't need me losing it. But now her eyes appeared focused. She wasn't staring; she was scanning. At something in particular.

"May I borrow the binoculars, sir?" she asked.

Parson handed her the Zeiss. She looked through it and turned an adjustment ring.

"See anything?" he whispered.

"An animal," she said. "Maybe a dog."

"You're sure it's not a person?"

Gold nodded and gave the binoculars back to Parson. She paused, brushed her hair back with her hands, and tied it in a tight knot.

Beyond the second field, the land flattened into a valley divided by a narrow creek. The stream was visible as a dark gully only in short stretches where the water ran fast. In most places snow overlaid ice that had formed across the surface. Parson chided himself for not noticing the creek earlier. The last thing he and Gold needed was to break through and fill their boots with ice water. Near the creek there were depressions in the snow, straight lines at right angles to the stream. Old irrigation canals, he supposed.

Where the stream narrowed, a jumble of boulders and tree trunks lay across it in what passed for a bridge. A few branches remained attached to the logs, and they stuck up to about waist height. Parson guessed someone had left the branches there for handholds. Afghans were poor but not stupid.

He placed his boot onto the first log and pushed down to test it. The tree trunk held firm, so he stepped onto it cautiously. When he took hold of a branch, it broke off in his hand and left him with a flight glove full of snow, ice, and rotten wood.

Parson kept his balance only by stumbling down onto a rock.

He knew if he fell into the water now and couldn't find anything dry enough to burn, he might as well put the Colt to his temple and pull the trigger. He remounted the logs. He felt the whole mass shift under his weight, and water purled around the soles of his boots. Parson stepped onto a boulder, then another log, then finally to the opposite bank.

Gold removed the magazine from her rifle. What the heck is she doing? thought Parson. She pulled back the bolt, ejected a cartridge from the chamber, placed the magazine and bullet in her pocket.

"Catch," Gold called. She tossed her rifle across the stream. Parson caught it by the barrel with his left hand. Now Gold could cross the bridge unencumbered. Why didn't I think of that? wondered Parson. Gold picked her way over without slipping. She took the weapon, reloaded it, and let the bolt slam shut.

CHAPTER FIFTEEN

Parson and Gold moved away from the old farm and orchard, and the pines thinned out, leaving nothing but knee-high thorn-bush crackling with ice and snow. There was no place to hide. Just a white plateau rimmed with ridges, as if the Hindu Kush went on forever.

Gold had the binoculars again. Now and then she stopped to survey. Parson took that as a good sign. She was back in the game. He watched her drink the last of a water bottle and then pack it with snow. She seemed careful about her fingers, but she didn't ask for help. Gold pocketed the bottle and kept hiking. No sounds but their breathing and the crunch of their footsteps, and the whisper of steady flakes.

After another hour of walking, Gold said, "I wonder if they've engaged yet."

"What?"

"If they've moved on that cave."

"We can find out," Parson said.

He had been conserving his batteries, so the

radio was off. He dropped his pack, pulled out the 112, and turned it on. Inserted the earpiece.

"Razor One-Six," he called, "Flash Two-Four Charlie."

No answer. Parson repeated his transmission. Still nothing.

Something broke the squelch, the radio's hiss interrupted like someone on the other end had pressed a transmit button. Then more static.

"Razor One-Six, Flash Two-Four Charlie."

Electronic buzz. Then another squelch break, with sounds in the background. A finger on a talk switch again. The rattle of gear. Two shots: *pa-pop*. One more.

Static again. Then a finger on the button once more. A voice in the background: "Covering fire!"

Then Cantrell, voice steady: "Flash Two-Four Charlie, Razor's in contact. Call you back."

Parson looked at the radio, wanted to ask more. Knew he shouldn't, so he removed the earpiece.

"What did they say?" Gold asked.

"Not much. They're in a firefight."

Gold did not answer. She just looked out ahead. Across the snowfield, Parson saw the light wind twisting whorls of fine granules across the surface. It made the ground appear to move, and the visual illusion dizzied him a little. Black dot in the distance. Parson raised his rifle, adjusted the scope, looked through it.

A wolf stood in snow up to its shoulders, several hundred yards away. Hard to see him through the snowfall, even with magnification. The creature looked toward Parson and Gold. Stared as if frozen. Then loped along like a dog jumping through high weeds. Vanished into the terrain.

"See that?" Parson asked.

"I believe I saw him a while ago."

Parson didn't think much about it. Wildlife was the least of his problems. Getting spotted by the enemy was his greatest. Not seeing bad guys didn't mean they weren't seeing you. And out in the open like this, we wouldn't be hard to find, Parson thought. Especially with Gold in ACU gear and not winter camo.

White-coated evergreens stood in the distance, beyond where the wolf disappeared. Short ones that offered little concealment, but better than nothing. Parson checked his compass and saw that they lined up with the course he was tracking, so he used them as a marker and headed straight for them.

It took longer than Parson expected. He and Gold forded the deep snow step by step. The two of them eventually came to the wolf's tracks, holes left by his paws as he'd leaped along, and feathery marks where his tail had dragged. And three other sets of wolf tracks. Parson guessed he and Gold had seen the wolf pack's straggler.

They hiked on toward the trees. A little closer now. Pines seemingly wrapped in white felt. Parson shivered, and his toes had no feeling.

He checked his compass again, its floating dial rotating in oil. Snow pellets struck the compass face and shattered, the white molecules skating across the glass. Parson had a hard time holding the instrument steady. He read his course under the lubber line, checked it against the trees and other landmarks. Tried to think. Very little magnetic declination here, close to one of the earth's agonic lines. Closed the compass and kept moving.

Parson began to make out a sheer cliff rising beyond the trees, close enough to vertical that it wasn't all covered by snow. A rock face black as a gun barrel. No climbing that in our condition, he thought, even if we were equipped. Just have to move around it, watch the heading and pace count, and try not to fuck up the navigation.

He didn't want to stop and study his map out in the open. When they finally reached the copse of pines, he felt better about calling a halt. Parson kneeled in the snow beside a tree, unzipped a thigh pocket to reach for the map the SF troops had given him. Heard a noise. Rasp of paws on snow crust. He looked up as a wolf bolted away, kicking up crystals. Fur the color of smoke. They had come within yards of the animal without seeing it.

Parson opened the map. Snow fell into it and collected in the creases. The map shook as he held it. Parson was trying to save his GPS batteries; he could count on only about fifteen hours even in warm weather. He turned on the unit just long enough for it to initialize. The GPS fix checked with the map. Parson turned off the receiver and placed it back in his pocket.

He surveyed the terrain and decided to pass west of the cliff. That direction amounted to the least bad option; any path he chose went uphill. And he based that call purely on slope, not on tactics. He had no idea where the enemy was.

The snow sounds changed from hissing to ticking. Some of the flakes that struck his coat bounced rather than shattered. More ice in the snow now, and it came down in ropes. Maybe some warmer air aloft, Parson guessed. Probably not good news. Brittle snow would make more noise as they walked.

As they rounded the cliff on the side of the mountain shielded from the wind, the snow on the ground became shallower. The accumulation barely reached the tops of Parson's boots. The walking came much easier after hours of slogging through deep snow. Limestone talus crumbled under his soles like terra-cotta, and when his feet slipped they scraped away snow and rocks to reveal frozen earth the color of dried blood. Gold plodded along in the snowshoes he'd given her. She left oval tracks that paralleled his own. He wished he had a second set of snowshoes. Right now he lacked the materials and energy to fashion another makeshift pair.

Parson stopped to catch his breath on a swale of level ground. Beyond, the land rose still higher to elevations hidden by mist. He noticed another set of wolf tracks. Fresh. No glimpse of the animal itself. He pointed at the prints. "I suppose they're moving because they can't find their usual food in the storm," he said.

"The one I saw did look pretty scrawny," Gold said.

Parson slipped his rifle sling from his shoulder and carried the weapon across his chest. He figured it would take a pretty hungry wolf to attack two adults, but he could use the M-40's stock as a club if he had to. Didn't want to fire unnecessarily, even with the silenced weapon. He wondered whether his course happened to follow the wolves or if it was the other way around. If they were hungry, they sure weren't going uphill for nothing. Smart bastards if they were circling him, checking him out.

His own hunger pangs started again. He shifted the rifle to the crook of his right arm. Without looking he reached behind him with his left hand and opened a side pocket flap of the backpack. Felt for a chocolate bar from the MRE he'd opened earlier. He unwrapped it, stuffed the trash back in the side pocket. Broke the bar in half. It was frozen and it popped like a .22. Parson handed one of the halves to Gold.

He bit into his own piece and made shallow teeth marks. Bit down harder. When the chocolate shattered, it had the taste and consistency of hard plastic. He crunched it and swallowed. Didn't enjoy it but knew he needed the calories. He had more MREs but didn't want to stop now.

Parson hiked on, climbing, thinking about food. He had heard of people in bad situations entertaining themselves by planning imaginary meals. Steak medium well. A Guinness. Big slice of tomato. It just depressed him.

He tried to think of something else. What's good here? Well, Gold's here, sort of in one piece. She was useful and didn't talk much. This would be so much worse with a yammering idiot or a whiner. And if she wasn't whining now, she never would. Parson wondered about her wounds, and he decided to take a chance and ask.

"How are your hands?" he said.

"Still hurt a little."

That worried Parson. If she admitted any pain at all, it must be awful.

"I bet you hate those ragheads as much as I do now," he said.

Gold didn't answer for a long moment. Then she said, "This is hard to forgive, but I have to try."

Forgive? Was she serious? "I couldn't forgive them in a thousand lifetimes," Parson said. What was that saying he'd heard from infantry guys? Let God forgive them. We'll arrange the meeting.

Gold looked straight at him. "Hate will hurt you more than it hurts them," she said.

Parson wondered if Gold—or anyone—could really have that

kind of inner peace. After torture, no less. Maybe she just had to play mind games with herself to do her job.

"I gotta hand it to you, Sergeant," he said. "I don't see how you do it."

"They're not ragheads to me, sir. Muslims were perfecting algebra when we were burning witches."

Parson wished he had more of her knowledge. She could probably give one hell of a background briefing. But that would have to wait until they were safely back at Bagram. In the unlikely event that ever happened.

The icy snow began to form a crust on top of the powder that had already fallen. It broke like a membrane and crackled underfoot. Parson tried to walk quietly, but it was impossible. Doesn't matter, he decided. If the bad guys can hear me, I can hear them.

He did not hear the wolf. It just materialized out of the fog, three steps in front of him. Hair raised along its spine. Lips curled in a silent growl. White fangs. Yellow eyes.

Parson expected the creature to run like before, but it stood motionless. Then it sprang like it could fly.

Flash of teeth. The wolf hit Parson in the chest and knocked him backward. As he stumbled, he smelled wet dog odor, but sharper. The animal bit hard. Parson felt canines through his sleeve, pain in his arm like the scrape of a nail. Ripping cloth.

The animal jerked Parson to the left. He swung the M-40. No leverage, just a weak blow to the wolf's side. Parson went down on one knee.

The animal whirled, snapped at Parson's throat. Mouthful of razors. Parson jammed his elbow into its chest. Felt the thrashing muscles. Why wasn't Gold helping?

The body armor did him no good now; it just slowed him down. He swung the rifle again. Wider arc this time. The stock cracked against the wolf's head. The predator leaped back up like pain meant nothing.

Parson swung once more. The butt of the weapon slammed into the animal's muzzle. The wolf yelped. A tooth dropped from its bleeding jaws.

Before Parson could swing again the wolf had him by the leg of his flight suit. Yanked him all the way to the ground. Pounced for his throat again. Parson blocked with the M-40 in his left arm, pulled his boot knife with his right.

The animal moved like quicksilver. Red teeth in Parson's face, dripping and snarling. The wolf's foul breath was like a dog's but sickly tart, like it had fed on carrion.

Parson sank the blade into the wolf's neck. Twisted. Stabbed again. The animal sprang back. Parson brought up the rifle with one hand and fired.

The bullet caught the wolf in the chest. The creature fell into the snow, one hind leg kicking.

Parson turned to see Gold on the ground, a wolf on her arm. It had her sleeve in its teeth, and it was twisting its head side to side. She jammed the barrel of her AK into its cheek. Fired. Spray of blood and fur. She sat up and fired as another wolf flew at her. It fell beside her in the snow, blood gushing from the wound in its neck.

Parson pulled the Colt from his survival vest. Thumbed the hammer. Another wolf came toward him at a hard run. Parson pulled the trigger. Thought he missed, but the wolf crashed into him dead.

He turned, looked, waited for the next attack. No sound but the whimpers of a dying wolf.

Then he saw another one, running away down the mountain. It stopped by a boulder and looked back. Maybe four football fields away.

Parson holstered the pistol and racked the bolt on the M-40. Twisted the sling around his left arm for a steadier hold. Kneeled and aimed. Centered the crosshairs just above the wolf's eyes. Not a critical shot now. No more point in being quiet, either. So let's just see how good this weapon really is. He pressed the trigger.

The wolf's head exploded. Parson lowered the rifle, ejected the empty brass. Chambered another round. So that jarhead armorer did his job, he thought. This thing is accurized and cold-barrel zeroed true as Gospel.

"You all right?" Parson asked.

"I think so." Gold checked her legs, pushed up her sleeves to examine her arms. Parson saw nothing worse than deep scratches. He raised his own pant legs and pulled off his gloves to look at his hands. Same as Gold, scrapes and punctures bleeding only a little. The skin across his knuckles was cracked and sore from the cold. Lucky. We probably should get rabies shots when and if we get back, thought Parson.

He pulled his knife from the neck of the wolf he'd stabbed. He wiped the blade, clicked it back into his boot sheath. It seemed everything in this place—inhabitants, climate, terrain, flora, and fauna—wanted him dead. But he wasn't angry with the wolves. They were killers by birth, not by choice. Just doing what predators do. That, Parson understood. He even felt a bit guilty about that last one he'd shot at long range. It hadn't been entirely necessary, but now at least he knew more about what his rifle could do.

"Keep a good watch for a minute," Parson said. "Be ready to shoot."

He dropped his rucksack, took out his first-aid kit. Opened the Betadine, unscrewed the cap. Gold held her weapon with her right arm while Parson painted the scratches on her left arm and hand. She neither flinched nor looked down at her injuries while he worked. She shifted the rifle, and he repeated the process for her other arm and her ankle and calf. Then he treated himself, put away the first-aid kit, pulled on his gloves, hoisted the pack and M-40.

"We'd better go," he said. No telling who or what the sound of gunfire would attract. He hadn't wanted to shoot, but the wolf attack had given them no choice. Nothing for it now but to move. They left churned and bloody snow, cartridge casings, dead wolves behind them.

Parson's heading took them higher, but not across the spine of the ridge. He knew that was good in some ways. Keeping near the top but not on it placed them at what the Air Force survival school called the "military crest," where they would not be silhouetted against the sky. But there wasn't much sky to see now. Just mist roiling with snow and ice pellets, as if the air so full of hard particles had scoured away the horizon itself.

After a time, the map led them over the real crest. By then the fog was so thick that Parson didn't worry about getting spotted. When he cross-checked his position with the GPS receiver, he noted that the elevation was above eleven thousand feet. Might as well use the altitude to some advantage, he thought. Parson pulled out his radio and turned it on.

"Razor One-Six," he called, "Flash Two-Four Charlie."

"Flash Two-Four Charlie," Cantrell answered, "Razor One-Six reads you loud and clear. Delta."

The code word by itself, not even used in a sentence. Cantrell sounded exhausted. Parson changed frequencies and called again.

"You guys all right?" he asked.

"We have some KIA," Cantrell said. "And some wounded."

So that's why he was past caring about radio procedure, Parson thought. He paused, unsure what to say. "I'm sorry," he said. "Are you still at the same location?"

"Affirmative. Contact's over."

"We'll come to you. It's just a couple miles now."

"Keep your radio on, then. Call me before you get to my perimeter."

"Copy that. Flash Two-Four Charlie out."

Parson left the earpiece in his ear. If these guys were bloodied and on a hair trigger, he sure didn't want to blunder into them. He led the way downhill, placed his feet carefully. The snow was thicker on this side of the mountain. While he was still within a few hundred yards of the top, he noticed what looked like two perfectly straight, leafless limbs jutting from the snow. Too symmetrical not to be man-made. He lifted his rifle and looked through the scope.

Gun barrels. Some kind of artillery.

"Don't move," Parson whispered. Gold stopped a yard behind him.

He clicked off his safety and scanned with the scope. Combs

of snow along the artillery barrels. The rest of the mechanism covered by accumulation. No one in sight. No tracks.

"It's okay," Parson said. "Just an old triple-A piece." Some kind of small-bore antiaircraft gun, he guessed. A weapon designed to be towed by a vehicle. Rotted tires topped with a plume of snow. Parson wondered how they ever got it up here. Maybe behind horses.

"Did something like that shoot us down?" Gold asked.

"No, it was a missile that got us. But this thing could ruin your day, too."

He wondered whose it had been. Maybe Taliban, maybe Northern Alliance, maybe mujahideen back in the 1980s. He saw why they put it here. In clear weather this spot would have commanded a good view of the valley below. A gunner could have made short work of a helicopter or low-flying airplane.

Parson slipped his way downhill and examined the weapon more closely. Rust exfoliated from the steel like dry bark. So this thing had been here a while. He wondered why they'd just left it. But then he imagined a Soviet helicopter popping up from the ridge behind him, catching the gun crew unaware. A two-second burst of fire from a Hind could have made short work of a triple-A emplacement.

"Why do people fight so hard and long over hellholes like this?" Parson asked.

"Free will," Gold said.

Parson moved around to the front of the weapon. Those mute barrels might point up at the sky for the next thousand years, he guessed. He steadied himself on the incline, then shuffled farther down the slope. Glanced back at Gold to make sure she was close behind.

When Parson stopped to rest a moment, he noticed a patch of dry bracken sticking up through the snow. He placed his fingers around some of it, felt it crumble in his flight glove. Held his hand above his head and watched the tinder drift in the breeze. He noted that the wind had not changed direction in at least two days. That meant no change in the weather anytime soon.

CHAPTER SIXTEEN

Visibility improved a little as Parson and Gold descended the ridge. The mist opened up enough for Parson to discern the mountain spur tapering off toward the north. A white expanse dotted with thornbush and stunted trees. The surface crust reflected what little light there was, giving off a pale glow. Icy snow pelted his face like grit in a sandstorm. They didn't have much time left before dark, and he fought the urge to rush.

Parson stopped to size up the landscape. He thought he knew how to find the SF team. His current heading would take him toward what looked like a hogback along the next ridge. Easy to imagine a cave among the rock formations there. But he couldn't see well enough to be sure. Of course, he wouldn't see Cantrell's men until they wanted to be seen.

He guessed they were still above nine thousand feet. Below he saw an area that looked like easier walking. Steep but no boulders or brush in the way, just a slope thick with virgin snow. He started to take that route, but something at the back of his mind worried him. Why would there be a swath so smooth in terrain so rugged? Because that's a damned avalanche chute, he told himself. You're so tired you're getting stupid. You better think fast and move slow, or tomorrow won't be your problem.

Farther below, he made out the narrow channel of the avalanche track, and beneath that, the runout zone filled with what looked like lumpy snow. Probably lumpy because of boulders and debris that had piled up there over the years.

"We want to stay away from there," Parson said.

"What's wrong?" Gold asked.

"Anytime now, all that snow up here," he said, pointing, "is going to wind up down there."

Parson picked his way parallel to the ridgeline, away from the slab of snowpack poised to blast its way downhill. Something will kill me someday, he thought, but not that. As he walked, the topcoat crunched under his boots like broken glass.

He glanced back at Gold. She held her rifle close as she followed him, one step at a time. At a point when he paused to choose the path for the next several yards, he looked over his shoulder and saw her watching him, waiting for his decision, silent.

The body armor he'd taken from the insurgent weighed on him and he wanted to ditch it, but he still had enough self-discipline to keep it on. Too valuable a piece of gear not to use. He wished Gold would wear it, but she had turned it down every time he offered.

Parson eased his way down among the leafless scrub laden with snow. When he finally reached the saddle between ridges, he found ice fog hugging the ground. Snow to his knees, mist to his waist. From the lay of the land, he suspected a primitive road ran through where he stood, but the snow made it impossible to tell. All roads in this part of Afghanistan were long since impassable because of the blizzard. Normally, Parson would have avoided any line of communication like a road or a river. But now, between the storm and the insurgents, everywhere was dangerous. His situation made him think of the bomb-sniffing dogs he'd seen back at Bagram, never at rest, judging every breath they took for the whiff of a threat. At least he and Gold had the ice fog to cover them. When he kneeled, the mist hid him completely. He pulled out his electronic gear.

Parson took a GPS fix and saw he was only a half mile from the position Cantrell had given him. He turned up the volume on his radio.

"Razor One-Six," he called. "Flash Two-Four Charlie."

"Flash Two-Four Charlie, go ahead on Delta." Crisp as a landline. Parson changed frequencies.

"We're nearby. May we come on in?"

"Affirmative. I'll tell my guys weapons tight."

Parson kept on his GPS and started up the next ridge. He saw no one, but uphill he made out a cornice of rock that seemed to correspond to Cantrell's location. As he approached, a black-gloved hand waved, motioned for him to continue. He found Cantrell and Najib behind a limestone ledge. Blood on Najib's parka. Smears on his shotgun. Not his own blood, apparently.

"Didn't expect to see you again," Cantrell said. "This must be Sergeant Gold."

Gold nodded. Took off her gloves, checked her fingers. The bandages showed yellowish stains from the antiseptic and blood.

Her hands trembled slightly. Najib watched her, offered the drinking tube from his CamelBak. She drank and passed it to Parson.

Cantrell examined Gold's hands, then looked at her with
something like reverence. He called over his medic. Gold took off
her coat and pushed up her sleeve while the medic gave her an
injection. The lines around her eyes seemed to soften as the morphine took effect.

"Did you recapture the mullah?" Gold asked.

"No," Cantrell said. "We killed several of those assholes. They
killed two of our men and wounded two."

Parson saw the bodies of two insurgents slumped among the
boulders. Blood on snow. Casings everywhere. A dead black horse
down the slope, its coat wet with melted flakes.

"We thought we had them cornered in this cave," Najib said.
"But there must be another exit. The cave is empty now except for
our own soldiers."

Parson looked around and at first recognized nothing as a cave
entrance. But he eventually found a jagged hole in the rocks, not
nearly as big as he'd imagined. The snow made it hard to tell, but
Parson thought the opening was hardened with a row of rough
masonry. Icicles hung from the top edge like fangs.

Some of the troops were inside the cave. The medic tended
the wounded. An M-4 stuck by its bayonet into the ground served
as a pole for an IV bag. Plastic tubing ran from the bag and disappeared under a green blanket covering one of the injured men. Off
to the side lay two other troops, ponchos pulled over their faces.

"Any idea where the insurgents went?" Gold asked.

"Unless they have something else below ground, there aren't
many places they could have gone," Cantrell said. "They can't keep

an old man and their wounded out in this weather for long." He opened a canvas map case and pulled out a topographical chart. "We're here." He pointed with the stub of a pencil that had been sharpened with a knife. "The nearest villages are here and here." Parson judged from the map's scale that reaching any of those villages would take more than two days' walking.

"My men are searching for the other exit," Najib said. "We will track them down from there."

"You're going to follow them again?" Parson asked.

"Task Force says take that mullah at all costs," Cantrell said. "They'll send help when they can."

Cantrell withdrew a black-and-white photograph from his map case. Printing along the bottom read: NATIONAL GEOSPATIAL INTELLIGENCE AGENCY. A satellite photo.

"I think the corner of this picture corresponds to where we are," Cantrell said. "This village is the closest, and it doesn't look demolished."

"How old is that photo?" Gold asked.

"About three months."

Parson could tell little from the photo. Just an image taken from so high that the mountain ridges looked like folds of wrinkled corduroy. But he noted that it must have been shot on a perfectly clear day. On that day, anyone in his situation would have had a chopper ride within hours if not minutes.

He shivered hard, and he couldn't feel his feet. He stumbled over to the cave entrance, ducked through it, and sat down near the wounded. Inside, it felt only a little warmer. He opened his ruck and found an MRE. Cut open the package and pulled out the heater pouch. Unscrewed a water bottle and dripped water up to the pouch's fill line, which wet a packet of anhydride powder.

When the chemical reaction began, he wrapped the pouch in his handkerchief so it wouldn't burn him. Then he placed the pouch and handkerchief beside him, untied his flight boots and took them off. Peeled away the filthy socks. His toes were a glossy white. When he pulled off his gloves, he saw that his fingers were, too.

"You'll lose them if you don't warm them up," the medic said. "But don't heat them too quickly."

Parson pressed the handkerchief bundle against his bare feet. The more his toes warmed, the more they hurt. It seemed this was a race between the enemy and the elements to see which would get him first.

He looked at the wounded troops. One stared at the cave ceiling, eyes unfocused. The other's eyes were closed. They both looked a little younger than Parson, maybe thirty. Because of their blankets, he could not tell anything about their wounds, but they were obviously in no shape to move. He guessed Cantrell would have to divide his soldiers, leaving some here with the wounded until a medevac helicopter could reach them.

Parson wondered whether these two guys would make it. He didn't know a lot about Special Forces, but he did know that each of these troops was fluent in a language, and expert in a particular field such as demolition or communications. Damn shame to lose that kind of talent. He admired the quiet dedication of these snake-eaters. They did a job given all sorts of fancy names by politicians: The Global War on Terrorism, Operation Enduring Freedom, The Long War. But the troops had simpler names for it: My first deployment. Second deployment. Third and fourth.

The sound of voices speaking in Pashto came from farther back in the cave. Parson reached for his Colt, but then saw that no one else reacted. Flashlight beams played against the walls. Three of Najib's ANA troops emerged from the depths of the cavern and reported to their commander. Dirt covered their uniforms. When Najib spoke back to them, Parson thought he sounded resigned.

"They have found a hidden exit," Najib said. "The enemy escaped through a passage to the other side of this ridge."

"I'd like to run after those sons of bitches now," Cantrell said, "but it would be a goat fuck trying to chase them with night-vision goggles. We'll start out first thing tomorrow. Reeves and Obaidullah will stay here with Simpson and Jones."

Tough bastards, thought Parson. They're going to pursue what might be a larger force after already taking losses. Parson knew he had to decide whether to wait here with the wounded or go with Cantrell. The book answer was to stay and live to fly another day. Do what you're trained for. But these guys saved my ass, he thought, and I can move and shoot and do what they tell me to do. Gold's probably going to want to go, too. Guess we'll just push our luck till we all get killed.

Through the cave entrance, Parson watched the snow fall diagonally. The light receded until he could no longer make out the flakes. He sat with his knees upbent, holding the heater pouch around his toes. Unfolded the handkerchief and placed his fingers inside against the pouch. Like his toes, his fingers ached as they warmed. When any of Parson's extremities thawed out enough to feel sensations, the first one that came back was pain.

He didn't really feel like eating, but he knew he had to. He looked through the MRE he'd opened and found a packet of Sloppy Joe filling. Sliced it open and dug at it with the long-handled plastic spoon. No way to warm it now, because he'd used the heater for something more important. It was like eating leftover beef soup right out of a refrigerator.

Gold sat beside him and handed him a steaming canteen cup. He didn't see any fire, so he guessed she'd figured out some way to warm up water with a ration heater. He was too tired to ask how she'd done it. Parson inhaled the vapor. Tea. He sipped and felt it all the way down. He offered it back to her, but she shook her head. She opened some cheese spread and ate it right out of the packet.

"I've been meaning to ask," she said. "Did you ever confirm what happened to that family that took us in?"

"We found them dead outside."

Gold closed her eyes. She didn't speak for a while. "Terrible things happen both to the just and the unjust," she said finally.

Parson tried to imagine how she must feel about all this. Learning their language and culture, learning to think like them, trying to distinguish between the good, the indifferent, and the truly evil.

"I still can't believe you don't hate any of these people," he said, "after what you've been through."

"That wouldn't make it easier. It wouldn't make my fingers hurt any less."

"But you must be mad at the ones who did that," he said.

"Sometimes."

"You have a tough job, Sergeant Gold," Parson said.

"Sometimes."

"Are you going to go with these guys in the morning?" he asked.

"It's up to Captain Cantrell," Gold said.

When Cantrell heard his name, he sat next to them. Parson realized their presence meant another decision for Cantrell, an added layer of complexity to a mission already hard enough.

"What do you want us to do tomorrow?" Parson said.

"Do you think you can keep up with us?" Cantrell asked.

"We're a little worse for wear, but we won't slow you down."

"In that case, I can use two more sets of eyes."

"We'll try not to get in the way," Parson said.

When Gold finished eating, she got up and spoke to Najib and some of the ANA soldiers. Parson wondered whether she was asking questions, giving advice, or making small talk. Her tone seemed authoritative but kind. Parson thought Pashto had a soothing lilt to it when the words weren't shouted or spat in anger. Or maybe it just sounded better when she or Najib spoke it.

Gold unrolled two cold-weather sleeping bags. She unzipped one and placed it beside Parson. It took the last of his strength and wakefulness just to roll over into it and zip it back up. He didn't even remove his survival vest and body armor. Just pulled the .45 out of the vest's holster and kept his hand on it. He faded into sleep as he watched Gold zip up her own sleeping bag a few feet away.

It seemed only seconds later when Gold shook him by the arm. But when he finally got his eyes to focus on the luminescent dial of his watch, he saw he'd slept six hours. The SF troops were already on their feet. Gold handed him a water bottle. He sipped, then swished water, swallowed. Cantrell offered a small toothpaste tube. Parson squeezed some onto the tip of his index finger and brushed his teeth with that. He wiped his hand on the leg of his flight suit, rolled up the sleeping bag, and gathered up his gear. He took a last look at the wounded troops and their guardians left behind. They did not look back at him.

Parson and Gold followed Cantrell and some of the men deeper into the cave. Flashlight beams played across the cave walls. Most of the soldiers had lights mounted on their M-4s. Occasionally a red dot appeared in the middle of a bright pool of white light as the troops checked their laser sights.

One light beam stopped on the body of an insurgent. Somebody wounded yesterday who'd crawled this far, Parson guessed. No one commented. The flashlight beam moved away and the troops pressed on. Parson shined his own light around as well. In two places he saw brick defilades built up from the cave floor. Perfect places to take cover and shoot in the event of a running firefight through the cave. Maybe it's a good thing the bad guys had an escape route, Parson thought, or else the battle yesterday might have been a lot bloodier.

Empty crates and ammunition boxes lined the walls. A PKM rifle in the dirt. Discarded clothing and clay cookware. Yellowed and sodden manuals, some in Russian, some in what looked to Parson like Arabic, some in languages he could not even guess. Just behind him, Gold shined her light on some of the books, paused, and touched one of them.

"Dari," she whispered, "and Serbo-Croatian."

Farther on, Parson saw a barbell with fifty-pound lead weights on each end. Probably a terrorist training camp for years, he thought.

The passage narrowed until the troops had to crouch. Parson felt the air grow colder.

"Lights off," Cantrell whispered.

Parson switched off his light and plunged into total darkness. He had his night-vision goggles in an outside pocket, ready for this moment. He turned them on and looked through them. In the black of the cave they offered poor resolution, but he saw the soldiers in front of him kneeling, nearly crawling out a narrow exit. Some had to remove their rucksacks to get through.

When Parson's turn came, he took off his pack and handed it through the hole to a soldier outside. Opened the bolt on his rifle and passed it out, too. Lowered himself to his knees and felt the hard stone floor of the cave, sharp pebbles grinding under his hands.

It was like crawling into a deep freezer. The cave was chilly, but the wind outside hit him with a whole new order of cold. Parson estimated the breeze at fifteen knots. That could make twenty degrees feel like minus five. He pulled his woolen watch cap down tighter and placed his parka's hood over his head. Took his pack and rifle and reloaded the weapon. The frigid air seemed to burn inside his chest.

He saw Cantrell whisper something into his radio. A few minutes later, Najib and some of his men emerged over the ridge and out of a night that still seemed black and thick as oil. Parson guessed they had come around the mountainside to maintain overwatch while the rest of the troops took the route through the cave.

The snow sissed against Parson's clothing, flakes driven by the wind into Gore-Tex fabric. The troops stood motionless while Cantrell and Najib examined the tracks left by the insurgents. New snow had softened the edges of the footprints, but the trail was still discernible. The two men stooped, peered through NVGs, conferred, gestured. Najib led the way along a couloir that ran downslope.

Parson worried momentarily about avalanches again, but here the incline seemed too shallow for that particular peril. Not that there weren't enough others. He felt he was already on borrowed time.

Gold stopped to buckle on her snowshoes, then took several

running strides to catch up. She seemed strong enough. Like herself again.

With dawn, the darkness lightened to the color of tin and stayed that way, as if the night had congealed. The troops no longer needed their NVGs, and Parson stowed his own goggles. Now that he scanned the landscape with the naked eye, he saw that this side of the ridge offered little more cover than the opposite slope. Just a white expanse broken by occasional stunted camelthorn, gnarled branches sheathed in rime. The mountains loomed like swells in an ocean of snow.

Parson tried to count the sets of footprints the team was following. It looked like at least twenty, but it was hard to say. Perhaps more than his own group. The only good news was that he saw no horse tracks. If the insurgents were all on foot now, that brought the odds from impossible to merely bad. He saw no blood around the footprints, either, but that meant little in the continuing snowfall. So maybe they had wounded and maybe they didn't.

He looked more closely at the footprints. A few showed longer toe drags. That meant they were carrying something heavy. Perhaps larger weapons, perhaps an injured fighter, perhaps an elderly mullah.

The trail led through a pass marked by a creek that seemed to smoke as if it flowed with acid. Vapor from a hot spring, Parson supposed. The footing near the stream became tricky because of strange ice formations. The troops picked their way through a field of frozen spikes and pyramids a little shorter than knee high. Parson nearly tripped over these ice spears several times. He had no idea what hydrology could have produced such an obstacle, but what interested him more was that the guerrillas' footprints led straight through it. Not around it where the walking would have been easier. Like they were making a beeline for something.

Apparently Cantrell and Najib had the same idea. They stopped, and Cantrell opened his case of maps and photographs. He unfolded a topo chart.

"They're heading almost due east," Cantrell said. "That doesn't take them toward any village I can see."

"Unless they have another cave complex," Najib said.

"God, I hope not."

Gold looked over their shoulders, perusing the map and satellite photo.

"Where do you think they're going?" Parson asked. "You've talked with some of these people."

Gold said nothing for a moment, just looked at the tracks trailing off into the mist and snow.

"Pakistan."

CHAPTER SEVENTEEN

Parson followed a few paces behind Najib and Cantrell, shivering. Katabatic wind blowing downhill pushed the flakes sideways across the valley. Parson slung the M-40 over his shoulder and unzipped his parka long enough to tie the drawstring tighter around his waist. He hoped Gold was wrong about the bad guys heading for Pakistan, but he'd never known her to be wrong about anything. That was a long way on foot, but these lunatics seemed willing to endure anything for jihad, martyrdom, and their seventy-two virgins.

And if they made it to the border, what then? They'd probably disappear into Waziristan's tribal areas. It wasn't like terrorists hadn't done that before. No chance of getting them there unless a Predator happened to fly right over them. The B-2s could nuke the whole fucking region, as far as Parson was concerned. Well, maybe not. Muslims like Najib and his men were all right.

A *crack*-BANG interrupted his thoughts. Parson dropped flat to the snow. The echo rolled through the mountains like thunder.

He heard no scream, no moan. Either a miss or a very clean kill. He wanted badly to raise his head and look, but he knew that if he did he might draw the next round. The bullet must have come close for him to have heard the supersonic snap before the explosion of gunpowder.

Parson held his breath. Waited for another shot. Coppery taste in his mouth. Bile and fear. He did not need to see anything to know who had fired. A single, disciplined 7.62-millimeter shot from that infernal Dragunov.

Silence. He kept his head down and turned it as slowly as he could will himself to move. From the corner of his eye, he saw disturbed snow where Cantrell had hit the ground. No real cover, Parson thought, just concealment in the white powder. There's very little between us and that Dragunov that would stop a bullet.

"Careful," Cantrell hissed. "If anybody has a shot, take it."

Parson had been carrying his rifle with its forend in the crook of his elbow when he hit the ground. Now he was lying on top of the weapon with the scope grinding into his solar plexus. Not in a position to do him a hell of a lot of good. He thought of the old saying about never feeling more foolish than when your weapon's not in your hands when you need it. At least he saw that the muzzle was clear and not plugged with snow or dirt. His wrist ached from the fall.

He came to the sickening realization that he, Gold, and the rest of the troops were now pinned down by a patient and skilled adversary. The son of a bitch was obviously taking his time, waiting for someone to screw up and give him a good target. Very unlikely the team would get out of this without losing someone.

And even if they did, Marwan could harass them with sniper fire indefinitely, covering his group's retreat.

Parson dared not move any of his limbs. As it was, he saw the watch on his left wrist. It ticked so slowly that for a moment he thought the second hand was broken. Pinprick sleet fell with the snow now, and it seemed he heard the impact of each separate ice grain. He wondered whether he'd hear anything if a slug hit him in the head.

"There's an outcrop to the northeast," Cantrell whispered. "Maybe three hundred meters. I think that's where the shot came from."

From the corner of his eye, Parson saw Cantrell roll to his right, M-4 held tight against his torso. A burst of dirt and snow erupted beside the snake-eater's head. Then the slamming report of the Dragunov.

Cantrell popped up behind a low boulder. Compacted snow sloughed from his uniform. Another shot came. The bullet glanced off the rock, sprayed Cantrell with grit and ice. Parson heard the growl-whine of the ricochet.

"Yeah, that's where the fucker is," Cantrell said. "When I open up, rush to cover, then give me a mad minute on that outcrop."

Before Parson could wonder what that meant, he heard the cackle of Cantrell's rifle on full auto. The troops leaped from their burrows in the snow, kneeled behind trees, rocks, and brush. Then they all began shooting at once. The rifle fire rose into a crescendo like the roar of something enraged. Fountains of brass poured from their ejection ports.

Parson scrambled to Cantrell and dropped prone beside the boulder. Aimed the M-40. Through the scope he saw the strikes of bullets: flying rock and snow, shuddering branches, splinters.

He did not see any clear target. He fired anyway to add to the general effect. Cycled the bolt, fired again. Parson suspected he was wasting ammo, because anything near that outcrop had to be dead by now.

Then the firing stopped. Parson's ears rang. Dully, he heard the shush of wind and snow, the metallic clicks as men changed magazines. Their weapons gave off whorls of gun smoke that vanished into the gusts but left an aftertaste of burned powder.

"Nobody move," Cantrell said. The SF commander took binoculars from around his neck and peered through them.

"See anything?" Parson asked.

"Not a damn thing."

Through his scope, Parson saw no movement on the outcrop or anywhere around it. No body, nothing. It was as if the sniper fire had come from something that slithered away unharmed.

He looked around and saw what Marwan's first bullet had done. An ANA trooper lay crumpled on his side. A trickle of blood ran from the entrance wound in his chest.

The team watched and waited for about half an hour, as the dead man seemed to stare into the distance. Parson spotted Gold behind a tree. Cartridge casings lay scattered to her right. She apparently had emptied her AK.

Najib ran to the dead man in a low crouch, shotgun held in his left hand. Pulled off his right glove and, with two fingers, closed the man's eyes. Said something in Pashto, placed a poncho over him. Parson wanted to say something, too, but he didn't know what. Instead he did the only thing he could that might help. He turned on his GPS, and when it initialized, he stored their current position, marking the location of the man's body.

"All right," Cantrell said. "They have my attention. Captain Najib, I suggest we try to flank them from the north."

Najib watched the snowflakes, seemed to study the wind. "This will take longer now," he said.

"We'll just have to be careful," Cantrell said. "But if these assholes want to dance, we'll dance."

Parson wondered why the move to the north, but he didn't want to ask stupid questions of soldiers in combat. Eventually, as he followed Najib's slow stalk across the valley, the answer dawned on him. The wind had picked up to around twenty knots now, right out of the north, and walking into it brought tears to his eyes and numbed his face. And when we turn to try to engage those bastards again, Parson realized, we'll be coming out of the north ourselves. Any sniper trying to pick us off will have to watch and aim directly into that bitter wind. Nobody could stare into this shit long without his eyes blinking and watering.

When they reached the outcrop, the troops fanned out to look for bodies or blood trails. Parson found a single set of footprints leading to and from the firing position. Empty casings. Shards of wood, bark, and chipped rock left by the team's hailstorm of bullets. Not one drop of blood.

"I thought we had him there for a minute," Cantrell said.

"Marwan has expert training," Najib said, "and the mullah has long experience. They are not soft targets."

"And they think heaven is on their side," Gold said.

The team angled away from the outcrop, continuing almost due north now. The troops moved about three steps at a time. At each pause, they scanned into what looked like a wall of white and gray: snowy landscape and low clouds, steady patter of flakes. When they saw no threat, they moved up a little and looked again.

The painstaking advance left Parson shivering. He wasn't walking fast enough to generate much body heat, but he suspected he shivered as much from dread as from cold. Any moment could bring the crack of another high-velocity, boat-tail bullet. And if Marwan recognizes me, Parson thought, he'll nail me first just on principle. I'll just have to see him before he sees me.

Parson recalled what Marwan's men had done to Nunez, what they'd nearly done to him and Gold. The just-missed chance for payback. He wanted to shout, stab, shoot. Now he could only watch and wait. And take another three steps. He wished he had some sort of emotional circuit protection, like the breakers in the airplane that tripped when the load got too high. But he had no such thing, and the wiring of his mind could only burn.

Najib guided the team along an escarpment that paralleled their course. But where the ridge made an odd cut toward the south, he had no choice but to cross it into the next valley. The troops followed Najib at an angle through a cove that opened onto a steep incline pelted by snow granules. It occurred to Parson that the soldiers had done in slow motion what his own crew would have done in the airplane: fly low through a valley for terrain masking, and then cross a ridge at a low spot on a forty-five-degree angle.

The gritty snow must have been falling on this slope for some time. Sleet and ice pellets lay scattered over the snowpack like shattered crystal. It seemed to Parson that every fold in these mountains had slightly different weather, usually worse than the ridgeline before it. He couldn't see all the way to the foot of the massif; darkness was coming on, and blackness seemed to have pooled in the valley below. Night didn't fall in the Hindu Kush. It started on the low ground and worked its way up.

Cantrell called a halt and gathered the team around him. "I didn't want a firefight with these assholes at night," he said, "but since they've slowed us down, every minute counts. I don't know if they have NVGs, but just in case, take off any glint tape you're wearing."

Parson had a square of tape Velcroed to his shoulder. He peeled it off and slipped it into a pocket. No need to worry about identification by friendlies now. Gold and the men around him were the only allies for miles.

Najib gave orders in Pashto. Gold raised her eyebrows as if she was impressed. Two of the ANA soldiers stepped forward. They detached the ACOG sights from their M-4s and installed some other kind of scope. Thermal sights, Parson guessed. That's good luck or damn fine planning. The night belongs to whoever has the best gear and the biggest balls.

Cantrell and Najib consulted their maps and photos, and Parson turned on his GPS long enough to get a current position. Wordlessly, he offered it to them with coordinates displayed. Najib pointed to a spot on a satellite photo and nodded.

"Sergeant Gold tells me you are proficient with that M-40," Najib said. "If you see a target, do not hesitate to use it."

"I won't," Parson said. He doubted he'd get that chance to-night, since his weapon's scope was a daylight optic. But this was becoming a running skirmish that could go on day and night until the storm lifted enough for an air strike. Here, motherfuckers, have some napalm. All right, no air strike, he thought, since we can't fry the mullah. So this is man-to-man, bullet by bullet. We can do that, too.

Parson's nose ran because of the constant cold, and now the wind made it worse. He sniffled, tasted the salt on the back of his throat. Dabbed his nose with the back of his glove. The wind didn't seem to be dying down with twilight, either. That just made things a little more miserable. But at least the snake-eaters seemed to know how to turn misery into advantage. You had to give them that.

"Let's not keep our friends waiting," Cantrell said. "Pick your targets carefully. Remember, we want the preacher alive."

Not an easy task at night, Parson realized. You can't recognize a face at any distance with NVGs or thermal optics. They'll have to pay attention to which one moves like an old man. Just like with flying, he considered, everything's more complicated after dark.

The team followed the crest toward the east, moving in a column formation. Najib led the way, with each man covering a sector of fire to the right or left. These special ops guys are leaving nothing to chance, Parson thought. Just because we're hunting the bad guys doesn't mean the bad guys aren't hunting us.

When it got so dark his scope was useless, Parson slung his rifle over his shoulder. He drew his pistol and carried it in his right hand. Placed his NVGs around his neck. The Colt's weight reignited the flickering pain in his wrist. He shifted the .45 to his left hand. If he fired now, he'd be shooting blindly in an attacker's general direction, which he could do with either hand. And if he had to do that, things had really gone to hell.

Parson walked with his goggles switched on, and he raised them and looked through them every few steps. The soldiers had monocular night optics mounted on head straps, and they could scan with their hands free, weapons ready. Eventually, Najib and Cantrell halted. They kneeled and pulled a poncho over themselves to check the map by flashlight. No light visible to the naked eye leaked from their poncho, but when Parson watched them with NVGs, the rip-stop nylon glowed like a giant, misshapen firefly. Snowflakes falling onto it shimmered like green glitter. Then the light flicked off and the two men emerged.

"Time to turn south, fellas," Cantrell whispered. "Take it easy; look for them with IR. You know the drill." Najib spoke in Pashto. Repeating the order, Parson supposed.

Parson had little experience with infrared equipment, but he knew thermal scopes could penetrate snowfall and fog better than NVGs. They didn't amplify trace light; they sensed heat. Marwan and his goons might know how to use concealment and stealth, but anything at 98.6 degrees would contrast sharply in this god-awful cold. He hoped he'd soon see some of them brought to ambient temperature.

The team crept to the ridge crest. The soldiers watched the region below for several minutes. Then Najib nodded at Cantrell, raised his arm, and swept it forward. At that signal, the troops spread out and began descending the slope, pausing often to observe with their night optics.

It felt good to have the wind at his back for a change. Grainy snow spattered against the back of his coat with every gust, and Parson was glad he didn't have to take those ice nettles in his face and eyes. His NVGs revealed nothing except sparse trees, stunted branches bending with accumulated snow.

The troops reconnoitered for hours, and Parson was beginning to wonder if the insurgents had changed direction. But when Najib stopped and raised his fist, the team froze. Parson still saw nothing. He clenched his jaw to stop his teeth from chattering. No one moved or spoke for at least two full minutes.

Cantrell and Najib gave a series of hand signals that Parson could not follow. One of the American soldiers moved up, whispered with Cantrell. Parson watched the man remove the wrapping from a chemical lightstick. The commando hiked some distance from the team and kneeled by a thornbush. He tied a length of parachute cord to the lightstick, then wrapped the stick in a bandanna. He bent the lightstick enough to crack the glass vial inside, and two chemicals mixed to form a red luminescence. The soldier adjusted the bandanna to better hide the glow, then left the concealed lightstick hanging in the bush. He unrolled cord as he returned to his teammates and crouched beside Cantrell.

The troops began moving into positions behind trees, into low swales, taking whatever cover the landscape provided. Cantrell motioned for Parson and Gold to get down in a draw defiladed by a stone ledge. Parson still saw no enemy through his NVGs, but when Cantrell loaned him a thermal scope he saw two men a couple hundred yards away, each holding a Kalashnikov. Their infrared figures looked like a photo negative come alive, human shapes limned in white, surrounded by darkness. Their Pakul hats were dipped into the wind to help shield their faces. So they were on guard, but not really guarding. Chilled into complacency.

Parson handed the scope back to Cantrell. He caught a glimpse of the snake-eater's face in the backglow of the eyepiece. Cantrell wore a faint smile, as if he liked the odds he had created for himself.

Cantrell took a final look through the IR scope, gave it to Parson again. Then he raised his rifle and spoke softly into his MBITR.

Two quick shots ripped the night. The two guards fell. The soldier holding the parachute cord jerked it. The lightstick tumbled out of the bandanna, and the enemy opened up on it.

A storm of bullets slammed into the mountainside around the chem light. One round struck the stick itself. Glowing liquid sprayed like a splash of Saint Elmo's fire.

Gun blasts sputtered in the darkness. The SF team popped off one or two rounds at a time on semiauto. Aiming, Parson supposed. The other side tore through full magazines.

Parson looked through the thermal scope again. One of the sentries lay still. The other raised himself up and leaned against a tree. He held his rifle as if it were too heavy to bring up and fire. Then he dropped it. He placed his hand to his chest, stumbled, held on to the tree with that same hand. Seen through the IR lens, his hand left a glowing smear on the bark. The insurgent fell facedown into the snow. His handprint remained on the tree, but as Parson watched, it cooled and faded until no sign of the guerrilla's touch remained.

The firing died to sporadic crackles, then stopped altogether. Parson hoped someone had hit Marwan this time, but he doubted the terrorist leader was one of the two men he'd seen shot. Marwan would not have been standing watch like a private, certainly not like an inattentive private.

Cantrell murmured into his radio again. Some of the soldiers stood up and stalked forward. Others remained in place to cover them. Then the ones who had moved up crouched with weapons ready to guard the advance of their comrades.

In leapfrog fashion, the team crept ahead without any opposition now. Just a cold wind that lifted the powder from branches and mixed it with the flakes still falling, so that the trees themselves seemed to generate snow. The thermal scope didn't show the effect, but when Parson switched to his night-vision goggles, the larches appeared to send forth billows of emerald dust.

Najib checked the two bodies. No ID, no money or wallets, just their weapons and old Soviet-style ammo vests with pouches for AK-47 magazines. He handed a full mag to Gold, who placed it in a pocket of her field jacket. One of Najib's ANA troops reported to him in Pashto, and Najib shook his head.

"We get any others?" Cantrell asked.

"Negative," Najib said. "I saw no drag marks, either."

"Well, we thinned 'em out a little," Cantrell said. "Let's just keep the pressure on them until we can get some help."

But help isn't coming until the weather lifts, Parson told himself. The combination of low barometric pressure, temperature/dew point spread, and moisture content means we're fighting this part of the war by ourselves.

He looked straight up with his NVGs, hoping to gauge the cloud height. That gave him nothing but vertigo. It appeared the whole universe consisted of chartreuse fog and snow, not falling but floating into a world dissolving into mist. Dizzy, Parson stumbled and went down on both knees, nearly banged the scope of his M-40 against a rock. Shit, let's not do that again, he thought. I'm disoriented enough as it is.

Gold helped him to his feet. He thought he saw her smile slightly, as if she was amused that his equipment and his inner ear could not apprehend all of Creation.

The team followed the insurgents' tracks through most of the night. The footprints continued east unswervingly, and Parson decided Gold was probably right about where the bad guys were headed. They want to tag home base, he figured, where it's relatively safe.

Cantrell and Najib showed no intention of stopping for rest.

Looks like we'll just eat on the move and sleep when this is over, Parson thought. He'd heard of special ops troops training in scenarios that kept them awake until they began to hallucinate from sleep deprivation. So this was why they did that. With all that's riding on this mission, he realized, exhaustion is just another field condition. One more thing to overcome in the protection of civilians sleeping soundly, warm, well fed, and oblivious.

Parson scanned the terrain with his NVGs to get his bearings again. Noted where Gold was. Checked for Najib and Cantrell up ahead. Tightened his boot laces, placed his rifle across his arm, and pressed on.

CHAPTER EIGHTEEN

It was still dark when Najib and Cantrell stopped to check their map again. Parson joined them under the poncho that shielded their flashlights. He turned on his GPS to offer help, but he could tell that Najib was so proficient at old-school land navigation that he needed no assistance. About thirty years of living in these mountains didn't hurt, either, Parson thought.

"We should turn north and flank them again," Najib said as he closed his compass.

"Might as well," Cantrell said. "The wind hasn't changed."

"Is it a good idea to hit them again from the same direction?" Parson asked.

"If they do not expect us to do that," Najib said, "then it is exactly what we wish to do."

That made sense to Parson. It also meant another approach with the wind and snow at their backs and in the enemy's face. But not before the

team faced into it themselves for a while. When they began moving again, Parson turned his head against the whipping snow, tried
to shield his cheek with the hood of his parka. That helped a little,
but Parson still felt the stings of white pellets turned by the wind
into projectiles. He wondered how his face could be so numb yet
still sense the prick of every grain of snow and ice. He tried wrapping a handkerchief around his nose and mouth. The moisture of
his breath made it freeze into the shape of his face.

The lead weight of fatigue began to form behind his brow. He
wanted nothing more than to slump into a drift and sleep, but
he realized that the team could not stop now. Even if they did, he
knew that if he slept without taking the time to build a proper
snow cave, he would never wake up.

The sky to the east began turning from deep black to ice gray.
Parson hoped dawn would perk him up some, but, if anything, it
made his eyes more heavy-lidded. His wearied mind began to
wander. He wondered if the families of his crewmates had been
notified by now. Probably not. He doubted that would happen
until the bodies were recovered. What could I have done differ-
ently? he asked himself. He went over the events of the last few
days, especially the day of the shootdown. Then he forced himself
to stop. Better focus on the here and now, he thought, or you'll
get yourself or somebody else killed.

He saw Gold watching him again. Parson stopped to remove
his rucksack and put away his NVGs. Then he shouldered the
pack and kept walking.

A glance upward told him vertical visibility still amounted
to nothing. Overcast loomed just above like a sodden tarpaulin.
The team was passing through treeless country now, a valley that

looked like a moonscape blanketed by snow. Boulders littered the terrain, stones the color of burned metal on the sides not covered in white.

The troops watched their sectors of fire, each trigger finger extended across each trigger guard. Parson saw nothing to suggest an enemy close by, but he didn't trust his instincts when he was so tired. He felt he was moving into some stage of fatigue he'd never experienced before, with strange effects like a poison. He had a metallic taste in his mouth, as if he held a dime on his tongue. Despite the cold, his flesh became sensitive, as if his flight suit were made of sandpaper. Gold and the Special Forces troops looked like they were holding up all right, but the skin sagged under their eyes.

When the team turned to the south, Parson tried to make himself alert, to will himself away from exhaustion. Heading south meant a move to intercept the jihadists again. A firefight could happen at any time. He felt the wind against the back of his head.

Najib stopped and seemed to look at something for a long time. The soldiers froze. Parson crouched and shouldered his rifle so he could look through the scope. Eventually he found what Najib saw.

In the distance, a spot of red highlighted the snow. When the team moved closer and Parson looked through his scope again, he saw some kind of bloody mess. It had to have been recent or else new snow would have covered it. Something solid in the middle of the red slush. Parson supposed the wolves had killed an animal. Maybe they'd fed on an ibex or some farmer's goat.

Cantrell and Najib whispered to each other and moved up a few steps. Gold borrowed the binoculars, then handed them back to Parson. When he glassed the scene from a closer vantage point, he saw that the dead thing was a man.

The troops spoke to each other through their MBITRs, took positions, set up a perimeter. Now Parson was confused. He'd heard no shots. But then, that body didn't appear to have been killed in a firefight. Even from a few hundred yards it looked like something slaughtered. It seemed every day Afghanistan showed him some new horror.

Najib moved up with his shotgun poised to fire. Parson zoomed in with the binoculars and watched him crouch near the body. Najib turned to his side and placed his fist over his mouth, closed his eyes. Looked again and shook his head. He spoke into his radio, and Cantrell joined him.

As Parson neared the other two officers, he heard Cantrell say, "That is so fucked up."

Then he saw why. The body had been disemboweled and beheaded. Parson heaved, but didn't have enough in his stomach to vomit.

Entrails spilled from the belly like purple ropes. The corpse's hands were tied behind it with a long, black cloth. The head sat in the snow upright, eyes closed, mouth gaping. Flakes were starting to gather in the hair and on the eyebrows. Blood had melted snow into a puddle of red slush.

"He was Taliban," Gold said.

"How can you tell?" Parson asked.

She pointed to the bound hands. "That was his turban."

Cantrell began walking around the scene, examining tracks,

looking at the surroundings. Najib huddled with his men, speaking in Pashto.

"So who besides us is after these guys?" Parson asked. He thought some militia, maybe the Northern Alliance or whatever they called themselves now, had caught a straggler from Marwan's gang.

"Nobody," Cantrell said, hands on his hips, eyes on the ground. "There's no other set of footprints. No shell casings, nothing."

"They did this to one of their own?" Parson said. "Why?"

"Dissent in the ranks, perhaps," Gold said.

"So somebody got made into an example," Cantrell said.

"This is why Marwan needs the mullah," Gold said.

"What are you talking about?" Parson asked.

"Even some Talibs oppose what he wants to do," she said. "The mullah can give him theological backing."

"Theological backing for using a nuke?" Parson asked.

No one answered. But that was answer enough.

"We believe the mullah was about to issue a *fatwa* approving a nuclear strike on a U.S. city, but he was captured first," Najib said.

Now Parson was starting to make some sense of why the Taliban might not all support Marwan. The Taliban had Afghanistan as their own little medieval paradise until 9/11, and then al Qaeda blew it for them. Guess they're afraid if we get hit hard again, he thought, we'll turn this place into the fifty-first state and never leave.

Parson looked at the mutilated corpse. It reminded him so much of Nunez. The sight of his crewmate, beheaded, came rushing back, a waking nightmare. But maybe Nunez and the others hadn't lost their lives for nothing. They had given him time to get away with the prisoner.

The mullah had been just cargo to Parson. Part of a job he did with his crew. Fisher was right all along, he thought. This mission is more important than any of us.

Cantrell gave hand signals to the troops out on the perimeter. The men prepared to move again. "Stay alert, people," he said. "If this is what they do to their friends, think what they'll do to you."

The team looped to the north once more and hiked in that direction for more than an hour. Parson thought he and his rifle could be more useful now in the daylight. He just hoped he could stay awake enough to think quickly and make good decisions. It was getting hard just to read his compass, something that should come as naturally as breathing. Yeah, he reminded himself, north is still three-six-zero, dumbass.

The enemy had to be close, but Parson could not see where. Snow fell harder, with mist rolling over the ridges. He guessed any transmissometer reading would have shown visibility at less than a quarter mile.

The valley opened into a bowl-like plateau walled by mountains, with a gentle rise bulging across the otherwise flat plain. Beyond the rise, Parson saw the top of a gnarled sapling less than a hundred yards away. It grew from the hill's opposite slope, and the rolling ground hid most of its trunk. A goshawk flapped out of the tree and circled over the troops. Parson wondered why the bird would fly around like that in such sorry weather. Because something disturbed it. Parson froze.

Najib looked at the raptor gliding above. He held up his fist. Everyone stopped. The hawk screeched, and its cry echoed across the plain like the screams of the damned. Moving only his eyes, Parson checked for the nearest cover. Not much to choose from. A rock no bigger than a C-130's tire. Scrub brush. Those bastards are probably just on the other side of that rise, Parson thought. Najib motioned for the team to take cover.

Parson dropped behind the rock and tried to make himself as flat as possible, part of the ground. He dug the butt of the M-40 into the snow, with the barrel along the side of the rock. With his left hand, he held the sling near the forward swivel and pointed the rifle toward the hill. Scanned through the scope. His eyes were so tired that the reticle went fuzzy. He blinked and forced himself to bring it into focus. Thought he saw movement behind the hill.

He placed his finger on the trigger. The brittle handkerchief across his face was getting uncomfortable, but he welcomed the extra camo it provided. No clear target for him now, just that bare tree and the stinging snow. He felt pressure on his chest from this extreme prone position. Bent his right knee and slid his leg up a bit, and that helped some.

In his peripheral vision, he saw a couple of the snake-eaters in similar positions. He wondered what to do next. Well, Najib had said to use the M-40. A snowdrift near the sapling appeared to move. No, just a trick of the fog. A pair of stones at the base of the drift. Nothing to get excited about.

But Parson didn't like those two rocks. Couldn't make his tired mind reason why. Because they're windward, he thought. They should be drifted over. Something, maybe a fallen branch, between them. No, they're gloved fists. Holding a rifle. White parka, white shemagh. And that's where the chest should be, Parson estimated with his crosshairs.

He fired. Felt the recoil, heard the crack of high velocity. Spurt of blood. The gloved hands released the AK and the body slumped forward. Parson saw that he'd hit the man somewhere in the upper torso. A fatal or at least incapacitating wound, apparently, because the body did not move.

He expected the insurgents to open up, but no shots came. Maybe they were waiting for someone to stand up and give them a target. Marwan must have schooled them on how to fight a little smarter. Parson remained flat to the ground.

But now he had empty brass in his firing chamber. Raising his arm to rebolt the rifle could give away his position. He was alive because they didn't know exactly where he was.

Parson considered what to do. Then he turned his rifle, slowly, slowly, onto its right side. That put the ejection port toward the ground. Using his right knuckles, he lifted the bolt by millimeters until he felt it release. Hooked two fingers around the bolt, tugged it. That hurt his wrist, and he ground his teeth. He gave the bolt a short jerk. That hurt even worse. But it made the extractor pop the expended cartridge onto the snow. The casing gave off an odor like metal hot from welding.

Parson put the heel of his hand against the bolt and pressed it forward. He heard satisfying steel-on-brass rasps that told him the carrier had picked up a fresh round. He closed the bolt, turned the rifle upright, peered through the scope again. All right, he thought, who else wants to play?

Nobody. Nothing rose along the rise except the batting of mist. Parson expected rifle fire to sputter at any moment. He heard only faint whispers among the troops. Then the single cough of one of their M-203s.

The grenade sailed from its launcher just a few feet from Parson. It arced over the rise like a burning cigar stub tossed away. When it exploded, the ground jolted his chest as if he'd been kicked.

He looked through the scope again. He saw twigs missing from the sapling, lashed by shrapnel. Drifting smoke. Nothing else. Cantrell low-crawled through the snow toward the jihadist Parson had shot. Parson forced himself to watch closely and help cover Cantrell. If an insurgent came over that rise to fire at the SF commander, the team would have only about half a second to shoot first.

Parson's crosshairs floated just above the crest of the hill. If it moves, it dies, he thought. But nothing appeared except the scouring snow. It ground at what little of his face remained exposed, and ice collected between his fingers as he held his weapon.

Cantrell reached the corpse. He stopped, seemed to watch and listen. Got up on his knees and pointed his rifle. Swept with the barrel. He did not fire. Then he slapped the ground beside him in apparent frustration. Snow sprayed from underneath his glove. He motioned for the team to move up.

Parson picked himself up off the ground, careful about his rifle's muzzle. He didn't think he had lain sprawled long enough to get cramped, but his legs tingled with the return of blood. His toes had been numb for days, and now they had no feeling at all. Time flowed strangely in combat, he decided. Sometimes it trickled away like water; sometimes it froze up and clotted like slush.

He stumbled forward, examined the man he'd shot. It wasn't Marwan. That disappointed him a little, but he hadn't expected to take down Marwan that easily. He did not remember the face of the dead guerrilla from among his former captors. A steel-wool beard and cheeks tough as the leather of a knife scabbard. A scar across the bridge of the nose, punctuation in a life story now ended. Probably just some ex–goat herder who'd volunteered for martyrdom. Parson almost felt sorry for him, poor ignorant bastard and his short and miserable existence. But he also wondered, What might this guy have done to me if he'd had the chance? When Parson looked over the hill, he saw lines of bootprints leading away. No other bodies, no blood trails.

"Fuckers gave us the slip again," Cantrell said.

"All save this one," Najib said. "Major Parson has improved the odds somewhat."

Not by enough, Parson thought. If this comes down to attrition, we'll all freeze to death before anybody wins. He looked at Gold. She shrugged. Then she took a water bottle from her pocket, drank, handed it to Parson. He didn't feel thirsty, but he took a few sips anyway and returned the bottle to her.

"How are your fingers?" he asked.

"Better. What about you?"

Parson wasn't sure what to say. What about me? "I'll manage," he said.

"You're doing all right."

Parson took that as a compliment. He was impressed that after all she'd been through, she was thinking outside of herself enough to keep an eye on him.

The insurgents' trail led out of the plain and into a pass lined by hoodoos: looming pillars of rock carved by millennia of wind, rain, and snow, and by the narrow river that spluttered through the gorge. The terrain made Parson nervous. He didn't have to be an infantryman to see that every few yards offered a perfect kill zone for an ambush.

The tracks led to a spot where the insurgents seemed to have stopped and stood for a few minutes. Sets of bootprints faced each other. Other marks suggested gear moved around.

"What the hell are they doing?" Cantrell asked.

"The mullah's tired," Gold said. She pointed to a drag mark among the tracks leading away from the spot. Something about a foot and a half wide had plowed a smooth path through the snow. Parson had to think for a moment. An improvised litter. They must have rolled a blanket between two sticks to make a stretcher to carry the old man. Good, he thought. That'll slow them down.

The team followed the tracks and drag mark along the river. Parson scanned the bluffs above him, though he knew the first sign of a trap would be a bullet or an RPG. Couldn't see much but clouds, anyway. Scuds of fog flowed over a lobe of the ridgeline and sank downhill like silt. He tried to listen closely, but the rumble of water over a cataract downstream made the effort pointless.

The gurgle of the water's passage and the sissing of the snow seemed to blend into a slow rhythm, hints of song. In the dark of his fatigue, Parson imagined it as music. But the tune did not bring comfort. It came in a minor key, something dire and mournful, like an ancient ballad of war. Then his mind lost the pattern, and the sounds separated back into mere snowfall and splashes.

The lack of sleep hurt more now. The lead weight expanded inside Parson's head. Every sound annoyed him; every thought required physical effort. It felt like the worst hangover and the highest fever he'd ever suffered.

He wondered whether the others fared any better. Gold scanned the terrain around her as she hiked. Still alert, then. The snake-eaters looked like this was all business as usual. Parson hoped he could keep it together and not let anyone down.

Snow pellets ground like grit as they fell against the left side of his hood. When he checked his compass he saw that the wind had shifted several degrees, but he didn't know whether to trust that reading. Canyon walls created all kinds of backflows, swirls, and eddies. Doesn't matter anyway, he thought. We just have to follow the enemy's tracks until someone else gets killed.

The tracks angled close enough to the river that Parson could see the current rushing white across rocks. He was hungry enough to wonder whether the stream held any fish, but he knew the team couldn't stop for that. Fishing was a survival skill for a noncombat environment.

He remembered one particular time when he'd gone fishing. Another survival situation, of a sort. It was after his father's death in the Gulf War. He went to the San Juan River, where cold waters flow through the New Mexico desert. One afternoon he saw a school of big rainbow trout rising to take insects on the surface. He paid out flyline and made a long roll cast to put a Royal Coachman near the feeding rainbows. It fell short, so he waded nearer. Another cast, and it, too, fell short. He waded ahead, keeping his eyes on the rising trout. He felt the breeze and smelled the earth scent of the riverbanks, and he tried to think of nothing else. But something felt wrong with his footing as he waded ahead. He looked down, and through Polarized sunglasses he saw that he was standing on the edge of a deep pool cut by the current. Another step would have drowned him. He could swim, but not in flooded chest waders. He backed away from the pool, more sure than ever that even in the quietest, most peaceful settings, it was a world of danger and loss.

The insurgents' trail veered away from the river and up a ridge to the north. The bootprints beside the drag mark turned sideways and choppy in places, apparently where the insurgents carrying the mullah had struggled to haul him along. As Parson slogged uphill, he wished he'd picked up a walking stick somewhere. But only stunted hawthorns grew on this incline, nothing with branches big enough for a staff. A crusting of snow clung to Parson's legs and formed knots of ice around the zipper tabs of his lower pockets. Najib and Cantrell stopped to study the map again.

"They wouldn't go uphill in this shit without a reason," Cantrell said.

Najib examined the chart. Snowflakes speckled it, and he blew on it to clear them away. "They are heading northeast now," he said.

"I don't see any village in that direction," Cantrell said.

"There is none," Najib said. "The only thing I can remember in this region is an old fort. Perhaps they have cached supplies there."

Gold looked over their shoulders. "What do you think?" Cantrell asked her.

"That would give them a good place to rest," she said. "And fight us off."

Najib folded the map. "In better times I have fished the river down below that fort," he said. "I caught an enormous Pabdah

catfish, and my mother made it into *korma-e-mahi,* a fish stew."
Najib looked into the distance and spoke softly, as if he knew he
was describing something that could never happen again.

Without another word, he picked up his shotgun and moved
on. As he led the troops along the guerrillas' trail, the slope lifted
them into the clouds. Mist enveloped them in the dying light.

CHAPTER NINETEEN

Just before full darkness, Parson noticed fine snowflakes spiraling down like white dust motes. That was an improvement. All day, pellets had come straight at him, hard and sharp, little ice flechettes driven by the wind. He removed the handkerchief frozen around his face. The stiff cloth had started to chafe at his cheeks, causing more discomfort than it prevented.

Something was changing in the storm system, but he dared not hope for flyable weather. Ice fog still drifted across the peaks. When Parson looked through his night-vision goggles, the mist glowed like ectoplasm.

Gold walked near him. He couldn't see her well when he wasn't using the goggles, but the crunch of her boots comforted him. He slung his rifle over his shoulder and carried his pistol in his left hand. Parson was so exhausted he couldn't remember why his right wrist hurt.

He thought he heard more boots next to him, the snow crackling with the footsteps. Then a voice that said, "Hey, nav." Despite the darkness, when he looked around he saw his crew.

Fisher tromped along with his helmet in his hand. He still wore that little unauthorized patch across the pen pocket on his left sleeve, the one that read: FDNY. Jordan kicked at the icy crust and smiled when some of it sprayed onto Parson. Luke and Nunez threw snowballs at each other. They wore only their flight suits.

Parson stared, too tired to be startled. "Aren't you guys cold?" he asked.

"Nah, we're fine," Fisher said.

"What are you doing here?"

"Just came to say hello," Nunez said.

"And thanks," Luke said.

"That's it?" Parson asked.

"What do you want?" Jordan said. "A bottle of Crown?"

"Maybe later."

"I'm afraid we can't stay that long," Fisher said.

"I thought I'd never see you guys again," Parson said.

"New assignments," Jordan said. "You know how it goes."

"We'll catch you at debrief," Luke said.

"Hey, this is Sergeant Gold," Parson said. "She's—"

Parson turned toward Gold. When he looked back, the crew was gone. Swirling clouds, unbroken snow.

He took a knee, breathed hard. Felt his throat clench. Gold touched his shoulder.

"Did you see them?" he asked.

"Who?"

"You know. My friends. From the plane."

"You're badly sleep-deprived," she said. "It makes you see things."

Parson didn't know how to take that. Did she mean it makes you see things or *see* things? He didn't believe in ghosts, but in every ghost story he'd ever heard, the dead returned to make a demand or issue a warning. The crew did nothing but offer moral support. And that was just like them.

"Don't fuck with me," Parson said.

"I'm not," Gold said. "Let's go, sir. This mission is about what we can do for the living."

Snowflakes twisted to the ground like cold pinfeathers. Parson felt them settling on his eyelashes. He blinked and then strained to stand, every tendon and muscle fatigued. With nothing left to move him but his obligations, he shifted his Colt from his left hand to his right, felt the twinge of pain. Switched on the NVGs and looked around to get his bearings. He saw Najib and Cantrell conferring in the lee of a boulder. When they moved on, he turned off the goggles and followed.

The team crossed the ridgeline's summit. Atop the peak, with nothing on either side except blackness, Parson felt deprived of his senses, as if all that existed was the cold and the ground where he stood. Whenever the soldiers stopped, the silence was so pure he heard only his own breathing.

Scanning through his goggles, he noticed that the troops were no longer following the insurgents' trail. The tracks and drag mark were long gone now. How long ago had the team diverged from the tracks? He had been too tired to notice. But he realized Najib and Cantrell had gambled that the jihadists were, in fact, headed for the old fort. And the team evidently planned to approach it from a different direction than the jihadists. Parson marveled that the SF soldiers could still think tactically.

The troops halted once more for a map check. While Najib and Cantrell examined their chart again, Parson scanned with his NVGs.

The cloud ceiling was well defined. It glowed overhead like a layer of cotton. Still too low for flying these ridges, but at least it wasn't hugging the ground. Good visibility underneath. Parson saw where the slope dropped away beneath him and flattened into a vale of rolling hills.

As he turned a focus knob, a meteor blazed out of the overcast and punched into the valley floor like a tracer round. Parson had witnessed meteor showers during clear weather, but he'd never seen a shooting star in the soup before, and he'd never watched one strike the ground.

"Did you see that?" he whispered to Gold.

"I did."

Then it must have been bright for her to see it with the naked eye. Parson wished she could have seen it on NVGs.

The team descended the slope a few feet at a time. Parson stumbled through the snow-covered limestone scrabble, trying to stay alert enough to watch his footing. He knew going down a mountain could be more dangerous than going up. Especially at night, in a blizzard, too tired to tell reality from illusion, and cold beyond reason. He could concentrate on only two things: follow the others and don't drop the weapon.

The troops stopped their descent about halfway down the incline, then began moving parallel to the ridgeline. They looked through their NVGs as if they expected to see something. But when Parson scanned through his own goggles, he saw nothing other than terrain. That didn't surprise him. The stone and mud-brick buildings of Afghanistan had a way of blending into the landscape even without a coating of snow.

The ridge tapered off to a finger that led onto an open vista. Through the goggles, Parson saw why someone might put a garrison there. It wasn't the highest ground, but it commanded a good view of the region. And just like Najib had said, there was a river down there, providing a good water source.

The soldiers stopped. Parson and Gold kneeled by Cantrell.

"Do you see the fort?" Parson asked.

"A few hundred meters this side of the river," Cantrell said.

At first, Parson didn't recognize anything man-made. He had trouble steadying the NVGs because of his shivering. But eventually he discerned what looked like right angles among the wrinkles of snow. So Najib had been right. The guy was dependable, Parson thought. You had to give him that. Muslims who fish can't be all bad.

Parson was about to turn off the goggles when a light source blossomed in the lower edge of his field of view. The shades of green shifted as the NVGs' electronics adjusted. Then the bloom went away and the pixels darkened to a deeper emerald.

"I just saw somebody light a lamp or something," Parson said.

Cantrell looked through his own monocular. "I don't see it now, but I believe you," he said. "They probably lit it and then covered it up. Stupid."

"What now?"

"While it's still dark, we'll set up to hit them."

Cantrell spoke as if he were talking about getting into a deer stand before light, not sizing up a battle he might very well lose.

The men gathered around Cantrell and Najib. They spoke in low tones, gestured, double-checked their weapons and radios. The comm sergeant hooked up the Shadowfire, and Parson saw Cantrell whispering into the handset.

He figured Cantrell was making a fairly routine call to Task Force. Cantrell was where he was supposed to be, doing what he was supposed to be doing. But Parson knew his own status remained that of a downed and missing flier. Isolated personnel. He decided to check in with search-and-rescue. He pulled his GPS receiver and Hook-112 from his flight suit pockets, hoping his body heat had kept the batteries from getting cold-soaked. He removed his pack, opened the flap, and felt for his flashlight. He held the light down inside the pack, covered its lens with three fingers, turned it on. Placed the GPS and 112 inside, and opened his fingers just enough to allow a sliver of light onto the switches.

His hands were numb, so he took off his right glove. When he placed his right hand near the shielded glow of the flashlight, he saw that the skin at the tips of his fingers was turning whitish purple. He knew then that he might lose some of those fingertips.

Parson fumbled to turn on the equipment. His fingers had no more feeling than if he were pushing the buttons with a stick. He exhaled into his fist, but that didn't help. When the GPS powered up, the thing took forever to figure out where it was. Parson worried that its batteries had grown weak, but finally it showed present coordinates. Gold had to plug in the radio's earpiece for him, though he managed to press the transmit button by himself.

"Any aircraft," he whispered, "Flash Two-Four Charlie."

"Flash Two-Four Charlie," a British voice answered, "Saxon is on station."

"Can you tell me conditions at Bagram and relay a message to the AOC there?"

"Affirmative. Stand by."

Parson imagined his English counterpart pulling a Mont Blanc from the pen sleeve of a heavy RAF flight suit. Hurry up, Nigel. Put your tea in the cup holder and copy my location. God, to be in a warm place like that flight deck.

When Saxon called back, Parson gave his coordinates. He said nothing about the fort and what the team was planning.

"Saxon has your numbers," the British flier said. "Bagram weather is ceiling nine hundred, visibility one-half mile. Temperature minus ten Celsius, winds two-zero-zero at fifteen knots."

Better than anything Parson had seen for days. "Flash Two-Four Charlie copies all," he said.

"Are you ready for extraction if Bagram can launch helos?" Saxon asked.

"Negative," Parson said. "Still low weather at my location. I'll call you when it improves."

"We'll be here, mate."

"Flash Two-Four Charlie out."

After Parson put away his radio, he looked up to see the SF troops and ANA soldiers inspecting gear, dividing up into squads. The Afghan troops prayed together. One placed his bare hands around a small book, then wrapped the book in a silk cloth and put it in his pocket. The Americans shoved fresh batteries into their laser sights and NVGs. Whispers and soft clicks. Faint whine from something electronic.

The soldiers melted into the darkness as they moved to positions closer to the fort. They walked so quietly that Parson could not hear them after they got about four steps away. When he watched them through NVGs, they seemed just spectral flickers growing smaller with distance. Some vanished altogether on the far side of the fort ruins.

Cantrell and one of his riflemen kept to the higher ground for an overwatch position. Parson and Gold stayed near Cantrell. Working together, they dug into the snow behind a rock shelf above the valley.

"We'll give them the business just before dawn," Cantrell said.

"You might be able to get some help by then," Parson said. "They just told me the weather's improving at Bagram."

"There's usually some kind of close air support standing by for us whenever visibility allows."

Parson wished he could foretell the outcome of the next few hours. He held to no superstition; he'd never flown with any of the usual good-luck charms like a rabbit's foot or a girlfriend's scarf. No talisman could help; it all came down to talent, competence, and chance. He didn't discount some force guiding the latter, but he doubted anybody could fathom the intentions of that force.

He placed his hands inside his parka, hoping to save at least some of his fingertips. The numbness had given way to a stinging sensation, and he knew that wasn't good. He closed his eyes and immediately fell asleep.

The cold woke him, his own shivering. When he checked his watch, he saw he'd slept about forty minutes. Nothing close to what he needed. His fingers hurt worse.

He fumbled for his NVGs and turned them on again. The snowfall was lighter now, and when he looked through the goggles he could make out the fort's arches and towers. When Najib had said "old fort," Parson envisioned something from the Soviet war. Now he realized Najib thought in timelines far longer. This thing had been old when the British evacuated. Each wall had rows of embrasures. For firing muskets? Or maybe even crossbows, Parson thought. He picked up his laser range-finder and pressed the button, forced himself to hold it steady. The nearest tower was 856 yards away.

"Who built that thing?" he asked Gold, shivering.

She shrugged. "They call this country the graveyard of empires," she said.

Sure as hell it has been the graveyard of too many people, Parson thought. Maybe us, too. He wondered whether Marwan's band had joined more insurgents there. Until now, the two sides had been about evenly matched in numbers. Now there was just no telling.

"What would you do," Parson asked, "if you knew you might not live to the end of the day?"

"You mean like today?" Gold said. "I'd do the best I could at whatever I was doing."

She would, thought Parson. The idea of getting killed didn't bother him much. He believed he'd already outlived his luck. But the idea of getting captured again sickened him. That's just not happening, he thought. I have plenty of ammo now, and I'll save the last round for myself.

He wondered how that would be accounted in the hereafter. You weren't supposed to take your own life. But in this situation, you weren't doing it because you *wanted* to die. He decided the accounting was unknowable, like the number of jihadists in that fort.

Cantrell began whispering into the headset microphone connected to his MBITR. Parson could not hear the transmissions coming back. But he did hear Cantrell's final order: "Fire at will."

CHAPTER TWENTY

Rifle fire crackled as the soldiers killed sentries and lookouts. From his position hundreds of yards away, Parson saw figures running toward the fort, heard the thud of an explosion that breached a door. Viewed through night-vision goggles, the blast sent out globules of light like a spattering of burning oil. Then came the popping of AK-47 rounds and replies from M-4s. Deep booms of Najib's shotgun echoed underneath the rifle chatter. Najib must have already gotten inside, Parson thought, if he was close enough for that weapon. Shouts in Pashto, Arabic, and English.

Parson dropped his goggles and scanned through the rifle scope. Still not full daylight, just a suggestion of dawn. He wanted to fire, but nothing was clear but the reticle.

Another staccato wave of gunfire rippled from the fort. "Too much shooting," muttered Cantrell. "This isn't going well." The SF commander made a radio call, repeated it. No answer, apparently. Then he picked up his M-4.

"Fuck this," he said. "I'm going in there. If you see any good targets, nail 'em."

Cantrell and the SF soldier who had remained with him took off at a trot down the hill toward the fort. They stopped to fire, then ran on. Parson could not see what they shot at. The two of them disappeared behind a crumbling wall.

"Let's get down to that fort," Parson said. "We aren't doing any good up here."

He took off his pack, stuffed his radio and extra ammo into his pockets. Then he pulled himself over the rock shelf and began running down the slope. He slipped and slid in places, but he never lost balance. Gold followed close behind, plowing through a mantle of dry snow light as foam. She held the AK tight across her chest.

A breeze kicked up out of the west and stirred the top layer of powder. The white ground seemed to undulate in the gray light. It made Parson a little dizzy, but he gripped the M-40 and ran, panting.

Rifle fire crackled in fits, but Parson no longer heard the bass slams of Najib's twelve-gauge. Between the shots, he heard the murmur of the river below. He reached the fort, stood with his back to the cold wall. He motioned for Gold to follow him. Parson moved left and came to a wooden gate blown open.

The body of an insurgent lay inside the courtyard. A wounded ANA soldier nearby rolled onto his side and gestured. Parson and Gold started toward him, but the man pointed to the east wall. Shots echoed from inside.

The two of them scrambled in the direction the man pointed, though Parson wasn't sure what to look for. They came to a mud-brick staircase open to the courtyard, the steps scalloped from years of wear. As Parson climbed them, he nearly tripped on the uneven footing, which was made even more precarious by a coating of snow. The steps led onto a row of battlements. When he reached the top, he heard the crack of a shot. A bullet smacked into the bricks beside his head. Grit sprayed into his nose and mouth. He tasted salt and lead as he dropped to the walkway behind a masonry ledge. Decent cover now but no room to move. He peered through a chink in the bricks, trying to see what had happened to Gold. She had been right behind him.

A wisp of blond hair showed through where mortar had fallen away from the low wall of the staircase. She was down on the stairs, not thirty feet away.

"You all right?" he shouted.

"Yeah, I think so."

Another slug glanced off the ledge right in front of him, showered dust and snow into his eyes. The ricochet moaned into the distance. Damn, somebody can shoot, he thought. Marwan, probably. Parson wanted to get up and run to Gold, but that would be suicide. He tried to make himself act rationally. Don't do something foolish, he told himself. Think.

He turned over and lay flat on his back with the M-40 across his stomach. He pulled off his watch cap and slipped the multitool from his survival vest. Unfolded the tool to open its pliers. Draped the watch cap across the pliers. He lifted the pliers to raise the cap above the brick ledge. Almost immediately, a bullet struck the jaws of the pliers and tore the multitool and cap from his hand. The broken tool clattered against the opposite wall. The shock of it hurt Parson's frostbitten fingers, and he shook his hand, clenched his fist. He still didn't see the shooter, but now he had a better idea where the rounds were coming from.

Parson looked back toward Gold's place on the stairs. Now he saw not just a wisp of hair but her face. She pointed two fingers at her eyes, then pointed across the courtyard with her index finger. She mouthed the word "Marwan." Then she shouted, "Run!"

Gold sat up, propped the rifle on the staircase wall, and fired a long burst on full auto. Parson got up and ran along the battlements. Chips of brick crumbled from a row of bullet holes that followed behind him. Whoever was firing now, he thought, it wasn't Marwan. Marwan would have known enough to lead him.

He looked to see Gold running behind him, still firing. They came to another set of steps under a brick archway. He ducked inside the stairwell, slung the rifle over his shoulder, and drew his Colt. Gold changed magazines.

"Did you get him?" Parson asked.

"I just pinned him down for a second."

Another rattle of automatic fire came from somewhere in the courtyard, and an answering burst rippled from downstairs. Parson wasn't sure, but he thought the weapon downstairs sounded like an M-4. He took a chance.

"Hey," he yelled. "Americans above you! Don't shoot!"

"What the fuck are you doing?" Cantrell's voice.

"One of your Afghan guys sent us this way. I don't know why."

"Najib's hit. I can't see him now." Cantrell fired again.

Parson caught a whiff of something. Cloves and wood smoke. If that's cooking, he thought, this is an established camp.

He stumbled down the stairs and found Cantrell sweeping his barrel right to left, covering some of his men as they crossed the courtyard.

"Marwan's up there somewhere," Parson said.

"No shit." Cantrell bled from a graze wound on his neck. Parson looked beyond the courtyard to the fort's opposite wall and the angles of stone that made up its stairways and passages. A hundred hiding places for a sniper.

"I'll look for Najib," Parson said.

Parson ran down a hallway lit only by dim daylight where the outer wall had crumbled, either from some battle ages ago or from age itself. He wasn't sure where to go, and he was starting to feel useless as he searched randomly. Gold followed close behind. He paused at the opening in the wall and looked out. Dark clouds still spitting snow. Crest of a white hill. Bloody tracks. More ruins a few hundred yards beyond the hill.

He wanted to run and follow the tracks, but he knew that would make him a target even the poorest marksman could hit, especially now that it was light outside. He continued several feet down the hallway until it ended in a jumble of bricks that opened to the fort's interior, onto the courtyard. Parson crouched behind the rubble. Two SF troops ran across the courtyard. Maybe they're getting the upper hand, Parson thought.

He and Gold charged across the quadrangle and up another set of steps. Climbed up to the parapets for a better view outside the fort.

"There he is," Gold said.

Two insurgents were dragging Najib by the arms toward the other ruins. He did not resist. Either unconscious or too weak to fight, thought Parson. Or maybe he knows it's actually harder to drag someone who's *not* struggling.

The insurgents tugged at him like pulling a sled. Parson slid the M-40 off his shoulder. Steadied his forearm on a parapet. Now he saw through the scope pretty well.

No time for the range-finder, but it looked like a good seven hundred yards. Some breeze. No time to adjust the scope for wind, either. Back to basics, then. Parson held the crosshairs a little left and high. Kentucky windage and Tennessee elevation. He exhaled, held his breath. Pressed the trigger.

The insurgent twisted to his right and fell. Parson couldn't tell exactly where the bullet had struck, but he saw red spatter on the snow. The insurgent lay still. His partner let go of Najib and took off running.

Parson cycled the bolt and slammed home a fresh round. The fleeing man's back bounced up and down behind the reticle. Parson fired. Missed.

The bullet made a hollow whack against the mud wall of whatever outbuilding those ruins had been. A sheaf of dry snow slid from the remains of the roof. The insurgent disappeared behind the wall.

Parson cursed and rebolted. The empty brass clinked off the battlement and flipped end over end, trailing smoke.

"Stay behind some cover," he said to Gold. He slung his rifle across his back. Sprinted down the steps and along the interior wall. Kicked open a decaying wooden gateway and ran toward Najib. Gunfire barked all around. Parson expected a slug to take him down, but he made it.

Parson crouched low beside Najib. The dead insurgent's

arm lay across the Afghan officer's face. Parson flung the arm off and was relieved to see Najib's eyes open and moving. He heard the crump of a grenade from the battle still going on throughout the fort.

"*Saarah dee,*" Najib whispered. Blood oozed from his legs. Parson saw maybe four entrance wounds. One leg was so mangled it was hard to tell.

"I don't speak Pashto, buddy," Parson said. "Let's get you to cover."

Parson fired three pistol shots toward the wall where the insurgent had run. He didn't see any enemy there now, but he wanted to keep their heads down. Then he grabbed the collar of Najib's anorak and began pulling him back toward the main fort. Through clenched teeth, Najib made a noise closer to growl than speech.

"I know it hurts," Parson said. "I'm sorry."

Three shots snapped close by, from the fort. Parson flattened himself over Najib. But when he looked toward the fort he saw that the shooting came from Gold. Smoke wafted from the muzzle of her rifle as she aimed. She was inside an archway, laying down covering fire. Parson dragged Najib a few feet, then fired a round or two. Dragged, fired. He considered lifting Najib into a fireman's carry, but decided that would make a target too big to miss. Dragged and fired some more. When the Colt's slide locked open, he ejected the empty magazine. Pulled a new one from his vest. Dropped it. He cursed his frozen fingers as he scooped the magazine from the snow and rammed it into the pistol. Released the slide and fired again.

He pulled Najib inside the archway. Gold kneeled to examine his wounds. "See what you can do for him," Parson said.

Parson hoisted his M-40 in his right hand and gripped the
Colt in his left. Without looking back, he headed down the hallway, not sure what he should do next. When he came to another
opening in the wall, he saw Najib's shotgun lying in the snow just
inside the courtyard. That gave him an idea. Najib's Benelli had
blood on its stock and a bullet hole in the receiver. Probably not
working, but that didn't matter. Parson holstered his pistol, reached
through the rubble, and picked up the broken shotgun.

Parson watched the courtyard, judged when and where to
make a break. He did not see anyone, but he still heard firing from
rooms within the fort. He ran for the nearest steps. Climbed back
up onto the battlements, this time along the south wall. Dived for
cover among the ramparts.

With the shotgun in one hand and his rifle in the other, he
crawled in the snow along the walkway. He came to an embrasure that faced into the courtyard. Designed for a bad day when
the enemy gets inside, he thought. Just what I need now.

He pointed Najib's shotgun through the embrasure, far enough
to be visible, not far enough to seem an obvious ruse. Then he
picked up the M-40 and crawled a few yards over to the next gap
in the battlements.

This section of the fort remained fairly intact, with alternating
merlons and crenels where archers could take cover and shoot.
Parson placed his rifle barrel through a crenel, the muzzle barely
visible. From here he could cover the whole courtyard and much
of the fort's structure. If only he had a target. He saw no one,
though he still heard sporadic firing.

He watched and waited, looked out into the courtyard and
back at the broken shotgun. It drew no fire. He looked through
his rifle scope, panned across the battlements. Nothing. Come on,

you bastard, he thought. You can't miss something like that shotgun barrel.

Even if Marwan didn't shoot, Parson hoped he'd look at the decoy long enough to get distracted. Maybe slink around to maneuver for a better shot at it. But nothing moved. The rest of the firefight had seeped down to the lower rooms. Muffled shots pounded in the recesses below. Parson saw nothing outside but snowfall. Sparse now, letting up.

Damn it, he's gone, Parson decided. So the watch cap worked but not the shotgun.

He raised himself, crouched low with his rifle, and trotted along the parapets. They led to a narrow chamber, perhaps a barracks for guards centuries ago. He stepped inside, hoping he'd find interior stairs. Paused to let his eyes adjust to the gloom. Webs of frost on the walls. Trash on the floor, an empty water bottle with a Farsi label.

He nudged the bottle with his foot. Felt cold metal at the back of his neck.

"Do not move." The voice turned Parson's blood to ice. "Put down the rifle. Slowly."

Parson's hands sweated, though his fingers had little feeling. His gloves felt as if they were filled with cold mud. He did not even exhale.

"Go on," Marwan said. "Put it down."

Parson lowered the rifle. His trembling made the weapon rattle as he placed it on the floor. As he stood back up, he saw the barrel of the Dragunov in his peripheral vision.

"Do not turn around," Marwan said. "Did you really think you could fool me twice?"

Parson did not answer. His .45 was holstered in his survival vest, under his parka. No way could he pull it fast enough. He thought to run. No, he'll shoot me. At this range the bullet would pierce body armor.

"There are stairs to your right," Marwan said. "Walk."

Parson shuffled to the stairwell as if in a trance. Tried to form thoughts.

"We have unfinished business," Marwan said. "You are going to suffer for your treatment of our spiritual leader."

Then maybe I want him to shoot me, thought Parson. I'll go for the pistol and make him shoot me.

Like the other stairways in the fort, the center treadway of each step had worn down nearly to the next step. Parson lost his footing and tumbled into darkness. He felt his head and limbs striking a misery of stone. As he lay at the bottom, his wrist and elbows throbbed. But no bones seemed broken, not that it mattered anymore.

He grabbed his twisted ankle. Through the leg of his flight suit he felt the silver pommel of his boot knife. And he decided to live a little longer.

Parson put his hand under his flight suit, onto the knife handle. Groaned as if in more pain than he really felt. Kept his hand in place as if massaging an injury. Marwan avoided the stairs' eroded center and descended with the poise of a gymnast. Parson felt the Dragunov's muzzle against his cheek. Perfect.

"Get up," Marwan said.

Parson grabbed the barrel with his left hand and wrenched it to the side. Marwan fired. The muzzle flash lit the dungeon like lightning. Parson yanked the rifle toward him and swung his elbow into Marwan's face. Kneed his groin.

The Dragunov clattered to the floor. Parson felt both Marwan's hands choking him. He tried to stab him in the chest, but the Damascus blade scraped body armor. Parson slashed higher.

Marwan shouted a word Parson did not understand when the blade entered his armpit. He let go of Parson's neck. Then kicked his chest. Parson's own flak jacket took the brunt, but the blow sent him reeling against the wall. His vision tunneled, particled. Then cleared.

He shifted the knife from his right hand to his left and dug for his pistol. A kick to his knees knocked his legs out from under him. Parson fell onto his side and dropped the knife. Marwan reached to the floor for his rifle.

Parson tore open his coat and drew the Colt. He could not seem to make his frostbitten thumb pull the hammer. Marwan pointed his Dragunov just as Parson cocked the .45 and pulled the trigger.

The shot sounded like an explosion within the stone walls. The flash illuminated Marwan as the bullet hit his armor. Photo of a man with rifle, falling. Parson pulled the trigger again.

Nothing. Parson tried to clear the slide, but it wouldn't move. Jammed.

Marwan began to pick himself up. Parson dropped the pistol and swept his hands across the stone floor, looking for his knife. Felt the blade slice his left thumb through his flight glove. He grabbed the antler handle and hurled himself at his enemy.

Parson drove the knife through Marwan's throat and slammed him against the wall. The blade penetrated to the hand guard. Air whistled through the severed windpipe. Parson twisted the knife as the two men slid to the floor. He jerked the blade up, left, down. Pain in his wrist again. Warm blood on his face.

Dust floated in a narrow beam of milky light from the stairwell. Marwan's torso spasmed. Parson felt him exhale through both mouth and wound, and the dying man's chest did not rise again. One of his hands clenched as if he still had fight left in him, but then the fist just trembled with the stray impulses of muscles shutting down for good. In the dimness, Parson thought he saw Marwan's eyes fix on him. Parson could not tell the exact moment they ceased to see.

CHAPTER
TWENTY-ONE

Parson's flight gloves were already ruined with blood, so he used one of them to wipe his blade. Then he put the boot knife in its sheath and pulled the glove back onto his hand. The glove felt sticky and he wanted to take it off, but it was too cold to do without it.

He picked up his pistol, climbed the stairs, and found his rifle where he had left it. Hoisted the M-40 by the sling. Out on the battlements in the daylight, he saw better what was wrong with the .45. An empty casing was caught in the slide. He took cover behind the parapets, racked the slide, and cleared the jam. The offending cartridge casing dropped into the snow, and the next round fed into the firing chamber.

Thinking to clean his gloves, he picked up a handful of snow and rubbed it between his palms. Didn't seem to help. His war couldn't get any more primal now. Personal combat with brawn and edged weapons, against an individual enemy despised by name. It would have been good for the snake-eaters to take Marwan for questioning, but there was nothing Parson could do about that now. He doubted they'd get the mullah alive, either.

Especially not with all the shooting. Shots still thumped from other rooms in the fort. A grenade sailed into the courtyard. When it exploded, shrapnel raked the battlements like grapeshot.

Insurgents poured into the courtyard. Bursts of fire from somewhere beneath him cut most of them down. Parson ran along the parapets, hoping to get a better idea of what was happening. He leaped across a hole blasted in the stone walkway, landed hard, banged a knee. Four ANA troops ran through the courtyard.

More shots came from outside, just beyond the walls. He looked over the parapet to see Gold and Cantrell on the ground, shooting at insurgents fleeing the fort.

Parson shouldered his rifle and looked through the scope. One of the insurgents, a tall man, had his arm around a shorter, stooped man, helping him lope through the snow. Perhaps the shorter man was wounded. Then Parson recognized him as the mullah.

Gold ran forward a few yards. She dropped to one knee and pointed the AK, elbow resting on her thigh. Parson watched the mullah and the other insurgent through the crosshairs.

Gold's rifle popped once. Parson saw a puff of dust between the insurgent's shoulder blades. The man fell and took the mullah to the ground with him. Hell of a shot at that distance with open sights.

The mullah flailed in the snow and pulled himself from under his downed follower. Snow wadded onto his baggy *shalwar kameez* and dusted his beard. The old man staggered to his feet and pulled at his helper's rifle. The sling was wrapped around the body. The mullah jerked at the weapon but could not free it. He let go of the rifle and tried to run. He limped, but he moved fast enough for his boots to kick up powder.

Gold and Cantrell gained on him anyway. Then Parson heard rifle fire from somewhere beneath him in the fort. Snow sprayed up from the ground between Gold and Cantrell. Gold dropped to the ground and returned fire. Cantrell also turned and opened up. Then he ejected a magazine, slammed in another, and emptied that one. Parson leaned to see where the shots had come from, almost directly underneath him in the fort. The insurgents remained inside. No target for him there.

About a mile distant, past Gold and Cantrell, beyond the river, he saw men on horseback. The mullah was headed in their direction. The old man stumbled, fell, then got up and ran again.

Parson saw just one option. He watched the mullah through the scope, put the crosshairs on his torso. The old man had caused enough trouble. Parson had always enjoyed the hunt, but this time he'd enjoy the kill. Too bad not to have hollow-point bullets. Expand and fragment on impact and rip that motherfucker's guts out.

The mullah was damn near a thousand yards away now. Parson looked up from his rifle to check the wind. Still a little breeze, not much snow falling. Then he saw Gold looking up at him. Remembered why they were here in the first place. A mission to transport a prisoner. All right, Sergeant, he thought, you brought me this far. I'll do it your way.

He put his cheek back on the stock, lowered the reticle to the mullah's pumping lower legs. Pressed the trigger.

The bullet kicked up snow between the old man's feet. Parson swore, rebolted. He expelled air from his lungs, steadied the M-40 on a parapet. Aimed again, a little higher this time. The mullah was getting near where the land pitched downslope. Time for one more shot, if that.

Parson squeezed the trigger so slowly that the recoil surprised him. The old man crumpled. Then he sat up and held his right calf with both hands.

Through the scope, Parson watched the riders and horses. Six of them. One with a rocket launcher. Another with a belt of grenades. Out of range. If I just had a Barrett rifle, he thought.

The firing around the fort subsided to sporadic crackles, then stopped altogether. The riders galloped away. Where they were going, he could not tell. Three of them followed the riverbank, and the other three just disappeared. Parson didn't know how the raid had gone, but every insurgent he saw was dead, wounded, or fleeing.

He watched Cantrell and another SF troop lift the mullah by his arms. They brought him back to the fort a few yards at a time, checking his wound, giving him water. No slaps or punches. When they put him down, Gold spoke to him in Pashto without raising her voice.

Parson found his way through the fort to where he had left Najib. Cantrell's medic was tending to him. Najib's face had a gray cast, and his eyes were closed. Tan granules lay scattered around his legs from where the medic had poured QuikClot into his wounds. A pulse oximeter clipped to one of his fingertips glowed red from its LED.

"How is he?" Parson asked.

"I've done all I can. If he doesn't get to a hospital this morning, he'll die."

Parson looked up at the sky. A canopy of clouds stretched

from peak to peak at the higher elevations, but he guessed the valley's ceiling at better than three thousand feet. It would be tricky, but that's why helicopters had radar altimeters.

"Let's go home," he said. He took his GPS and 112 from his coat pocket and switched them on. Keyed his radio. "Saxon," he called, "Flash Two-Four Charlie."

The answer came immediately: "Flash Two-Four Charlie, Saxon. How are you down there, mate?"

"Better. Weather's better, too. Can you have the bartender call me a cab?"

"Affirmative. Ready to copy coordinates."

Parson gave his numbers. After an agonizing wait, the Brits called him back: "Flash Two-Four Charlie, Bagram wants your nine-line."

Dear God, thought Parson, we're actually getting out of here. He couldn't remember all the items in a nine-line medevac request, but he knew enough to get the aircraft to him.

"Saxon," he said, "I'll remain at the previous coordinates. One critical patient. A few other wounded. I also have a whole A-team that needs a ride. We'll mark the pickup site with smoke."

Parson checked his watch. He wasn't sure how long it would take the helicopters to reach him, but if the crews were locked and cocked, they could get airborne within minutes. Cantrell tramped around in the snow and decided on a fairly flat LZ not far from the fort. Najib couldn't be carried much farther.

Cantrell deployed his troops in a perimeter to guard the landing site. Parson selected a knoll high enough to overlook the LZ and much of the fort, and he waited there with rifle and radio. Half an hour went by. No radio call, no sound of aircraft. He keyed his 112.

"Saxon, Flash Two-Four Charlie. Status report, please."

Before the answer could come over the airwaves, he felt it in his breastbone. The beat and slap of rotors. Cantrell grinned at him and gave a thumbs-up. A new voice came on the radio, vibrating as if speaking through the blades of a fan.

"Flash Two-Four Charlie, Komodo Eight-Six. We're a flight of two HH-60s inbound your position. Please advise."

Parson already had his compass out. He turned it around backward, pointed it toward the noise, read the reciprocal. He was so tired he did not trust himself, so he checked it twice.

"Komodo," he called, "Flash Two-Four Charlie hears your aircraft. Fly heading two-four-zero."

"Copy that. Two-four-zero."

A moment later, the helicopter called back: "Flash Two-Four Charlie, when did you kill your first elk?"

Parson thought for a second. He had reviewed his authentication statements just before takeoff, days ago.

"When I was twelve."

"That checks."

The rotor noise got louder and Parson calculated the direction it came from more precisely. "Komodo," he said, "adjust heading two-one-zero."

"Two-one-zero. Any bad guys down there?"

"The ones who aren't dead have scattered."

"That doesn't sound good."

When the Pave Hawks broke through the cloud deck, Parson thought they were the most beautiful thing he'd ever seen. Spinning rotors. Refueling probes extending from their noses. Miniguns jutting from the sides. Two lethal wasps against a pewter sky.

Cantrell held out an MK-13 smoke flare and removed the

orange cap. He pulled up the ring attached to a lanyard. Twisted the ring to break the seal. Yanked hard.

There was a loud crack, then reddish smoke boiled from the end of the flare. Cantrell held it aloft like an Olympic torch. The smoke spread into the valley and hung low.

"Flash Two-Four Charlie, Komodo has you in sight."

"Copy that. Be advised we also have wounded to pick up at another site."

A hot shower. That's the first thing Parson looked forward to. He'd eat everything in the chow hall at Bagram and sleep for two days. Then he'd make sure command knew what Gold, Najib, and Cantrell had done. He wanted them to receive the highest decorations they could get.

The first Pave Hawk began its approach to the LZ. It did not hover; instead it made a gliding approach, keeping forward momentum to stay ahead of the snow cloud kicked up by its rotor wash.

Cantrell snuffed out the flare in the snow. To signal the chopper, he held his arms over his head, then swept them downward and crossed in front of his body: Land here. As the helicopter descended, tendrils of red smoke left from the flare curled over it. The Pave Hawk slowed as it neared touchdown, and the snow cloud behind it caught up to it and enveloped the tail boom. The aircraft rocked slightly as it settled onto the ground, and the billowing snow obscured it completely. Then its rotors changed pitch and slowed, and the snow cloud dissipated. Two pararescuemen hopped out carrying a litter. Interphone jacks dangled from their helmets as they ran toward the wounded.

Parson surveyed his surroundings, tried to remain aware of every detail. He lay on his chest, propped on his elbows in the snow, just fifty yards or so from the fort. The SF troops were settled into overwatch positions around and behind him. Some he could see, and others were too well hidden. Cantrell kneeled by the helicopter that had already landed, rifle up to guard the aircraft, which sat with engines at idle. Parson noted that the aircraft was well within range of his rifle, no more than a hundred meters to his right. That meant he and Cantrell commanded an interlocking field of fire on anything coming from the fort that threatened the Pave Hawk. The snake-eaters on the perimeter could handle bad guys from outside.

The second helicopter descended to about five hundred feet, then began orbiting the area. A helmeted flight engineer manned the minigun that jutted from the cabin window. A black visor covered the engineer's face. With gloved hands, the crewman pointed his weapon down at the fort.

Parson saw no insurgents. He got up on one knee. This would all be over soon.

Two troops hoisted the mullah through the side door of the helicopter on the ground. The pararescuemen lifted Najib onto the litter and loaded him aboard. The Afghan troops put two other wounded men inside. Gold walked behind them. She turned and looked at Parson as she climbed aboard. The second chopper descended and began its approach. When the helicopter entered ground effect, a snow cloud formed in the vortex of tortured air and began following the Pave Hawk.

A smoke trail spewed from the fort's battlements like a smudged pencil line drawn straight to the landing helicopter. God, not again, thought Parson. The RPG struck the tail rotor. Shards of metal punctured the chopper's skin as the tail rotor disintegrated. The stricken aircraft began to gyrate, spinning in the opposite direction from its whirling main rotor. The snow cloud behind the chopper flattened, then encircled and enclosed it as if the ground itself had erupted and swallowed the Pave Hawk in a white maw.

A voice came over Parson's 112, straining like the pilot was lifting something heavy: "Two's hit. I got no antitorque. Two's going in."

Four insurgents stood on the parapets. One aimed a grenade launcher. Parson shouldered his rifle and shot him.

The wounded helicopter gained a few feet of altitude. Parson saw parts of it through the whipping snow: a rotor, the nose, the broken tail boom. Still spinning, it lurched toward the fort. One of the remaining insurgents rose up with the grenade launcher.

Parson chambered another round and made a snap shot. The bullet chipped masonry in front of the insurgent holding the launcher, and the man dropped behind cover. Cantrell fired a burst from the M-4. His rounds kicked up a spray of dust from the merlon shielding the insurgents.

For a moment, Parson saw the pilot inside the spinning helicopter. He was holding on with one arm and reaching across the cockpit panel with the other as the copilot fought the controls. The chopper spun into the ground between Parson and the fort. Torque from the rotation rolled the Pave Hawk onto its side. The main rotor shattered when it chopped into snow and dirt. Blade fragments tore through the air. A five-foot section sliced into the ground next to Parson like a broadax.

As he ran toward the wrecked helicopter, he heard its engines whine to a stop. He hoped that meant somebody inside was uninjured enough to pull fire handles. Damn fine job setting that thing down if they could continue to function and run the shut-down procedure. Things were bad enough without an explosion.

Rifles chattered as the SF troops tried to keep the insurgents pinned down. Parson slung his M-40 over his shoulder and climbed onto the side of the chopper. He smelled the burned steel odor of overheated turbines, but to his relief, not the sharp fumes of raw fuel.

A pararescueman inside was helping the pilots unbuckle their harnesses. Shouts and curses. Parson offered his good hand and helped the crewmen crawl through the upturned side door. The two pilots, two pararescuemen, the flight engineer, and the gunner all carried M-4 carbines. They dropped to the ground with their weapons at the ready, and each took cover behind the wreckage. Nobody seemed badly hurt. One of the pilots took off his helmet and slammed it into the snow.

"Son of a bitch!" he shouted over the rotors of the other chop-per. Sweating face. Trimmed black mustache.

"They're up in that fort," Parson said. "I think they got more RPGs."

"Great," the pilot said. "And we can't get all of us out of here in one Hawk."

"I know it."

Parson looked over the wreckage and saw the insurgent with the grenade launcher peek up. Cantrell fired a burst. A miss, but the insurgents stayed crouched behind the wall. Parson couldn't see what the bad guys were doing, but it looked like they had a second launch tube, some kind of shoulder-fired weapon. An SA-7 missile, probably.

Aboard the first chopper, the gunner swiveled his minigun

toward the insurgents. The spinning bores fired a storm of bullets that tore into the side of the fort. The slugs threw up red dust but struck none of the enemy.

On his 112, Parson heard Cantrell talking to the first helicopter's pilot: "Take as many as you can," he said. "The rest of us will keep them pinned down when you take off."

"Roger that. We'll get another aircraft to you ASAP."

Parson turned to the downed helicopter crew beside him. "You guys take this flight out," he said. Their job was saving lives. No point keeping them here as targets. Then he looked around him, across the snowfield. Those damned riders could be anywhere by now.

Gold jumped down from the side door of the first Pave Hawk and ran toward him. She held her rifle with both hands and turned her face against the snow and gritty ice kicked up by the rotors. A lock of her hair had come untied, and she brushed it from her face as she knelt beside him. Something about the angle of the gesture, the profile of wrist and hand, struck Parson as a moment of beauty. Simple grace in the middle of hell.

"What are you doing?" he asked.

"If you want my place on the chopper, I can wait here with Captain Cantrell."

"No," Parson said. "Go back to Bagram while you can."

"Are you sure? You could escort your crewmates home."

That made him pause. They deserved a last ride with someone who had known them. Their families deserved to hear the story straight from him. He looked at the waiting Pave Hawk, heat waves shimmering from its engines. It could lift him out of this nightmare within seconds.

Cantrell squeezed off two rounds. No guarantee the insurgents would stay pinned down forever. No telling if more were coming. Time for another decision.

"Get back on board," Parson said. "You can make sure the right people ask the mullah the right questions." His crew deserved a job seen through to the end.

"You're certain about this?"

"Charlie Mike, Sergeant Gold. Continue your mission."

Parson thought he saw a hint of a smile.

"You're starting to sound like me," she said.

"Maybe that's a good thing." Parson said.

Gold put her hand on his left forearm where his parka sleeve overlapped his glove. She squeezed just for a second without looking into his eyes. Then she jogged back to the first helicopter and the flight engineer slid the door shut. Parson doubted he would ever see her again. He hoped he had done right by her. If he had, that was enough.

"Can you leave me an extra weapon?" Parson asked the helicopter pilot beside him. "I might need more firepower than this bolt action."

The pilot handed Parson his M-4 and two magazines. Parson shouldered the carbine and opened up with covering fire as the downed crew ran to the other aircraft.

The howl of its turbines rose. When its blades changed pitch, waves of snow shrouded Parson and bathed him in white. The flying snow swirled with exhaust smoke and became a gray soup that smelled like overheated oil. He heard Cantrell fire a burst, then he felt the rotor wash roll over him, a cold, pulsing wind. The chopper rose from the ground, and the smoke and snow cleared enough for him to see the aircraft lower its nose and accelerate.

An insurgent stood with the launch tube. Parson fired and the man went down. Couldn't tell whether the insurgent was hit or just took cover. Parson dug his spare cartridges from his pockets. Two magazines of rifle ammo, one more magazine of .45s. Plus the M-4 and the ammo the helicopter pilot had left him.

The Pave Hawk grew smaller, and the thump of its rotors faded with distance. It climbed through the cloud ceiling and disappeared as though it had never existed. Now the mullah was someone else's problem. Whatever the old man knew or did or didn't do was between him and God and the government. Parson keyed his radio.

"Saxon, Flash Two-Four Charlie," he called. "We need some close air support in here. Expedite."

A few moments later, the Brits called him back: "Quick Reaction Force is airborne and inbound. Flight of two Apaches."

Exactly what he wanted. He could vector in those attack helicopters and have them lay a couple of Hellfires into that fort. The insurgents said they wanted martyrdom. Coming right up.

Parson pulled the cold air into his lungs. It carried exhaust that smelled like a match just after striking, and it scored the inside of his chest. The snow had stopped completely now. Still a solid overcast above, but visibility underneath maybe fifty miles. The sky so smooth and still that pilots would fly through it with only their fingertips on the controls.

He set aside the carbine and picked up the M-40. Lay prone in the snow by the crashed helicopter, the aircraft now a permanent part of the landscape. His wrist throbbed with pain, though it was bearable. He could chamber another round if he had to. Little feeling in his fingertips, but enough to press a trigger. No feeling at all in his feet. He didn't like that, but it wasn't important now.

Parson scanned for horsemen approaching from beyond the

river. Then he peered through the rifle scope and watched for an insurgent to pop up. The crosshairs bounced with his shivering. He packed some snow into a mound in front of him. Rested the weapon across the packed snow. Crosshairs steady now. He hoped his batteries and ammo would last.

Past the fort, mountains backdropped mountains, ridge after ridge in the cold distance. He thought he knew which of those crests overlooked the wreckage of his C-130, but he put that from his mind. He listened to the hiss of his radio and waited for the sound of gunships.

The Story Behind

THE MULLAH'S STORM

When you write fiction, your best work may come from what scares you most: you take pen in hand and imagine the worst. When I first flew into Afghanistan, what scared me most wasn't the thought of getting shot down and killed. It was the thought of getting shot down and not killed.

For most aviators, an encounter with the enemy usually happens in the form of lights streaming up from the earth. It has an air of unreality about it, almost like a video game. If those lights don't hit you, they don't hurt you. But what if you had an airplane blown out from under you and you met the enemy on his terms, in his territory? What would you face on the ground? What would your buddies need you to do? Under conditions of extreme duress and hardship, would you make decisions you could live with later?

When I went to the Air Force Survival School years ago, an instructor gave a briefing I have never forgotten. He said, "Every Air Force flier shot down in Vietnam, captured, and dragged to the Hanoi Hilton sat right here in this auditorium and thought, 'It won't happen to me.'"

I still think it won't happen to me. But if it did? *The Mullah's Storm* is an imagining of that fear.

The book's action begins with the downing of a C-130 Hercules in Afghanistan, at an indeterminate time in the war. It could have happened in 2001, or it might not have happened yet. A shoulder-fired missile blows my main characters out of their normal world and onto a journey that forces them to disregard personal safety and even personal loyalties for the sake of the mission.

My fears have become reality for some service members, and the characters in *The Mullah's Storm* are composites of people I have known. One of those people was an early mentor and squadron mate who had served as a Marine Corps helicopter crew chief in Vietnam. He enjoyed target shooting, and I assumed such an avid marksman would also be a hunter. But when I invited him to go duck hunting, he declined. He said, "When I was shot down in Vietnam, I learned what it felt like to be hunted. I have never hunted anything since."

Although my colleague's Vietnam ordeal echoes through the book, the characters draw their motivations and mind-sets from veterans of the current wars. These service members, all volunteers, come from the best-educated military ever fielded. American troops have more skill and training than ever before, and their leaders have more confidence in them. They have more individual responsibility and, in extremis, more ability to act alone when necessary. They are not cynical, yet neither are they naive about their missions and the mistakes of those who send them on those missions.

Another difference with today's military is the greater contributions of women. Their presence as part of the team no longer raises eyebrows; in fact, it is taken for granted. My novel's female character, Sergeant Gold, was inspired by women with whom I have served. Those real-life military women include some of the best pilots, navigators, and flight engineers I've known.

Other characters are from a U.S. Army Special Forces team. As a C-130 flight engineer, I often had the pleasure of working with Special Forces. Sometimes we flew SF troops during their parachute training, dropping free-fall jumpers from so high that they had to breathe from oxygen bottles on the way down. In addition to their other military skills, each SF soldier is fluent in at least one foreign language. Those guys are very smart and very tough, and I've seen them face awful conditions with spirit and humor.

I could have set this novel, or one very much like it, in Iraq, or even Bosnia or Kosovo. But during airlift missions over Afghanistan, I was struck by the stark beauty of the country as seen from the air: the snows of the Hindu Kush, great distances of mountains unmarked by so much as a dirt path, cold and clear night air lit by a meteor shower, rural expanses so dark the stars appeared not as scattered points but as silver dust.

The book contains scenes of violence, and sadly, that reflects reality, both past and future. Afghanistan will likely never completely rid itself of insurgents and warlords, jihadists and opium traffickers. The Taliban will not show up on the deck of the USS *Missouri* to sign an instrument of surrender. Even if American forces were to end combat operations tomorrow, the country would need humanitarian assistance and airlift support into the foreseeable future. Whether U.S. troops stay or go, this will be a long war for the Afghans.

While the idea for *The Mullah's Storm* had been knocking around in my head for a while, it took an in-flight emergency to get me started on the actual writing. In August 2007, I was part of a crew flying a routine airlift mission into Osan Air Base, South Korea. On the way, we lost a hydraulic system and a generator. We declared an emergency and landed safely, greeted by the flashing lights of crash trucks. When we taxied to the ramp, the aircraft dripped a trail of hydraulic fluid.

After we shut down, we learned we'd be stuck for days, waiting for parts. So with time to kill at Osan, one morning I went to the Base Exchange and bought a yellow legal pad and a cup of coffee. I sat on a couch in aircrew billeting, and wrote at the top of the pad: "Chapter One."

ABOUT THE AUTHOR

Thomas W. Young served in Afghanistan and Iraq with the Air National Guard. He has also flown combat missions to Bosnia and Kosovo, and additional missions to Latin America, the horn of Africa, and the Far East. In all, Young has logged almost four thousand hours as a flight engineer on the C-5 Galaxy and the C-130 Hercules, while flying to almost forty countries. Military honors include two Air Medals, three Aerial Achievement Medals, and the Air Force Combat Action Medal.

In civilian life he spent ten years as a writer and editor with the broadcast division of the Associated Press, and flew as a first officer for Independence Air, an airline based at Dulles International Airport near Washington, D.C. Young holds B.A. and M.A. degrees in mass communication from the University of North Carolina at Chapel Hill.

Young's nonfiction publications include *The Speed of Heat: An Airlift Wing at War in Iraq and Afghanistan,* released in 2008 by McFarland and Company. His narrative "Night Flight to Baghdad" appeared in the Random House anthology *Operation Homecoming: Iraq, Afghanistan, and the Home Front, in the Words of U.S. Troops and Their Families.*